REVIEWS

"A galloping good read, filled with the savvy street smarts of this quirky and unpredictable heroine."

-American Rig Radio

Being inside the heroine's head makes Mud Blood an unusual kaleidoscope of characters, scenes and dialogue. You know it's 'just a novel,' but you have this weird sense of deja vu' as well. Read it, read it, read it. Del Monte's books always take on a life of their own, and you'll find yourself running into people who look like one of her characters or hearing bits of the same dialogue you just read last night.

-Terri Jenkins-Brady, Editor/Author

Masterfully written! I kept returning to the book cover to make sure it read 'novel.' Joan's rich, unmistakable literary voice leaps from every character, every scene, and every page. You will swear you know these people. And what a heroine!

-Gene Cartwright, Author/ifogo.com

"This author's mystery novel, DEATH HAD A YELLOW THUMB, adds spice, and turns her quest for saffron into fictional gold."

THE DAILY BREEZE

"Revenge is the subject of Del Monte's new book, PLONK GOES THE WEASEL, about a small town that gets even."

VALLEY LIFE

"I loved this author's idea of a small town of people who plan to get revenge because they feel used by a film company."

THE MIDWEST BOOK REVIEW

CRITICAL ACCLAIMS for JOAN DEL MONTE

DEATH HAD A YELLOW THUMB

"The centuries-old saffron mystique is a terrific device for a mystery—"

-The Literary Guild

"Joan Del Monte's DEATH HAD A YELLOW THUMB is an engrossing, intelligent and informative mystery, chock-a-block full of colorful characters, unforeseen twists, and fascinating history. Fresh and invigorating as the sea breeze in its setting, San Pedro."

-James Cass Rogers, Author, Venice to Avalon

"Hands down, DEATH HAD A YELLOW THUMB is a good read. Seem s like Joan Del Monte just gets better with each book she writes."

-Nadine Wheeler, Author, Tennessee

"This author's mystery novel, DEATH HAD A YELLOW THUMB, adds spice, and turns her quest for saffron into fictional gold."

-The Daily Breeze

PLONK GOES THE WEASEL

"Revenge is the subject of Del Monte's new book, PLONK GOES THE WEASEL, about a small town that gets even."

-Valley Life

"I loved this author's idea of a small town of people who plan to get revenge because they feel used by a film company."

-The Midwest Book Review

Also by Joan Del Monte

▼

Plonk Goes The Weasel
Death Had A Yellow Thumb

MUD BLOOD

Murder In The Sacramento Delta

A Novel

Joan Del Monte

iUniverse, Inc.
New York Bloomington

MUD BLOOD

Murder In The Sacramento Delta

iUniverse books may be ordered through booksellers or by contacting:

iUniverse
1663 Liberty Drive
Bloomington, IN 47403
www.iuniverse.com
1-800-Authors (1-800-288-4677)

ISBN: 978-0-595-48194-1 (pbk)
ISBN: 978-0-595-48925-1(cloth)
ISBN: 978-0-595-60288-9 (ebk)

Printed in the United States of America

Cover Design
By
Gene Cartwright

iUniverse rev. date 11/05/08

For Bob

PROLOGUE

The Sacramento Delta, California

1920

People are funny. They love a good fight. Years later Delta people were still talking about Billy Sun's fight with the fire chief.

The story went round that the fire that burned Isleton's Chinatown in 1920 started in the kitchen of Billy Sun's restaurant on the bank of the Sacramento River, because everybody knew Billy brought in illegals from his home in the Chinese province of Guangdong to work in his restaurant kitchen.

Billy was a prosperous man, a hard little man, who stood five feet four inches, his gestures quick and direct. Billy adopted an amenable nature. "You learn to move with the river current," he often said, "or you fall down and drown in the mud."

In the Delta in June, the tule fog hangs low, different from other fogs; it hugs the ground in streamers of white, and forms a barrier that blocks one's vision. People in the midst of a tule fog think the entire area is socked in, because they can't see their hands in front of their faces.

The day of the fire, it was hard to see what really happened. People whispered that Harold Ah Tye, angry about a gambling debt, threw a lump of lard on the hissing deep fryer next to his rival, Jum Gai, intending to frighten him. But the fat spattered on the dry wooden wall behind the stove.

A tired old man in a dirty white apron and grease-caked shoes was sitting in the corner near the stove. He saw the fire and yelled. Somebody threw water on the fire, which made it worse, and the restaurant went up in flames.

Shortly thereafter, the Isleton fire crew swung in, pulling a brightly polished wheeled water pumper. They started to unroll a hose.

"We need to pump water from the river," Billy shouted, running up the street. "I'll speak to the men."

Lifting his ham sized hands, the fire chief said, "Now, just hang on a minute. Any words to be had will be had by me. This is my fire department. I'm chief here."

"The fire's moving fast," Billy insisted.

He broke free of hands restraining him and tried to drag up the equipment. More Chinese arrived. Flames snatched the gold-painted roof braces and caught the underside of the roof, sparks flew in the air; then Billy's storage building located next door caught fire, and next was the big asparagus sheds lining the Sacramento River. The dry wooden shingles from the buildings curled, split, and began to fly in the air and drop on the surface of the river.

"I'm the person says if we stop a fire," the chief said. "That's my job."

"What are you going to do?" Billy asked. "Are you going to just stand there?"

"I'll tell you what I'm not going to do, is send in a volunteer fireman," said the chief, "put a man's life in danger, and have the building collapse on him."

Several volunteer firemen left the pumper and gathered round. So did some Chinese. They sensed an argument and they didn't want to miss a single word.

"Billy," the chief said, reaching down to put his hands on Billy's shoulders, "now you know there's nothing much we can do when these old rickety wooden buildings start burning. And if we use the new pumper, all that junk floating on the river, it will jam up the equipment."

"You've got the equipment! Hook it up!" Billy said.

"*Public* equipment!" the chief said, jabbing a finger at Billy.

"There could be people inside those buildings," Billy said.

"Now, Billy, nobody's inside."

"How would you know?" Billy asked. "You don't see them, right? They're Chinese."

"Well, I didn't sit and count them, but they scattered like roaches," said the fire chief. "You know this fire is your fault, bringing in all these men, guys who got problems with immigration. God knows what these people do. So you watch your manners." The fire chief gave Billy a look of concentrated malevolence. "You want taking down a peg or two, you people. Some folks in town think too many of your kind are moving in right now."

"I can't believe you're going to stand here—" Billy said.

"We can't help you here. We're leaving," the chief said.

He circled his hand above his head for his men to follow him. The firemen looked at each other. Then they pulled the pumper up the street, away from the fire.

The Chinese came out of the warrens of the poor, where the air was thick with the smell of latrines, incense, wok cooking, and the copper stills in which they made their gin. They tried to save their tiny businesses. They stood on the levee road, gasped in the acrid air, and passed buckets of water. Harold Ah Tye ran with buckets of water from the river until he fell gasping in an exhausted heap in the middle of Main Street. They stood and watched the buildings burn to the ground.

That night Billy Sun decided the Chinese needed to establish their own town.

At that point, because of the harsh Alien Land Law of 1913, which prevented immigrant Chinese from owning land in California, the Chinese could only lease the land. The California Legislature didn't get rid of the Alien Land Law until 1952.

Billy Sun chose Swan's Landing, a few miles south, named for the cranes that wintered in the Sacramento Valley. The non-English-speaking Chinese called the town "Swanee." Because the land flooded easily, the landowner leased them the town cheap.

Billy built levees, just like the ones the Chinese were familiar with from Guangdong. He set up a rotation of men. The work required the men to work in waist-deep water, with river currents and parasites. They slowly built up a ring of protection for Swanee. Then they planted pear orchards and asparagus.

Billy Sun wanted a written lease showing their rights to Swanee. He drew up a one-hundred-year lease that included a right of renewal. The document was executed and notarized. There were two copies of the lease; Billy Sun had one copy, and the landowner had the other.

The sand and stone levees worked. They held back the river for five decades, through the end of Prohibition and the Great Depression, through World War II, until the devastating Andrus Island flood in June 1972. The Andrus Island flood howled into the Delta from the North Pacific, made waves twenty-five feet high in the shallow sloughs, released three inches of rain an hour, and dumped a roaring, unstoppable wall of water on the Delta.

The buildings of Swanee withstood the flood, but people had to chop their way out of their roofs. Main Street in Swanee was flooded, and Billy Sun's copy of the lease was washed away and lost.

Which led to murder.

CHAPTER ONE

Venice Beach, California

2007

Oliver told me Fulton was peculiar when he first suggested we collaborate on a novel, but it wasn't until four o'clock in the afternoon on a hot Thursday back in mid-April that we both realized just how peculiar.

"I got this crazy call from Fulton on my service this morning," Oliver barked on the phone.

"Thank God," I said. "Where the hell is he?"

"That's just it," Oliver said, "he said he realized he was causing us trouble and he was sorry, but things had gotten so complicated with his life that he was going to have to go away."

"Away? What away? We're in the middle of writing a novel!"

"Did you talk to him today?" Oliver's voice was strained.

"I've been calling him for two days."

"Vera, there's a kill date of June 1 on this book offer," said Oliver.

"He's gone? Really gone?"

"What about his office? You never went to his office?"

"A big law office?" I replied. "We couldn't write there. The phone was forever ringing. We worked on the novel here at my house. If I got an idea, I left him a message on his voice mail over where he lives, with Florence."

"Vera," said Oliver, "if you don't finish this book quick, you'll get a big $2,000 kill fee instead of the book contract."

"Don't start," I said. "It was your idea I should collaborate with Fulton on a mystery novel. You wouldn't take no for an answer."

"And I'll get 10 per cent, $200. That's for eight months of work," said Oliver.

I hate it when he's right.

"What about Richard Spain?" I turned the visor around on my head. "You said he introduced you to Fulton. Maybe he knows where Fulton is."

"Christ, I hate to start up with Richard," Oliver said. "He calls me three times a day with what he thinks is some brilliant writing idea. His editor, Nancy Branscomb, she won't even return my phone calls. His writing isn't bad. It's sort of marginal, but I only took him on because I wanted to get Fulton and get into his files. You've got to find Fulton."

"Oh, come on. What the hell am I supposed to do? Print up a flyer: 'Missing, one male collaborator, Fulton Yee, Asian, five foot six inches, one hundred fifty-five pounds, balding, lawyer—'"

"Asian-American," corrected Oliver.

"Oliver, political correctness is a form of racism. See, the connotation is that you're superior and you have to shelter the poor slobs. Fulton preferred Asian. He always said that only the media, academics, or the politically correct use 'Asian-American.' Why speak a mouthful when one word will do?"

"Vera, this is your idea of a time for a smart remark?"

I switched the phone to my left shoulder. "Why would he have to go away?" I asked.

"There was the business about the rape tape," Oliver's voice lowered.

"What rape tape?"

"I don't know if I should discuss it on the phone. You never know—"

"Fine, don't discuss it," I said. "You don't like my flyer idea for finding Fulton, you find him." I slammed down the phone.

One thing about Oliver: he's polite but pushy, which is what makes him a good literary agent.

The phone rang again. After the second ring, I picked it up.

"I'm on my way over," he said.

He hung up before I could say no.

I was thinking hard. I would have to be very careful. When he had first suggested it, Oliver had loved this idea of collaborating with Fulton. Now I had the feeling he was going to try to offload the mess on me.

I peeled off a sweaty T-shirt that said "Venice Marina Christmas Run, a Holiday Tradition" and took off my cropped running pants and stood barefoot in my panties in front of my bi-fold closet doors. My toes were on the level with a pile of shoes, none of which I wanted to wear. I exhaled a vexed sigh. A dust bunny rose, a metaphor for the state of my closet. I had built a wardrobe that featured velvet and chicken feathers. I wondered how I got all these ill-matched clothes.

Easy, I thought. I hate being in a department store.

I did love to scavenge in thrift shops, pouncing on blouses and long skirts that catch my eye. I'm a sucker for vintage, and the occasional small bit of damage didn't bother me. I always feel more comfortable in clothes that are slightly worn, because I don't have to worry about staining or damaging them. When my closet gets too full, I recycle cartons of stuff back to the thrift shop. The truth is, I no longer dress as I used to when I worked in the outside world. The old sartorial care has left. But Oliver was a literary agent, and he dressed beautifully. He took me more seriously if I dressed in business clothes rather than my usual sweats. He probably didn't realize it, but he did react to what I was wearing. Now I needed to dress for some clout.

I own a simple black jacket without shoulder pads and one pair of black wool pants, with a faint pinstripe. The waistband still fits, which pleases me. I'd dress my feet in trouser stockings and oxfords.

I ran a wet comb through my hair and looked in a mirror. My hair is still thick and vigorous. The occasional gray strand is subtly dyed away. When I was younger, I didn't take much trouble with my looks, and it would be silly to start now, so I don't do much more than lipstick. I don't consider myself to be pretty, but I do have strong features. Some men respond to my looks, although not Oliver, of course. I work at keeping my body fit. I live in Venice, California, which is a good place to keep fit. There's a bike path, a running path, and on the canal, twelve feet outside my kitchen door, is my rowboat.

Eight months ago Oliver said, "I love your work. You've got a deft hand with the dialog. But frankly, hon, your structure sucks. Look, let me put you together with somebody for structure."

I'd had a modest success with the three mysteries I'd published—no bestsellers, mind, but each novel sold respectably more than the last. My name was above the title now, and people were coming up to me at book signings and saying they had read one of my books. I was what publishers call a "mid-list writer." That's not a compliment.

"Oliver, you know how I work. I work alone." I said.

"I got this criminal lawyer with a file cabinet full of gnarly crimes. Real gut stuff. He wants to write. He gave me a little taste of some of the stuff out of his files; I tell you, it's just terrific ideas. I loved them. Guy plays chess, very structured; he outlines everything, then outlines each chapter. I think it could be a blockbuster."

"So go tell him to write a novel," I said. "Sounds like he'd drive me crazy."

"Well, because he can't write worth a damn, Vera. That happens sometimes."

"Oliver—"

"Once, don't argue with me! Try it, just try it. I think it would be a growth experience."

My first mistake was not taping that conversation. Because now I had the distinct feeling Oliver had forgotten it, and the whole collaboration idea was suddenly going to be mine.

Oliver swung his Lexus into the parking pad of the house next door, slammed the car door, and trotted around the corner of my Venice Canals cottage.

"It's not my fault," he said.

"Right. It's my fault."

That's another thing with Oliver. When there's a problem, he first has to spend forty-five minutes explaining why it's not his fault before he'll do anything about it. So now I say it's my fault. That shortcuts the process.

Oliver Handlery was the Handlery of Mason and Handlery Literary Agency of West Los Angeles, California, but I never knew a

Mason and don't know if there ever was one. To his friends he's Ollie. I call him Oliver, and we're comfortable with that.

Oliver is the only man I know who wears a vest in Los Angeles. I always figured that's because he wanted to look literary when calling on publishers. The vest today was gray wool, accompanied by a light blue windowpane checked shirt and a dark blue tie. His rectangular, tanned face was the shape and color of a brown paper bag. He wore rimless glasses over alert brown eyes. His blond hair was tightly curled, and he stood about five foot nine inches and weighed a well-packed one hundred seventy pounds. His clothes looked crisp, even in the heat, and his body was West Coast fit rather than East Coast squishy. He wears a college ring but I could never remember the college, some small college on the California Central Coast. He has his pants made especially for him by a tailor, to show off his waist. He has the waistline of a twenty-five year old, which is pretty good since he's thirty-five, which he keeps reminding me is five years younger than I'll be next May 27.

The big four zero. Oh, God.

"Duck shit! Damn it," he said, scraping the side of a polished cordovan on the cement. "I don't know why you put up with it. I brought a release." He took a folded form out of his briefcase. "You're going to have to get Fulton to sign off the book. He's on the book offer; so there are copyright issues."

"Are you listening to me?" I asked. "Fulton is gone. I called his office, and the clerical staff is stonewalling me. Florence, the woman he lives with—"

"Yeah, that Florence," he said, jabbing a finger, "Call her again right away."

"She says he left in the middle of dinner four days ago. He walked out, and she hasn't seen him since. Says he went out at night a lot; it was part of being a criminal lawyer. And he told her specifically never to call the cops."

"Jesus, it's hot for April. You know, you could offer me something cold to drink," Oliver remarked.

Especially living where I did, I should know something about agents. Neighborhoods don't seem to stand still in Southern California. They improve or deteriorate. Venice was a community gone "affluhip," filling up with the creative rich. That included agents, writers, directors, and their entire cutting-edge group.

I like where I live, and that hasn't changed over the years: a beach bungalow on one of the canals. The house was my settlement from a divorce fifteen years ago. At the time it was nothing special, and my ex husband remarked to a friend that he thanked God I never had any business sense, because he got off cheap. But the value of the house had gone up exponentially in the crazy Southern California real estate market. I took pleasure picturing his anguish as he contemplated my growing equity.

It's my lair, my hiding place. I defend the space fiercely, even from the occasional male who drifts through my life. Having no house payments allows me to live the life of a freelance writer. I'm not doing the happy homemaker model, feathering the nest for a prospective mate. Virginia Woolf was right; I need a room of my own. I'm an independent woman, which means lonely.

Actually I need a whole house of my own. For reasons I don't understand, my muse comes to me at four a.m. This means I have to get up, put on a robe, turn on every light in the house, walk to my office, boot up the computer, and write down the idea. The idea has to be shot on the wing, because let me tell you, in the morning it's gone, exactly like a dream, where you remember a snatch of the dream or that you've had a dream, but not the dream. All in all, it's best I live alone. I like the idea that I have my own house. I think the concept of home profoundly matters to me and to all women; I have that room of my own.

My house is one of the larger beach bungalows, 700 square feet, built around 1910. The canal front door opens to a central living area. The walls are bead-board. A counter separates the dining area from the kitchen. A hallway leads to my bedroom and a bath and a small second bedroom.

The setting sun glinted off the canal surface, casting the line of houses across the canal into a reflected black silhouette. Oliver walked out on the wooden deck and sagged in an aluminum chair. I reached in the fridge of the four foot square kitchen and got him a Corona, a lime, and a paper napkin.

He tilted the bottle, took a long swallow, and then patted his fingertips together. He said, "Vera, let's be reasonable."

"That's exactly what you said when you came up with this collaboration idea."

"Did you and Fulton have some kind of goddamn fight? I hate to say it, but you have a fast lip, Vera."

"And remember, you brought him here. To my house."

"I only met him the one time, at lunch with Richard Spain," he said, "the day I brought him here."

"We weren't friends, just collaborators. He told me once he was sorry, but he wasn't any good at being friends. Said the criminal courts are not an environment where friendship flourishes. He said the life he lived stressed speed, competition and duplicity."

"You worked with the guy eight months. You must have some idea what the hell is going on."

"I found something out," I said. "Working with a collaborator is very peculiar, because the two of you are talking to each other about characters that are only in your two brains. So you're mingling a stream of ideas from two brains. It's sort of a mental joining. Like sex."

"Oh, Jesus, you didn't—"

"No, no, I didn't," I said. "I'm just telling you the way we worked. He told me the plot was all important; it had to fit perfectly. He said any drone could do the actual writing."

"He actually said that?" Oliver paused, the beer halfway up. "To you? No wonder he disappeared."

"And that was one of our better days," I said. "We'd be sitting at the table having a normal conversation, and suddenly he'd start asking questions, you know, lawyer questions. When he'd meet people here at my house."

"Well, he was a criminal lawyer—"

"Lots of people in Venice get nervous, you ask that kind of question. I started warning people when he'd be here."

My hip kinked. When I get stressed, there's this muscle in my butt located below my right hip bone that kinks and I start walking like Quasimodo.

"I called Richard Spain after I talked to you." Oliver's said. His eyes slid sideways. "Spain said shit may be coming down on Fulton; maybe that's why he disappeared."

"What's that supposed to mean?"

Oliver suddenly became very interested in the mist on his Corona bottle. He said, "See, Fulton was defending a guy accused of rape. Tried to rape some old lady, eighty or something. The police taped her testimony. But everybody in the neighborhood knew this old lady. She dyed her hair jet black, and she wore big hats and pants that were bright yellow and pink. She still drove, and she raised plants in her backyard to sell at the neighborhood weekly farmer's market."

"What has all that got to do with anything?"

"She was crying a lot, on the tape," said Oliver. "Said when she woke up the guy was standing by her bed. He was masturbating, with his pants down, and demanding oral sex. He was on something, sort of weaving around and cursing her. But she looked at him and realized he wasn't armed. And uh, she grabbed his penis, twisted and yanked, and held on with one hand. She grabbed his testicles with the other hand. He hit her. But still holding on, she got him to the porch, where he stepped out of his pants, and lost his footing. Then he got up and ran."

"Sounds like some feisty old lady."

"Anyway, he got away, but the police found his name in a wallet in his pants. They found him in severe pain at home."

"I'm glad to hear it," I said.

"And Fulton defended this guy," He said 'my client regrets his actions. He has no permanent damage, but he was in severe pain for days. He's already been punished.'"

"Oliver, what has this got to do with Fulton disappearing?"

"The tape was the main evidence in the trial. So naturally Fulton had a copy." Oliver said, setting down the Corona.

I picked some flaking brown paint off the doorjamb. I had a bad feeling about this conversation.

Oliver cleared his throat and continued, "So, a couple of months ago, there was this convention of defense attorneys, up in Sacramento. They have a young lawyer division. Some of the young guys had this party at night, you know, skits and stuff, raunchy stuff they make up about the judges. They put in raunchy stuff in general, I guess. And they put in other sexy stuff they come up with."

I didn't say anything.

"Fulton took the tape," said Oliver. "He played it at the party."

"He played it?"

"He meant it to be a joke," said Oliver. "I mean, Fulton thought it was a funny scene. Just picture it, some old lady's house, that's probably all dark and with doilies on the dresser; imagine all this stuff about the guy standing by her bed with his pants down, jerking off."

The phone rang.

"Yes," I barked into the receiver.

"I lost my sweater," my mother's voice was the voice of doom.

"Mom, I'm talking to my agent—"

"The pink one," she said. "My favorite."

"Did you ask Mrs. Caspia, the neighbor who looks in on you? You just had it yesterday," I said.

"No, I did *not* ask Mrs. Caspia. She's busy."

"Mom, I pay her—"

"She has her own family to take care of. The way my family should be taking care of me," my mother said pointedly.

"I'll be over," I said. "Later, I swear. But I can't talk now."

"I'm never going out," she said. "I'm never leaving the apartment again." She hung up.

"What's going on with your mother?" Oliver asked.

"She's in her seventies and starting to forget things. Right now I'm trying to figure out what to do about her and that scares the hell out of me. I don't want to think about it. I don't want to talk about it. Let's get back to Fulton."

"Somebody turned him in," said Oliver. "The Bar Association is investigating. But the old lady—the rape attempt did something to her mind. She's in a rest home now. Afraid to live alone anymore."

I stalked inside. Oliver followed. I replaced the phone in my second bedroom. This tiny second bedroom was the center of my existence, just large enough for my desk with my printer and an L-shaped return for my MAC computer. One wall held a bookshelf made of boards and concrete blocks, the bottom shelf overflowing with news clippings organized in a system that, if I'd tried to explain it, could probably have got me committed. The other wall held a large bulletin board crusted with index cards which I rearranged to construct the book I was working on. Index cards in my handwriting and Fulton's handwriting spilled out of the bulletin board and were scotch taped across the wall, like an addled snake.

I had perfected a skid in a wheeled stenographers chair across the board floor of the room from the computer to the reference books and back to the computer without getting up. I did the skid now. I booted up the computer.

"Look, I didn't know any of this before today," Oliver said, retreating three steps back to the kitchen where he put the empty beer bottle on the plastic drain board, "and I swear, Spain just told me. But I still don't think Fulton would split. I mean, he apologized. He told them he didn't intend to offend anybody. Don't you think he'd duke it out with the Bar Association?"

"I keep telling you," I said, "I don't know what he'd do. We just worked on the book. He did the structure, I did the writing. But he'd only give me the story three chapters at a time, as he worked out the outline."

"Vera, the publisher—" started Oliver. "You know, Fulton got that advance on the book by working directly through a friend of his, this Nancy Branscomb, the editor. They're old buddies from way back in college. I didn't sell the book. I read the contracts, of course, but only to protect you."

"Oliver—"

"The thing is, he told the publisher the book was finished. And now the publisher wants it delivered."

I looked at him evenly and said, "There's a problem."

"What?"

"The way he insisted we work," I said. "He insisted we shouldn't judge the characters before we got them down on paper. He kept talking about how we'd lose the quirks that happen with real people. They'd be cardboard."

"All right, Vera, so you adjust."

"Listen. Are you listening?" I asked. "The working arrangement was he'd give me the outline by sections only as we went along and then we'd argue. I told him that was a crazy way to work, but with Fulton you worked his way or no way."

"Okay, so then finish the novel using the outline—" said Oliver.

"He was fixated that I'd work better if he didn't tell me who the murderer was." I said.

Oliver was hyperventilating. He unbuttoned his vest.

He said, "I'm not hearing this. Please, please, you're not telling me you're almost through writing a murder mystery and you, the author, don't know who the murderer is? Is such a thing possible?"

"So now we're almost through the book and he disappears," I said. "And I can't afford to waste these eight months, Oliver. There's no way I can lose that kind of money."

"You've got a character in this book who is killing people. Fulton must have dropped clues—"

"That's part of the trouble. There are too many clues in this book."

"Vera, I'm sure if you had to wing it, you could," Oliver said.

"And show how the murderer trips himself up?" I asked. "That's the part that was in Fulton's head."

"Hey, Vera!" My neighbor, Sammy Chang, yelled over the wooden fence. "Somebody's Lexus is in my parking pad."

"Mine," Oliver said. "I had to park someplace."

"So I don't have the plot," I said.

"Well, for Christ's sake, did Fulton take it from one of his files?"

"He never said. It could have been from one of his files or a couple of files he put together. He could have been making up the book up as he went along. And believe me, I asked."

Oliver wiped his forehead with the napkin. His face was now bright red and suddenly dripping sweat.

He asked, "Vera, do you realize what you've done? This is a small business. Everybody knows what goes down." His hands were pivoting in the air like windmills. "I can't afford to piss off this publisher. You can't either."

"The Lexus! Move it, fella!" Sammy said, coming around the fence. "You're blocking my driveway."

Sammy was medium sized and medium everything with brown hair fading to gray, chinos and a T-shirt. The gap between his front teeth which dentists call a median diastema made his frequent grin infectious. But he was not grinning at the moment.

"A minute. I'm leaving in a minute," Oliver said. "There was nowhere to park when I came."

'You gotta move right now," Sammy said. "I teach my class in wok cooking tonight and I have to go set up."

"Wok cooking," Oliver said, rolling his eyes. "Obviously, the world would come to an end if we held up a class in wok cooking."

"It's very popular," Sammy said. "I call the course Wok Pan Sam. I have to limit it to twenty students, so many want to register."

"And another thing—" Oliver said. He reached for his keys and then swiveled back to me.

"For God's sake, there's more?" I said.

Sammy jabbed his right forefinger in the direction of Oliver's face. He said, "The other thing is, don't park in my space. My driveway is not for your convenience. Glad I don't have to wear one of those suits any more." Sammy nodded at Oliver's suit.

"The release—" Oliver said. He dashed for the porch and picked up the folded document from the table and returned. "The manuscript has both your names on it. They're not going to stand for that if Fulton's not around. He has to sign off the book. This is a lawyer, remember."

"You keep saying that," I said, "like a record. How the hell can I get him to sign off if I can't find him?"

"You have to find somebody?" Sammy's eyes swiveled from me to Oliver.

"You told me once you were a tracker," Oliver said.

"What?" I dropped into a chair.

"You told me once there are basically two types of writers. One is a researcher who knows what he's looking for, and then it's a matter of finding it and organizing it. The other is a tracker. He has an idea or suspects something. Then he tracks through the records picking up on stuff. It's serendipity. You said you were a tracker. The joy was, suddenly finding something."

"Oliver, for God's sake, that meant tracking information, not finding a lost criminal lawyer who doesn't want to be found!"

"That place I teach," Sammy said, walking back around the fence, "The Learning Warehouse? They teach a course in finding people, using public records. I met the detective who teaches it. He sounds like he knows what he's talking about."

"I can stall for another month, max; maybe stretch it to near the kill date, June 1," Oliver said, "And to do that I have to be in my office when they call."

Oliver followed Sammy.

"You have two choices." Oliver said. "You can blacken your name with me and with your publisher. Then forget about publishing any book in the future." He got in his car. "Or you can find Fulton. And find out why he disappeared. And find out who the hell is the murderer in your novel."

CHAPTER TWO

San Fernando Valley, Los Angeles, California

April 18, 2007

Sammy Chang was right about one thing—in Los Angeles you can take a seminar on how to do anything.

Given the Southern California fixation on self improvement, local universities had discovered their adult education divisions were cash cows. The key was to teach what people wanted to learn, without any hassles, no pre-registration, and no requirements. Now, private enterprises were offering more off-beat seminars. One of their seminar catalogs could provide an alien with a quick insight into the hot topics of the moment.

The Learning Warehouse produced a slick catalog in four colors on newspaper stock, with photographs of the teachers; and a compendium of courses for the upwardly mobile or the would-be self improver. The catalog was distributed free through vending stands at bus stops.

I had started taking buses into Westwood for my weekly office visits with Oliver. Parking in Westwood was now an outrageous twelve dollars. The catalog passed the time. The bus rider could spend his trip reading glowing descriptions of one day seminars in subjects such as "Making Your Home into a Bed and Breakfast;" or "Gourmet

Cooking." There was also a course called "Releasing Your Sexual Fantasies." I observed an illustration of a woman in high-heeled boots and black tights holding a whip. The subtitle read, "Erotic role playing in safety and privacy."

I couldn't resist poring over these courses, maybe as a contrast to my straight Catholic education. I generally had a copy in my canvas tote bag. In the Learning Warehouse's catalog I found the course Sammy told me about. "The Do It Yourself Private Eye" was taught at a detective agency that called itself "Bogie's Buddies," in North Hollywood in the San Fernando Valley. The course was offered Friday morning, April 18.

"In this class from an experienced private detective, you'll learn how to find people quickly, using public records," the blurb trumpeted. "Or," the suggestion was left evasive, "you can use that nosy eye to find out anything about anybody."

The detective agency had a large sign. Located on Magnolia Boulevard, the building was in a commercial area of North Hollywood that was rapidly turning Latino. Corrugated metal buildings marched to the sidewalk, with concertina razor wire perched right above the fences around their parking lots. The only trees in sight were two long-trunked palms. The bottom halves of their leaf balls were brown. The sound of salsa music came out of the open doorway of a discoteca, which was next door to two used bookstores left over from former days. A handmade sign on the door of one of the bookstores read, "All Packages Must Be Checked, No Exceptions."

Bogie's Buddies was a surprise. It didn't look at all like a detective agency out of a mystery movie. There were no battered desks, no frosted glass doors, no fedora hanging on a hook. Behind an expensive glass door framed in birch, the reception room was large and posh, maybe thirty feet by twenty feet. Painted in various shades of tan, it was filled with burgundy velour banquette sofas with throw pillows. Tables in front of the couches held magazines. Everything was curved, including the two walls, room dividers, the fronts of the banquettes, and the glass-topped tables.

The room was an elegant fit for the agency name, which recalled the 1950s and Humphrey Bogart. Two pretty girls sat behind the curved reception desk. Vague elevator music played softly in the background.

The whole effect was meant to soothe. The class waited for the teacher. I noticed the other students, including several retired people, a hefty young woman in a flowery polyester dress, and a muscular young man in Levis and ankle-high work boots. His sunburn was peeling, and his blond hair was tied in a bun. A contractor, maybe.

Fred Atkins, the experienced private detective named in the catalog, was tall and bony. He looked to be forty-five. He looked like he had been colored with a tan crayon, with his tan hair, tan moustache, and tan suit. I glanced at his shoes as he ushered a motley class of about twenty people upstairs to a large meeting room. Tan shoes.

"Right now I'm spending my time building a data base for the agency," the teacher waved toward a computer terminal sitting on top of a desk along one wall, next to a lectern. We selected folding chairs. "We have the best data base in Los Angeles. The Sheriff's Office, when they can't find somebody, they ask us to run the guy for them. Because even if you try, you can't live in our society without leaving a paper trail."

The meeting room, including the walls and floor, was all muted grays, and had a bank of double hung fixed windows and fluorescent lights over several gray metallic folding tables that sat six people each. So the whole room sort of glowed, no shadows. The room smelled of lemon carpet cleaner.

Fred stretched. Actually he unfolded and sat on the computer desk.

"Even if you try to change your name," he said. "Say you want to have the utilities put on because you rent another place under your new name. You give your real social security number or driver's license number. And then I've got you right there."

"For asset searches," he said, tapping the keyboard, "some companies only do them. They're under 'data information' in the yellow pages, but we wanted our own asset database. For liability trials. Well, there's no point suing somebody if you can't find any money." He laughed heartily. His teeth were tan.

"Let's introduce ourselves," he said, "Tell me why you're taking the class."

The group of students around the metal tables shuffled nervously, and moved their chairs. They didn't like that idea. The ratio of women to men was two-to-one. Farther down my table the hefty young woman in the flowery dress crossed her legs, her chair askew to the table. She flicked her right shoe on and off; showing the black leather of her high heel was scratched through to the white plastic base.

Several cool heads were able to avert panic.

"General information," they said when it came to their turn. After that everybody dutifully echoed "General information."

Fred said, "You want to locate a lover, an ex-spouse owes you support, a tenant ripped you off, or whatever, you have to find out about him."

He then distributed a handout, a booklet titled "Locating Methods," which was actually several pages stapled together.

"I can tell you that a prerequisite for finding somebody is a set of jumper cables and a good street guide," Fred said. "You're not going to get far if you're following somebody and you can't get your car started." He threw back his head and laughed heartily. "Most of the public record locations you'll want are on the downtown map page in the Thomas Guide. But some were moved to Norwalk."

He loped around the table, giving out yet another handout, titled "Find That Missing Person: A Step-By-Step Strategy."

The students turned to each other. To the right of me I could hear the muscular young contractor jiggling his work boots under the table. His rough hands were quietly clasped on the table like a child at school. His chapped lips formed a tight line. If this guy wanted to find you, you'd do well not to be found.

"What if they catch you?" said flowery dress, waving a hand.

"It's legal to snoop as long as you don't take money for it," Fred said. He returned to the lectern. "Once you find the sucker, it's easy to hide a video camera in something like a notebook. Preserve him for posterity, whatever he's doing."

"That's gotta be illegal—" the contractor said.

"It's legal as long as there's no audio." Fred said. "I've got a camera on now."

Pandemonium erupted.

"Wait a minute, I don't want pictures of me taking this course!" Flowery dress snapped her shoe back on her foot. She was about to bolt.

"Just for my records," Fred said soothingly, "to prove I didn't teach you anything illegal. Remember you can't represent yourself as law enforcement, so kill them with kindness. You ask."

"Ask who—" the woman with the flowery dress asked.

"Anybody you can find, Fred said. "Call the neighbors. Go see them. Most people can't keep their mouths shut if you ask them and then listen attentively. Nobody ever listens to anybody these days. So stand around. Look admiring. You won't believe how much info the good citizens will lay on you."

"A neighbor wouldn't know about his assets," the contractor said.

"Steal his garbage," Fred said. "That's legal. Look for credit card slips and receipts."

"How can you steal his garbage if you can't find him?" The contractor asked, unfolding his hands.

"That's why we're here. Remember professional associations," Fred continued. "Lots of people keep up state licenses; say they have a real estate license. Out here that's half the state."

"I just want them to pay their utilities." A small man across from me said. He was tightly flexed. His darting eyes displayed the nervous intuitiveness of a lemur. "Every time I foreclose on a house, the tenants haven't paid their utilities. Sometimes it's been six months. And the Department of Water and Power tries to force me to pay before they'll them back on."

The woman with the flowery dress tossed her head and shot him an irate look. She said, "Sometimes people just don't have the money."

"The clerks at Water and Power won't look in their computers and see that I pay my bills on time," the landlord said. "Oh no, that would be too much trouble for our civil servants. They make me bring them a copy of the deed to the house."

"Well, they have to know who you are," said the woman with the flowery dress.

"But some tenant, they just let him turn on the utilities," said the landlord. "They get real good, these deadbeats. They know all the laws to offload their obligations. They think they should be entitled."

"What makes you so big that you get to hound people for their old electric bills?" the young woman snapped.

"What about paying people?" the contractor asked. "To find somebody."

"For under thirty dollars you can find almost anybody, and think what you've learned about them," Fred said.

"I just thought, if I ever get engaged," the young woman said, twirling a strand of hair around her fingers, "so I'd want to know about the guy."

The landlord smirked and rolled his eyes.

"We investigate a lot of that, potential spouses," Fred said. The room was charged, like an electrical force field. "One couple, he hired us to investigate her, and we never told him she had already hired us to investigate him! I tell you, I love L.A.!" Fred hugged himself and laughed. His shoulders moved easily under his jacket.

"So then I can pay somebody," the contractor said.

"A whole cottage industry out there sells information, and it's just stuff they find in the public records," said Fred. "Deep Throat was right: 'Follow the money.'"

"Yeah, Deep Throat," said the landlord, his mouth twisting. "He turned out to be a toady who violated his government oath out of malice and spite. A sneak, not the great whistle blower. Another loser looking for his fifteen minutes of fame."

"If you're fast on your feet and good at it, you can make yourself fifty thousand a year as a process server." Fred said.

"Fifty thousand?" the contractor sat up straighter. "Process servers make fifty thousand a year?"

"I said good ones," Fred said, leaning back. "Let me tell you about an absolutely gorgeous process server I got working for me now. Real bright lady. One of our clients had a rug biz, and we couldn't serve the debtor who had ripped him off and not paid for the rugs. We tried for weeks, with regular process servers. Nothing. The debtor had a history of doing this. He was savvy.

"So my process server says, 'If I serve him, will you put rugs in my house besides paying my fee?' And the rug people said, 'You got it.'"

Fred continued, "You know what she did? She stopped her car in the middle of the street outside his house one night and knocked on the door. All teary, she said to the wife, 'Can I look at your phone book? I need to call a friend to come get me.'"

The contractor shifted his weight.

Fred said, "So then the wife lets her in and she says, 'My God, what a gorgeous place. Who was your decorator?' And the wife gets about three inches taller and said, 'I did it myself. This way for the phone.' And they come to the den and there was this man. And the wife said, 'This is my husband.' And my process server says, 'Well, here's your summons!' She hands it to him and runs for the door!"

"She got away?" I asked.

"Sure. She has what I call emotional intelligence," Fred said. "Being emotionally savvy is critical. It's as important as being blessed with a high IQ. You have to sharpen your feel for how your mannerisms affect others. And this process server acts confident."

"What," I said, "if you have nobody to ask about the person?"

"Find somebody," said Fred. "Who lived near him? Who lived with him? Get hold of a crisscross telephone directory, which Hanes publishes every year. Look in the big libraries. Look up the addresses next door to the last address of the person you're tracing. Give the neighbors a call. They sometimes keep in touch. Have they noticed anything? When did they see him last? Have they met any of his friends?"

A sweaty woman in a dark wool dress had been frantically taking notes. She took off her glasses and waved them for attention. She asked, "But would the neighbors tell you?"

Fred had been waiting for that.

"Well …" he said, hooking his elbows on the back of his chair and stretching his neck.

Somewhere in the back of my brain I noted the way he moved, as if all the disparate sections of him were knitted.

He continued, "I said it was illegal to say you were law enforcement. It's not illegal to say you want to buy his car and you said you'd get back to him. Now you've decided and you can't find his number. But don't stay around too long. Too much time allows the source to think and begin asking questions. Keep it fast. Then get going."

Uproar ensued. Hands waved with questions. The class was fascinated with searching, this bizarre new skill.

"Voter registration lists," Fred continued, "are public information. See who went with him when he voted."

The sweaty woman went back to writing.

"My favorite technique," Fred said, brushing his moustache with his forefinger, "is to say you used to work with him—the guy you're tracing— and now you're applying for a job and you can't remember your old supervisor's name to put on the application. You just need to contact your former co-worker. Ask if the neighbor would, by any chance have the phone number. I guarantee that one works almost every time."

The young woman was shocked. The sweaty woman, however, scratched a note.

The contractor muttered, "I'll never answer another phone question."

"Now a real good one," Fred said, "if you have his old address, try the local post office. Is his mail being forwarded? Submit a Freedom of Information Act request for the forwarding address. They've got to keep it for a year. Even better, if he was living with a woman, is her mail being forwarded? Lots of times he might not want to be found, but she figures nobody will check her. So she wants her mail from her auntie in Des Moines."

"Good," the sweaty woman said. She wrote so fast that she tore her paper with her pen. "You've had it, you prick! Rock bottom pond scum!"

The contractor jumped.

"Not you," she said.

But I knew this wasn't going to find Fulton if he didn't want to be found. Fulton wouldn't be stupid enough to leave a forwarding address.

"If he lives in a small town, you can call the tax assessor and ask if he owns any property," said Fred. "In L.A. they won't do it over the phone, but you can go down and look at the records."

"Tax assessor," the sweaty woman said. She was still tearing her notebook page with her pen point.

"Finally, you want to go down to the DMV," Fred said. "Look at his driving record. That's publicly accessible for insurance companies through an Automated Name Index, or an ANI. Make up an insurance business card, which is easy. And about these business cards; one of my best investigators keeps a portable printing press in his car, to crank them out. He just plugs it into the cigarette lighter, and makes a card for an insurance investigator, a building inspector, or whatever fits with his situation, and he's good to go. I'll tell you, I can give somebody a business card, whatever it says I am, he'll believe. I'm amazed at the authority a business card carries."

"You can get DMV information?" the contractor asked.

"It's not as easy as it used to be," said Fred. "The DMV tightened up after that actress got stalked. It'd be great to get his car registration, so it's worth a try. If you know where he parks for work, copy his plates. Registration might have an address. If he uses a post office box, get the information on the box. See if somebody else is on the box with him."

"You can find out who owns a post box?" the contractor asked as if he couldn't believe what he was hearing.

"Easy." Fred hardly bothered with the question. "Costs a dollar. The post office has a regular form. If he does business from the box, post office has to release the name. That's the law. So get any flyer, type his box number on it. Now say he's doing business from the box. If there's another person on the box, start checking his information, address, whatever. Maybe that's where your guy is holed up."

Uproar ensued again. The contractor folded his arms across his chest. He was looking more and more unhappy.

"Don't forget what I told you about filing the form asking the postmaster of the last address you have for the target whether he's left a mail forwarding address. Enclose a self-addressed stamped envelope," Fred said. "That's easy. That information is handy if someone is writing 'not here,' on envelopes when he's actually getting mail at the new address."

There was a stunned silence.

"I look for customer lists of their favorite magazines." Fred said, lolling his head. "You wouldn't believe how many deadbeat dads I've found just because *Sports Illustrated* sells lists of its customers and the wife tells me the guy waits for his copy every month."

"So he sends in a change of address for his magazine?" The landlord asked.

Fred circled the room. "Of course, if you're going put in some time on it, an official certificate of every birth, death, marriage and divorce should be on file in the locality where the event occurred. In

California, the vital statistics section of the state registrar has records starting in July 1905. Not on computer, of course. You have to dig."

Fred was right. I wasn't a detective. I was just me, a middle-aged writer. I was no more equipped to pick my way through these opaque civic records than I was to comprehend a computer manual, and I certainly couldn't fathom those. But I was determined to find out what happened to Fulton. I decided that single-mindedness would make me a formidable researcher.

"Look," I interrupted, "That'll take too long. I don't need so much economic stuff. I need to find the name of a murderer."

"What?" Fred asked.

"No, I mean in a book. I have to find somebody I'm writing a book with, about a murderer. This lawyer, Fulton Yee. I have to find him now. Fast," I said.

"Fulton Yee," he said.

"Right."

There was a collective intake of breath at my broaching this paragon, a popeyed interest from the other students at my embarrassing haste. Their ears reached for the details.

"Fast? Then you got a problem," Fred said. He hooked his leg on a chair and straddled it. He seemed to be able to fold like a jackknife. "You want to hire me to find him?"

"I want to see what I can do first," I said.

"Try on your own for a week," said Fred. "Then I'll check on you, see how you're doing. He was living with a woman?"

"She says she doesn't know where he is."

"The woman?" Fred said, chewing his moustache. "You might have to lean on her a little bit. Act sympathetic. Maybe she's pissed off. Doesn't like the way she's been treated, or the way she comes off looking. I'd start with her."

CHAPTER THREE

Crenshaw District, Los Angeles, California

April 22, 2007

"I knew you'd wind up coming over here, because on the phone you sounded like a pushy bitch." Florence Loring said. Her long pointy fingernails were enameled blue. She fanned them out so they wouldn't chip as she used the palm of her hand to unhook the burglar chain on the heavy oak door to let me in.

It was April 22. I did what Fred told me. I called Florence, the woman Fulton lived with, every day after I took the class at Bogie's Buddies. I wanted to try to get her to agree to see me. Finally I just decided the hell with it and showed up at her door.

The day was sunny, which is unusual for Los Angeles. Usually, April is gray. The beach areas get covered with fog and people yawn all the time because the leaden skies make them sleepy. The miniature pink Spanish haciendas that fill the city suddenly look like they're trying too hard. This was the fifth year of the Southern California drought, however, and the sun was shining that late Tuesday afternoon.

"I know you're angry," I said soothingly. "But I have to find Fulton, and I do have to talk to you."

Florence was a small Asian woman in her forties. Her shiny black hair was clipped short in the back and beautifully styled in a varnished swoop over her left eyebrow. Even at six o'clock at night, her makeup was immaculate. She wore a loose blue pants suit with a red silk scoop blouse and low heeled black kid pumps. She wore rings and a gold and jade bracelet. I was wearing jeans.

She remained in the entrance, not leading me anywhere. I walked past her and turned left on the dark oak floor, moving into a living room. A large arched window overlooked the street.

The single family houses on Santa Anita Avenue in the Crenshaw area of Los Angeles were fighting a losing battle against rows of intruding apartment houses. This block had only two small apartment houses but it still preserved several of its trees on the sidewalk. The arched front window was a thick, solid pane extending almost from the ceiling to about four feet above the floor. Measuring five or six feet wide, the window gave an unfettered view out in front of the house. As I looked to the left, I could see the lights of the small stores and a video rental shop nestled at the end of the block. Security bars laced the other windows.

The living room had a flat screen TV and a few pieces of furniture. It looked as if the residents were only camping out there. The room smelled of Carnauba wax on the polished oak floor. At the end of the living room, a wide archway led to the dining room. A bi-fold standing screen blocked part of the opening. A neat stack of empty carton boxes was next to it. Beyond the dining room, I could see the kitchen and a small service porch.

"Look, I need to find Fulton," I said.

"I told you on the phone, first I don't know where he is, and second, it's not my problem."

"All I want him to do is sign off this damn novel," I said.

"Which is not my problem either," Florence answered.

"How about his family?"

"I don't know them." Florence said. "He grew up in the Sacramento Delta. Maybe his parents are still there, but I never met them. He's working on something about the Delta now. Maybe it's for his family. I think you should go bug them."

"Something about the Sacramento Delta?"

"Yeah, he had stuff he was looking into in the Delta. But I don't want to talk about it. It's a Chinese thing. The Delta stuff has nothing to do with your book."

"Florence, you've been living together for months. You must have some idea—"

Florence closed her eyes in exhaustion and said, "You want to know how it was? I'm a real estate agent. Sometimes I buy a little house like this one and live in it and then flip it. So I picked this one up about a year ago, and Fulton didn't have a place to live right then, so I figured I could let him move in with me. He made me laugh. It was a temporary arrangement. Temporary is what I want."

"You don't have to tell me all this—"

"Because I've had it with permanent," Florence said. "I was married for years, and my ex-husband expected me to line up his shoes in the closet with their laces tied in perfect bows. One day I filled my car with all those damn shoes and dumped them at a charity. That was the end of that marriage. Now if a man turns out to be crazy, I throw him out and get somebody new."

Florence dropped into a low, overstuffed sofa covered in green velvet. She kicked off her shoes and put her feet on the coffee table.

"I'm wasted," she said. "The real estate market is down." She picked the *L.A. Times* off the table, glanced at the front page, and dropped it. "I don't know why I look at this newspaper," she said. "Not a damn thing in it doesn't make me mad. You see this picture on the front page of the old guy in a wheelchair? Somebody abandoned him at one of the pagodas in Venice Beach last month. They're trying to find out who he is."

"Look, Florence, right now I'm trying to arrange things for my mother," I said, "and she's old and sick; she forgets things, and that newspaper story horrifies me."

"It horrifies everybody. That's why it's on the front page."

"Nobody wants that old man—"

"Before my parents died a couple of years ago," Florence said, "I'd come home from work and my father would be waiting to tell me my mother's toes had turned black from her bad circulation. My boyfriend would be waiting to tell me his car had broken down again. The dog was jumping up and down because nobody had walked her all day.

And I used to feel like just turning around in the door and leaving. Never thought being alone without any family would have advantages, but it does now. I don't have to take care of some old person. I left and got educated at Long Beach State. Thanks, State of California."

"But a lot of people want to find Fulton," I said.

"No, you mean you want to find Fulton," she said.

She seemed to feed off the idea. She wanted to wax fat and act spiteful because of my need, but she'd never have been honest enough to say so. "Look, real estate gets pretty intense in a down market," she continued. "I needed somebody to make a joke, have dinner with me, maybe bounce me in a bed. But I'm not his nurse."

"What about his clients?"

She got up and strode to the folding screen in the archway between the living room and the dining room. She pushed it aside with a quick jab of her left elbow. She pointed at a desk and a phone lined up behind the screen, against the wall. She walked over and picked up a telephone message book.

"His office keeps calling here every damn day, yelling at me that people were left waiting in court without a lawyer. 'Where is he?' they ask. First three days I wrote all the calls down. Then I gave up."

"Could I take a look at the messages? I might find them useful." I said.

"Look, I'm trying to be helpful," she said, "but I'm exhausted." She handed me the message book. She walked back and collapsed again into the sofa. "I'm not looking for a job as his unpaid message service. And if I want people yelling, all I have to do is mention rent control at my office."

"You mind if I take his phone message book?" I asked, thumbing the narrow spiral book. The cover said "Carbonless Telephone Memo Record." It showed a photo of a telephone receiver and a phone memo message blank.

"Fine with me," she said. "Less for me to throw out."

"People don't just vanish. Not people with lives." I said.

"Well," she said, massaging the balls of her feet, "I can tell you that Fulton was tired. Said he wanted to stop representing small-time criminals."

"He wanted to quit law?"

"Said he was tired of families bringing in their wedding rings to pay his fee," she said. "And then he got mad when that kid showed up here the other night."

"Wait a minute," I said. "What kid?"

"Not a kid, really. A pudgy white guy in his twenties or so. Showed up here right in the middle of dinner. I make pork chops, I get the inch-thick chops and have them sliced and stuffed with bread crumbs and grated cheese. I cook them in wine. So Fulton didn't get to eat, and I didn't appreciate having that dinner ruined."

"Florence, the kid. What happened?"

"He was really yelling, very intense. Fulton went outside to talk to him on the sidewalk. After a few minutes I went up front, because the chops were getting cold." Clearly, the ruined chops were the focus of this conversation. "I saw through the front window that they were arguing, with their arms waving and all. And Fulton was shaking his head, to tell him 'no.'"

She tugged each toe and moved it in a circle. Then she massaged her arches again with her thumbs. She said, "And then Fulton said he had to go out. That was the last I ever saw of him."

"It doesn't make sense," I said, "to think he was thinking of quitting the law to write a novel."

"A novel never struck me as a thing he'd be doing. And about a week ago he suddenly started talking crazy, about chess." Florence said. Then she leaned back and closed her eyes.

"Chess?" I asked.

"Yeah, over and over. Something about playing a game of conspiracy chess. Whatever piece you're using has to be of equal or greater power than the other guy, because if you use a pawn to block a queen you're fucked."

"What?" I asked. This conversation was from a loony bin.

"You got me," Florence said. "I never played chess, but Fulton did. I play solitaire on the computer, is all."

"I've got eight months worth of work into a book. I'm going to lose it if I can't find him to sign off so I can finish it." I said.

"He had other things were important to him. Fulton was researching the history of the Chinese in the Delta. This guy named George Maxwell, a real racist bastard, wrote a bunch of stuff against the

Chinese in California back in the 1920s. So I thought Fulton would be writing an article about that, not a novel. I wondered if you two were just having it off." Florence said, looking at me sideways.

"He never seemed to need any extra in that department."

She turned to me and said, "He had me. Maybe he had a thing with that high ass editor, Nancy Branscomb. Now you. For your sake, let's hope the third time's the charm."

"Fulton and I weren't involved sexually."

"Doesn't really matter to me." She said, waving away my comment as if I were a bothersome gnat. "You want some white wine? Because I need some."

She rose and rummaged in the kitchen for a glass. She then poured. "Not cold." She said, shrugging. "I never have time to organize stuff in this house."

"Without him the novel seems stopped." I said. "Maybe it's me. It was his story. Maybe it was from his files. Could I take a look at the files he had here?"

"No, you certainly cannot," said Florence. "Those are legal files and I'm not going to get sued because you went through somebody's file. Those files are going to be dumped right back at his office. I'm tired and I'm going to bed early tonight. Fulton told me you two had a couple of real fights about how the writing was going. So you had your say. You weren't just sweetness."

"He kept trying things different ways," I said. "Then he'd want scenes taken out. Said every scene had to move the story forward. But some of my best scenes got thrown out. Gorgeous stuff. But Fulton insisted a vibrant scene was just a matter of rewriting."

"Sounds right to me."

"That was because he didn't have to do it," I said. "When he tried writing, his scenes came out dead. That happens with some people. But I don't know who's the murderer in my book. Maybe he was right about the structure being the most important part of the novel."

"You never did understand about Fulton, did you?" asked Florence.

"Understand what?"

"Let me tell you. Maybe you'll understand. I go on caravans for realtors. We see maybe fifteen houses for sale. One morning a week they take us around in a bus to look inside the houses that just came on the market."

"And?"

"It feels strange going through somebody's house when they're not there," said Florence. "You see pictures of the family, and the kids swimming trophies. You see their bathroom and kitchen. They sometimes got stuff set out on the kitchen counter defrosting for dinner."

"Florence, is there a point? What has this got to do with Fulton?"

"With him, I always got the feeling that everything looks fine, but there's nobody home. Like the houses on the caravan."

"Florence, the kid, the one came here. You know his name?"

"Couldn't hear what they were saying," Florence said, shaking her head.

"All right, then, I'm going to take this," I said, putting the phone log in my purse.

"Why not?" she said, waving a hand. "Go now. I'm going to box up all that loose paperwork. Then I'll put it all in the files that are going back to his office. This place is sold."

"Right." I said, standing up.

"I sold this place at an open house," said Florence. "Sundays are real estate open houses. But you've really got to keep an eye open at an open house. People pick up stuff. I went to look at some new models for a tract out in Simi Valley. All the decorator objects were glued down. The napkins were glued to the napkin holders. Oreo cookies were in a big glass jar in the kitchen. But the top was glued on. Just goes to show you."

"Florence, you check the police and hospitals?"

"You know they'd wanted me to file a missing persons report," said Florence. "You do that and they call you to come down and look every time they find some goddamn half-eaten body."

The deep left-hand drawer of the desk held suspended files. I wondered if one of them was the plot. I was going to make another plea for a look at the files but there didn't seem any point. I had lost her attention.

"That's enough, I want you to leave now," Florence said from the living room. "Look, a real estate agent has to size up people quick. Otherwise you waste all your time with flakes. So I'm pretty good at it. Fulton—he didn't seem like a person who'd spend time writing a novel. Of course, he didn't seem like a person who'd disappear either."

Florence didn't get off the sofa as I walked back through the living room and opened the front door.

"Florence," I said, "we're two women. You can tell me if something went wrong between you two. Something that would make him take off without telling anybody."

"Hey," she said, waving her wine glass, "The dude walked out on me, remember?"

"That's what I mean."

"If anybody's got explanations coming when you find that sucker," she said, "I figure it's me."

CHAPTER FOUR

Civic Center, Los Angeles, California

April 23, 2007

I picked out my one black suit, which had been left over from my married days. I put on my oxfords. I stopped in front of my closet's sliding mirrored door, then picked a silk charmeuse blouse. I loved that blouse, with its soft creamy color and a V-neck and full sleeves and small buttons that went from the elbow to the wrist. I considered a small hat, but decided that would be overkill. Instead, I got out a black leather attaché case. All this power dressing was for clout in attacking the civic workers in the warren of offices downtown. They behave differently if they're not sure who you might be.

The suit jacket restricted my movements. I wished I was in the soft flannel of my sweats. The first thing every morning I run three miles. I work at it, fighting gravity. I sometimes run the 180 steps that switchback up from Santa Monica Canyon to Adelaide Avenue in Santa Monica, moving through hillsides of wildflowers. From Adelaide I could look across the canyon to the ocean and fill my throat with sea air.

I theorized that exercise brought oxygen to my brain so I could write better. Somebody had told me that wasn't true. But when I slacked off exercise for a month, my writing would suddenly stop as my body descended into a pear shape. My computer screen would sit, white, mute, reproachful.

It was Wednesday, April 23. My time was going fast. For breakfast, I settled for an orange and a piece of string cheese. I threw the orange peel toward a paper bag full of garbage and missed, knocking it over. I started to pick it up, but then thought about getting stains on the suit.

Tonight, I promised myself. God, if my mother came over, she'd be complaining, on and on.

As if on cue, the phone rang. "I got lost," I heard my mother's voice, with barely controlled hysteria. "I walked to the Vons Supermarket and I got on the wrong block somehow coming back. I forgot how to get back."

"Mom, you didn't forget. You're back, right?" I said.

"And I was crying," she said. She started crying again.

"Okay, you went out," I said. "You got lost. You got upset. You found your way back to the apartment. That's happened before. If you can get rid of the part about getting upset, it's no problem."

"Vera, what's happening to me?" She asked, blowing her nose.

"Mom, if worst comes to worst, call a cab. Give him the paper with the address. It's right next to the twenty dollars I put in your wallet. You still have the twenty dollars in your wallet?"

"Yes," she said. "I don't know what to do."

"I'll be over later." I said and hung up.

I sagged and looked at the living room. It was a room where I could relax. There was a sofa in a neutral tan canvas and one large painting of a woman. The brightness of the air around the woman was suggested by stripes of color reflected from her dress. Other than my book jackets, there wasn't much more color in the room. It didn't feel like a hard day if I knew I could be in this room. There wasn't any TV. No magazines. It was just quiet. I could not have my mother invade my house. I could not!

Once I was in the car with my seat belt fastened, I still felt the vague sense of uneasiness that had been with me since I woke up. It just kept gnawing at me.

As I got on the freeway, the car radio station called the layered gray sky "early morning coastal fog", except that it wasn't coastal. The gray stretched inland to downtown Los Angeles, and it wasn't morning; it was getting toward noon. These clouds looked like they would last all day. Finally, it wasn't fog. It was smaze or haze or some kind of fiendish combination of opaque particles and wet air. I looked at the sky and hallucinated. I peeled back a patch of the gray to get at the blue sky I knew was up there, as if I could implore the rain to clean up the sky.

I punched a different radio station.

"—Los Angeles Police Department has set up a hotline," the announcer recited, "as a massive effort continues to identify the elderly man abandoned last month near a pagoda at Venice Beach—"

I turned up the volume. The pagodas were a few blocks from my house.

"—with a bag of adult diapers and a note saying he was an eighty-four-year-old Alzheimer's patient named Joseph. The note also said he was incontinent and required twenty-four hour care."

I didn't want to hear it. It reminded me of the decision I dreaded making about my mother. My mother hadn't been tested, but I suspected she had the beginning stages of Alzheimer's disease. Her frequent memory failures frightened her. They frightened me.

"Support groups for Alzheimer's patients from all over the country have poured in funds," the announcer concluded.

Would I ever be able to just leave my mother some place like that? Guilt swept over me at the thought. It was intense enough so the orange I had for breakfast repeated on me and I could taste orange again. She was a seventy-two year old widow who was fading. She had taken care of my grandmother after my grandmother's stroke. The grandmother I looked like. And a gaggle of my cousins had taken care of their mothers, putting on a happy face and burying their fierce resentment. They gave up their lives for the duration of their mothers' illnesses. She would expect me to do the same.

I punched another station. The radio extensively described the traffic on all the freeways I was not on. It didn't mention the Santa Monica Freeway, which I *was* on, and which was so backed up that the man in the next car was reading the *L.A. Times* sports section, propped up on his steering wheel.

From the freeway the few tall buildings of downtown Los Angeles huddled against each other in a comitatus relationship. Their backs were in a tight circle, as if they feared an attack from the surrounding two-story warehouses. I parked my car in a lot where I could pay by sticking dollar bills in slots in a series of metal boxes.

I noticed a cluster of large handwritten notes scotch taped to the dashboard of the sedan parked next to me. Curious, I read through the passenger side window. One note listed the name and phone of St. John's Hospital. One note listed Farmers Car Insurance and a phone number. One showed Amoco Gas and a sketch of an intersection. I walked around the rear of the car. The rear bumper had a sticker saying "Sexy Senior Citizen." The keys to the car dangled, forgotten, from the trunk lock.

Jesus, I thought. Aging and forgetting.

I walked toward the Civic Center and skimmed my notes from the course. I take great notes. I once supported myself in college by selling class notes.

The county maintains its records in a maze of rooms off marble corridors of a soaring height calculated to inspire awe in the citizen. Because the ceiling lights are thirty feet off the ground and the County economizes by using forty-watt light bulbs, people grope their way up the halls, grasping any passerby for direction. I kept my eyes down to avoid encouraging anyone with a baffled expression.

I first went to the County Assessor's Office, to see if Fulton's full name was on the title of the house on Santa Anita Avenue. Fred said he needed Fulton's full name, including his middle initial, to run him through the data banks at the detective agency. The tax records showed an acquisition date from a year ago and title held by Florence M. Loring, an unmarried woman. There was an address for tax bills on the site.

Damn! Florence had told me the truth.

The next stop was the County Registrar of Voters. There had been a city council election last year. Fulton liked insider gossip about the city council. It was a good bet that he voted. The room was downstairs. It had a musty basement smell.

"Go to the voter information list," Fred's handout said. "You want an index number for his last name. You'll get a microfiche with fifty names. Then you get a copy of what he filled out when he registered to vote."

Fulton's affidavit showed the Santa Anita address and "S" as his middle initial. I'd never heard him mention it. First piece of hard information I'd found, and I felt a surge of triumph. I wrote it carefully down on a yellow lined notepad. This was nitpicking work, but I enjoyed it. Fred said to look for other addresses, but I couldn't find any.

I pulled out Fred's handout and read, "An official certificate of every birth will be on file in the locality of birth. Write, giving full name of person, sex, birth date, and fee." I looked up California Vital Statistics Section, at 410 "N" Street, Sacramento. The fee for a birth certificate was eleven dollars.

What would that get me? It would show his parents. Would his parents be alive? Would he be with them?

Fred's handout was firm, "Most information given to you may sound immaterial. But little bits of trivial information, which are usually overlooked, can make the search a successful one."

He hadn't said anything about wearing comfortable shoes, and my feet were beginning to hurt. I looked for the code to see how recent the voter affidavit was. It was from a little over a year ago. I took down the document number. Then I pulled the affidavits before and after Fulton's file. Fred was strong on this. Somebody could have been with him.

The next name after Fulton's was Emma Sawtooth. I dutifully wrote down Emma Sawtooth and decided I'd take a chance calling her. But I'd first have to see if she was listed in the phone book. Which is not as easy as it sounds. Everybody in the courthouse carries a cell phone, and it was hard to find a working pay phone. I don't have a cell phone, but when I was there on jury duty a year ago I found one phone most people didn't know about. It was downstairs in the basement in a dark corner.

I lucked out. She answered on the first ring.

"I need to talk to Emma Sawtooth." I said

"This is Emma."

"I want to ask you about Fulton Yee."

"Why? And just who might you be?" She did not sound friendly.

"My name is Vera Moonachie and I was collaborating with Fulton on a mystery novel. Now I need to find him."

"Oh yeah, he told me about you," she said. "Good luck looking, I have to tell you. He never had a talent for being where he was supposed to be. Sucker made a life style of keeping me waiting in various places."

"We were collaborating on a novel." I repeated.

"You're lucky you caught me home," Emma said. "I work at a newspaper during the afternoons. I'm on my way out the door to work. Fulton and I don't see each other much any more. Ever since I told him to take his rape tape and bend over and insert it."

"Yeah, I heard about the rape tape," I said.

"That damn tape was the last straw," she said. "We hadn't been getting along. He needs a doormat. He only showed up when he wanted something from me. He'd ask to borrow my car and ask to use my writers group to bounce off ideas for his novel. He was a user. Did you try Florence?"

"She says she hasn't seen him." I said.

"You believe her?" Emma snorted.

"You think she's hiding him?" I asked.

"You know about her, right?" Emma said. "She's the broker at that real estate office the *L.A. Times* investigated about a year ago. They were running a scam. They'd lend money to homeowners down in South Central. Tell them the papers were just a formality. Well, what the old people were signing was a second trust deed on their homes. Florence ended up owning the house. She wound up in criminal court. That's how she met Fulton. He defended her. So, do I think she could be hiding him and lying about it? Yeah, I do."

"Could I come over and talk to you?" I asked.

"No, I just told you that I'm leaving for work right now. Didn't you hear? And my house is hard to find. I live in one of the canyons. But I run a writers group at the Ocean Beach branch library that meets Tuesday nights at seven o'clock. You should come. Fulton used to come. Maybe he'll show up. Other people in the group knew him, so you might pick up some information. You're welcome to come next Tuesday."

It was now two o'clock in the afternoon. Not having more breakfast was a mistake. I was starving. I was also getting a headache. So I went to the Vietnamese duck leg soup place, near the Civic Center, for hot soup and comfort.

Los Angeles is rumored not to have ethnic neighborhoods, but you could trace the waves of immigrants in the restaurants surrounding Civic Center, from the earliest Mexican places on Olvera Street to the Vietnamese restaurants now pushing the older Chinese restaurants out into Monterey Park.

I got tapped for jury duty a year ago. Since I was pissed off at the jury duty, I comforted myself by eating at every ethnic restaurant in the Civic Center area that looked interesting. I promise you, I could write a guide.

The Vietnamese duck leg soup place was on a side street. The front counter featured roasting pans full of dark glazed meat and chickens. Behind the counter were large open windows that provided a view into the kitchen. I could smell the pungent broth all the way out on the sidewalk.

A family operated this place. As teenagers shouted orders through the open window, men in the kitchen moved around each other, leaning and swooping with a ballet like grace in the narrow space. One would lift a mound of noodles out of a boiling vat and drop it in a large bowl. Another would top it with a roasted duck leg. At a separate counter a man dismembered cooked ducks with a cleaver, using what looked like a tree trunk section as a cutting board.

At large round tables with Lazy Susans in the center, patrons ate their food while keeping an eye on the action in the kitchen. Maybe they were watching for the inevitable collision, someday, of the cooks.

A candle burned before a red shrine in one corner of the dining room. A huge gilded screen of children wearing Chinese clothes while playing around a rolling food brazier covered another wall. Six dollars at this place buys a bowl of noodles the size of a washbasin, topped with the duck leg.

Each table had a little glass jelly jar filled with oil and red pepper flakes. I tried a spoonful from that jelly jar. Once.

I ate the soup and chewed at the duck leg bones. I felt a lot better after eating. I took Fulton's telephone memo book out of my purse. It was the kind of log with four phone memo blanks and a yellow duplicate to each page. It was almost full of messages. The most recent calls should have been at the end.

Three of the blanks on the last page had names with days and times of calling. I saw Emma Sawtooth, and Nancy Branscomb. Clarita Valdez was the last call.

I knew about Emma and Nancy. But who the hell was Clarita Valdez?

CHAPTER FIVE

Century City, Los Angeles, California

April 24, 2007

I hate people who are paid to smile.

The publishing company where Nancy Branscomb worked had a discreet name, archangel press, all lower case, one inch high, stenciled on a perfectly balanced glass door. A young receptionist wearing a black and white checked suit with a short skirt beamed another smile at me. She scrubbed a tissue at a speck on her desk, a slab of glass that matched the door.

It was Thursday, April 24. The waiting room had black leather couches. Before I sat down, I knew I'd be sticking to them after five minutes. Here I was, sticking to one now after an hour. I was on my second Coke from the vending machine near the ladies room in the hallway.

"I've been waiting for over an hour," I said.

"I'm so sorry," she replied. She flashed a well-practiced, brilliant smile. "This is an exceptionally busy time."

"No," I said. "That's not really the problem at all. Obviously, your job is to make her time more valuable. Keeping people waiting is a psychological ploy to enhance the value of the person people are waiting to see."

"That's funny," she said. "I mean, is that a joke?"

"No," I said. "In Beckett's play, *Waiting for Godot*, for example, we assume Godot's has high status because people are waiting for him."

"I don't think we have a Mr. Godot," the receptionist replied. Her eyes narrowed as if she were trying to recall. "But I could look on the organizational chart."

"Give me an index card." I said.

The smile widened, apparently because she finally had something to do she could handle.

"And a magic marker," I said.

I wrote down in block letters, "FULTON YEE."

"Take this to Nancy Branscomb," I instructed her.

She gave me a tiny frown. "Ms. Branscomb is still in conference."

"Do it," I said, shaking the coke and slapping my hand on the spotless glass slab. "Or I'm going to explode this coke all over your desk."

"You wouldn't—" she said, pushing back.

"You'll be sticking to the glass for three months," I threatened.

She backed away, keeping her eyes on me, reaching for the wall behind her. Then she turned and bolted down the hall leading to the private offices.

"Fulton?" Nancy Branscomb said, coming out of her office.

A tall blond man in matched denim and inlaid cowboy boots followed her. He looked ready to audition to play Kit Carson.

"Not Fulton," I answered, unsticking myself from the chair. "It's *about* Fulton."

"Oh," she said.

She looked around for help but the receptionist had retreated to the ladies room.

She waved me toward her office. The man trailed her back in. He was a real heartthrob. Over six feet tall, he was just beginning to put on some weight, a little pot under his breastbone. His hands and wrists were large. He had a good straight nose, but under it his blond moustache drooped in a scowl. His eyebrows were also blond and bushy. They looked like two more little moustaches.

A trophy man, I thought. The kind of man a woman could show off. Just that little, very little, touch of rough. To keep it interesting.

"You look familiar," I said.

"I'm Richard Spain," he said. He pulled a chair closer to Nancy, ignoring me. "We met once at Oliver Handlery's office. The agent."

Nancy Branscomb was in her late thirties. She was tall and tan. Her dark blue suit said couture and hung loosely from her body, as if she were very fit. She wore a bright yellow silk scarf under her chin. Her hair was dark and shiny and had been cut to swing by the side of her face. She wore the kind of gold jewelry you inherit.

"Vera Moonachie," I said, and offering my hand.

She made no effort to take it, so I sat in the one remaining chair in front of her desk that wasn't covered with manuscripts.

"Look, I really don't have much time to talk," Nancy said, "My fall book list is due May 6."

Nancy's office was all business, with pale green walls and furniture with hard edges. A computer was on her desk. Two black leather side chairs were available for sitting. Two walls of her small office displayed colorful framed book jackets. I noticed a small framed black and white photo of an old wood cabin.

But what really stopped me was what was on the floor behind her desk. It was a solid wall of manuscripts stacked one manuscript deep. Nearly six feet high, it reached from one side of the back wall across maybe ten feet to the opposite wall.

"I started stacking manuscripts six months ago," she said, following my glance. She revolved in her chair to face the manuscripts. "It was a joke, to see how high I could go. I think I'll reach the ceiling by the end of the year."

A solid wall of manuscripts. I noticed some of them were bound in black covers, while some of them were in the white cardboard boxes you get from printing places. Figuring a year's work for each manuscript, how many years were represented in Nancy's wall?

Well, you could find out, by counting one column and then multiplying by the number of columns.

"Odd name, Moonachie," Nancy said and swiveled back. "Oh, I know. You're working with Fulton. I read one of your books. Before you collaborated."

"I'm glad—"

"I didn't much care for it," she said. "You write in the first person, and I prefer third person. First person tempts the writer into too much autobiography; it's great for the writer working out issues, but unless you're Boswell, it becomes boring for the reader."

Jesus, I thought. I wasn't here for a literary discussion.

"And your writing is oddly dated," Nancy said and tilted in her chair. "For example, the term Asian American is preferred, rather than Chinese."

"Fulton was Chinese, and he said Chinese," I replied.

"Fulton has never been sensitive to acceptable language," she said.

"Nancy, you're just having a bad day." Spain said soothingly. "You say there are problems with my new book. But you know my writing grabbed you in the first book."

"You're right, Richard," Nancy said. She straightened her chair and turned to him. "The first book did it for me, all that psychological insight you had, the story twists, the humanity of your characters. But that sometimes happens with some writers. They say everything they have to say in one book. Then they have nothing more to say. You may be a one-shot-wonder. The lure could now be gone, and you've permanently blown it."

"This new book is high concept," he said, scooting his chair closer to her. "Just what everybody is looking for."

"In books we say, 'And then what?' And that's the problem. You have no narrative arc," she said.

"There may be some little problems—" said Spain.

"Richard, you're not hearing me," said Nancy. "You really are fixated on your own needs to the point where you don't accept incoming messages. No plot and too many clichés are not little problems. When I see them in a manuscript, it means I can weed that one out and go to the next."

It was strange that women like Nancy could gain the power they had over writers, could accumulate a wall of manuscripts for an in joke. They got the power because they wanted it so much. They were willing to work so hard. I looked at her tired eyes. And the whorls on the inside of her right thumb and index fingers were ingrained with print ink.

"Just tell me," I said. "You know where Fulton is?"

"I have no idea," Nancy said, shrugging.

"He's not at home," I said, "or at his office. Maybe we could go out for a hamburger or something—"

"I don't eat meat," she said. "I only eat one meal a day, and that's lunch. And I've already had it. Why would I know where Fulton is?"

"Do you know some of his friends?" I asked.

"Richard Spain," she said, nodding in the direction of the blond man. "Fulton defended a friend of Spain's, a real loser named Josh—Josh, what the hell was his name? Baggins, that was it. I keep thinking Bilbo Baggins, you know, like the Hobbit."

"Richard, do you know where Fulton is?" I turned to Spain.

"No, I don't. We're talking here, and I don't appreciate that you barged in by saying you were Fulton."

"Actually, we're finished," she said. "Yeah, Baggins." Nancy continued. "On drunk driving charges from an accident, a couple of years back."

"A real mess, too," Spain said. "Baggins swerved and hit a concrete divider and flipped onto the passenger side. I got hurt. The guy in the front passenger seat got killed in the accident. Fulton got Baggins off with community service."

"And you two became pretty thick?" I asked. "You and Fulton?"

"They became very thick." Nancy cut in. "And Fulton, poor scut, thought that was what friendship was."

I paused. "Are you saying these two were lovers?"

"What? Christ, no!" Spain said, exploding out of his chair.

"What did I say to give you that idea? Fulton is hetero. Well," she said, smiling. "I can verify that."

I looked at her and said, "I didn't know you two were intimate."

"Intimate?" she said mockingly, "I can tell from the word you're having trouble getting past the racial thing."

"It has nothing to do with racial differences. I'm just surprised he never mentioned it." I said.

"My father taught me to play chess and I was on the chess team at U.C. Davis. So was Fulton. We weren't close in college. We both spent a lot of time in the Sacramento Delta. My father had a fishing cabin on the Sacramento River there," she said, waving at the framed picture, "although our permanent home was in Hillsborough, of course. My family used it as a fishing shack. I've still got a cabin up there. In the Delta, Fulton and I moved in different circles, but we saw each other occasionally."

"Your father was a fisherman?" I asked.

"No, of course not," she said, frowning. "He was a business man. Before my father died, he and a man named Stix Chimineas were developing a huge project called The Docklands in the Delta. It was on the waterfront at Swan's Landing. My father used the fishing cabin to decompress. Actually, he started his own business in San Francisco, after his partners made him retire at sixty-five from the stock brokerage he started. He put up with retirement for about one month."

"So Fulton knew about the fishing cabin? Would he have gone there?" I asked.

"No, of course not. I told you that it was my father's place," Nancy said.

"Would your father have known where Fulton—"

"No," she said, staring down her nose at me. "I was supposed to join my father's business. He had it all set for me to go to Wharton. I was a cinch to get in because he was so active in the alumni group. But I got sidetracked into publishing. Nowhere near the money, of course."

"Your father built the cabin?" I asked.

"Actually, some writer built it years ago," Nancy said. "Dad had rented several places up there and bought it from him. He came back one time, the writer, wanted to see the place. He said he still loved the place. Long after we owned it. I was alone and had just taken a shower and was walking around in a towel. Thank God for the peephole in the door. I said, 'Can you remember a telephone number? Next time, call. All right?'"

"I know Fulton was talking to Florence about the Delta." I said.

"Fulton helped me out when I moved my stuff down here from the Bay Area a few years ago. One of my flights got cancelled. The moving truck filled with my stuff got here before me, and you have to meet the driver with a cashier's check. So Fulton was the only person I knew down here. I called him from the airport where I was stuck. He ran around and got a cashier's check so they could unload. I bought him dinner when I got here, and we just went on together for a while."

"You missed the moving truck with all your furniture?" My jaw dropped. "I'm too chicken. I'd have been here two days in advance. I wouldn't know what would happen to my stuff if I wasn't here."

"Well, things would have been all right," she reassembled her desktop. "They would have had to store the stuff until I could get here. But it was a lot easier with Fulton meeting them."

She leaned back in her chair.

That's what the rich have that I don't. They have the serene certainty that people will come forth to serve them. Nancy Branscomb had the ease that comes from growing up rich, the mask of patrician affluence. It never occurs to them to agonize over what people will think if they accept services, or if they'll be obligated to somebody, what. The free services are there for their acceptance. Of course.

I said, "I didn't know about your relationship, and he's been living with Florence."

"He just took up with her because he got in some stupid trouble with the Bar Association and he needed a place to live." Nancy said.

"Yeah, the rape tape. Oliver said shit was coming down on Fulton," I said.

I'd rocked her again. This was the way to do it with her—switch from one topic to another before she got two questions ahead.

She sat up in her chair and swiveled slightly.

She said, "That rape tape's a prime example of how far off base Fulton could be in his judgments of what was appropriate. He was either being a lawyer and asking rude questions—"

"Which is how he was with me," I added.

"—or he was accepting people completely," Nancy said. "There was no sort of middle ground."

"Nancy and I have to talk about my book now. We don't have any clue where Fulton is." Spain said. "You need to leave."

"He thought he was among friends at that lawyer convention dinner party, but he wasn't," Nancy said. "That's typical of his failings in judging friends. Somebody turned him in. And the problem with the Bar Association certainly could be a reason to disappear."

"You think?" I said.

"Well, Fulton apologized," Nancy said. "He wrote the Bar Association that he now felt his action was insensitive. While it may have been in bad taste, it was not a fit subject for regulatory oversight. The Bar Association disagreed. Then his office held up his money pending the Bar's investigation. That's how he wound up living with Florence."

"So you and Fulton—"

"We're just friends now. Anyway, neither of us has time to play chess anymore. And the sex is over. We sometimes get together, talk about what we're doing. That's if I have couple of hours free. But I haven't seen him lately," said Nancy.

"Funny, because Fulton told me he had no talent for friendship." I said.

"What Fulton doesn't have is an ability to keep friends in balance. Where do you think Fulton got the confidence about a year ago to actually write a book? I knew where that had come from." She nodded at Spain. "From Richard Spain. Spain thinks he's a major writer just because he published one book. He got Fulton to start churning his criminal case files for a mystery. Well, really, Fulton could never have thought of that to save his life. I'm looking at Spain's second book now, and it will never fly."

"Poor Oliver," I said.

She looked blank.

"Oliver Handlery," I added. "Our agent."

"Oh," she said. "Agents."

"You phoned Fulton. It was in his telephone log." I said.

"He called me about borrowing my car. I lent it to him, and he hasn't returned it. I can't believe he did that. It's really inconsiderate. That's why I've been calling him all week. I've got piles of work to do." She pulled a stack of glossy book covers toward her. "Your book has real problems, Richard."

His handsome face was sweating. He said, "But nothing you can't guide me through, sweetheart, right?"

"Richard, God knows I want a character with legs," said Nancy. "A repeat character or something we can put in a series, but this book is very different from your first. Now I need you both out of here. I'm working against a deadline for my book list, and I'm really out of time for this."

"And you called him at Florence's house because you knew he was living there," I said.

"Oh, her," she said, pushing away from her desk. "I mean honestly, a real estate agent. What did they have to talk about?"

"Real estate," Spain said.

"What?" Nancy asked.

"I heard Fulton ask her once to get him information on owners' records. He said he needed something from the County Recorder."

"Probably when he was defending her," she said. "You know she was brought up on charges of ripping off homeowners in South Central."

"I guess I'm the only person in Los Angeles who didn't know," I said.

I hate to feel out of the loop, but I'm not one of the crowd. No one told me anything. It goes with being alone, writing. I sit in a chair and look at my screen. I don't hear the poop.

"I don't think it was Florence's South Central case they were talking about," Spain said stubbornly, "because I heard him say something about the Delta."

"Whatever," she said. "Out."

Spain reached out his arms to give her a bear hug, but she waved her right hand, dismissing us.

"Anybody else you know I could ask where he is?" I asked.

"Try Emma Sawtooth." She said. She picked up a manuscript and put on her glasses.

"You think she'd know where he is?" I asked.

She shrugged and said, "He was humping her a while back."

"Have you seen her?" Spain said, wrinkling his nose. "She's thirty pounds overweight, and she refuses to shave anything. I can't deal with women who won't shave their legs. Send them in the woods and let the bears fuck them, is what I say. I guess she stopped being grateful for Fulton, because she threw him out, and he took up with Florence."

Still looking down at the pile, Nancy said, "Emma runs a writers group every Tuesday at the old Ocean Beach branch library. Spain and Josh Baggins go to the group. But it hasn't helped Spain's writing focus. You two can go together. Now, out!"

I passed the receptionist on the way out. She hunched her shoulders and kept one hand on the telephone until she saw me get in the elevator.

CHAPTER SIX

Ocean Beach, Los Angeles, California

April 29, 2007

The only good result of the five-year drought in Los Angeles was the twilights. At that time of day the glittering sidewalks caused the dust to rise above the city. It then mixed with the stale air that the air conditioners expelled and hung on the sky in a rose-colored wash. The city waited for the electric green streak over the ocean, which locals insisted preceded sunset. That streak was the subject of considerable dispute between those who insisted they had seen it and those who dismissed it as an urban myth.

It was twilight when I reached the Ocean Beach branch library on Tuesday, April 29. The library was located on the median strip of Venice Boulevard, which was currently being repaved over a layer of the vitreous china from broken toilet bowls. As part of a water conservation plan, Los Angeles mandates a massive toilet retrofit program. And 120,000 low-water-flow toilets have been installed in homes as a condition of sale. These toilets would use just one and a half gallons per flush instead of the conventional five gallons.

The vitreous china of the conventional five-gallon toilets is then broken into chunks and mixed with gravel to create roadbeds. Then all of it is paved over. Some future archeologist will come up with an imaginative theory about why Californians in the early twenty-first century broke their toilets to pieces with sledgehammers and used the pieces to make roads.

The Ocean Beach branch library was built in 1933. The high oak wainscoting and heavy wood doors were indicative of a less ecologically aware populace. One main beamed room contained an oval information desk. I could smell the dust, wood, and books. A spectacular large unused fireplace at one end of the room had a limestone mantel carved with a ship in full sail and the legend: "There is no frigate like a book to take us to lands away."

I grinned at the thought of the library commission's reaction these days to putting the word 'frigate' in a public building.

A small side room, called the Club Room, was used for public meetings. Emma Sawtooth had taped up a flyer with a computer-generated icon of an inkwell and quill and the words "Writers Group."

I glanced at the newspapers in the library rack while I waited for them to get started. The national papers had picked up the story of the Alzheimer patient as a human interest story.

"Robbed by Alzheimer's," the *New York Times* headline said, "A Man Is Cast Away."

The story reprinted the now famous photo of an elderly man smiling and wearing a baseball cap, seated in a wheelchair.

A babble rose from the Club Room, so I decided to enter. Chairs scraped as about twenty members of the Ocean Beach writers' group chatted, selected seats, and set out typed manuscript pages. The floors of the room were dark oak. All four walls were lined with oak book shelves. The room looked like the study in a fine old mansion. Richard Spain lolled in a chair on the opposite side of the table, holding a white canvas tote filled with pages. I took a seat at a heavy oak table.

Near me, a slender man with long supple fingers arranged index cards in uneven rows. He tried several chairs before settling. A fluorescent light fixture cast no shadows on the single long table.

"What's with the index cards?" I asked the slender man.

"I'm writing a cookbook," he said, waving at the cards. "I'm the chef at L'Escargot. But I'm not just putting in recipes. I'm putting in anecdotes about the famous chefs. I got a bachelor's degree in history at L.A. City College after I went back to culinary school, and I'm great on research. I'm writing the anecdotes in this class. I'm calling the book *You Must Be Joshing.* My name is Josh, so that's why I picked the name. Is that a great title or what?"

Looking closer, I could see he was in his thirties. He wasn't as young as I first thought. Standing about five-foot-five, he had a thin and muscular body. The deeply grooved puppet lines from his nostrils to his mouth saved his face from being pretty. His lips were thin, sharp, and nimble. He wore a black short sleeved T-shirt, black jeans and a single earring. His black hair had the kind of expensive haircut where the top is very long and curls behind his ears and looks ready to be cut again.

"I'm opening a new restaurant soon," Josh went on. "I want the book ready for the opening. Right now I have to carefully choose the anecdotes I want. It's like cooking. You have to choose exactly which ingredients to combine, and what does and doesn't work together. Then you have to pitch out the rest. You combine a lot of ingredients before a new recipe clicks. My way to be a chef is to want to be the best chef. It's not just giving 100 percent. You work until you reach your goal. I want the same with this book."

"Seems like a lot of cookbooks being published right now," I said. "Stiff competition."

"Well for a while, we had the dot com period," Josh said, waving his hands. "Money coming out of people's ears. Every chef thought he could write a cookbook. There were a lot of disorganized kitchens. I know because I worked in some of them. My kitchen is organized. I love the camaraderie, and the feeling when things are clicking and the crew is firing. It's like a jazz group making great music together just out of their heads, creating as they go along".

"You guys see this story on the old man who got abandoned? It's a good one for your clippings file," Emma Sawtooth said, holding up the newspaper.

Fulton's women didn't resemble each other. There was the athletic Nancy, the porcelain Florence, and now Emma. Emma was rotund, like a cloth covered haystack. Standing about five feet tall, she was bulked inside a serape. She wore the kind of clothing where everything tied with strings. She had dark supple skin, but her black hair, worn in a thick braid down her back, was beginning to be flecked with steel gray. Her deep gold-flecked eyes were amazing, large and liquid.

"Hi, I'm Vera Moonachie," I said, touching her arm. "I talked to you last week."

She carried three overstuffed canvas tote bags, and she rooted around in them as she spoke.

"Yeah, Fulton was collaborating with you."

"Collaborating? Must be strange to do that." A woman sitting next to Emma said. Her hair was tied in a greasy bandanna.

"Nancy Branscomb said you and Fulton were close." I said.

"Yeah, we played games a while," she said. She dumped one of the bags on the table in front of her. It flopped open: tissues, keys, newspaper clippings, and a paperback mystery fell on the table. "But he was a user. He had me do some of the rewrite on some scenes for your novel."

So *that's* why some of Fulton's scenes were a lot better than his usual writing, I thought.

"Have you heard from Fulton since I talked to you?" I asked.

"No," she said. "He called me a few weeks ago. Wanted to borrow my car. Said he had to drive up to the Delta. Said his old brown Mercedes might not make it. I told you, he only calls me when he needs something."

"You mean the Delta, south of Sacramento?" I asked.

"Yeah, he doesn't have any money now because of the Bar Association investigation. Anyway, I wouldn't lend the car to him. He borrowed Nancy Branscomb's car instead. She still doesn't have it back. That's where you probably need to go if you want to find Fulton. Go to Isleton in the Delta."

"Is Isleton where he grew up?" I asked.

"Somewhere near there," said Emma. "I don't know what he wanted up there. I'm getting worried about him. He's flaky about time."

"When I called, you were on your way to work," I said.

"I'm a copy editor for a newspaper," she said. "Goddamn sweathouse, that is. Do you know, we don't get a lunch hour? They tell you to take one, but you'll never be on deadline if you do. Miss deadline and you're out. Anyway, I had to check some facts with Fulton on one of his cases. That's how we got together. But he disappears."

"He does that," Richard Spain said, eager to get a word in. "Doesn't show up. Not even in court. No discipline. I'm an actor. One thing about acting; you learn to meet schedules."

"It's why we split up," Emma said, scratching the crown of her head. "I got tired of waiting."

"You two split up about a year ago?" I asked.

"Remember my spastic colon, Roz?" she said to the woman with the greasy bandanna. "Well, when Fulton left, the spastic colon left with him."

"Do you know exactly where he was going in the Delta?" I asked.

"Said he was going to some fishing cabin up there. After I turned him down for my car he told me he was driving there in Nancy Branscomb's car."

"That bitch," Richard Spain said.

"Nancy says she doesn't know where he went." I said.

"Hey, all I know is what he told me," Emma said, shrugging. "Stop milling around, all of you. Let's start class because we've got a lot to cover tonight. I wanted to show you this new book on writing." Emma extracted a bright hardcover book from one of the tote bags. "It's called *Writing from Deep Inside*. The author says you should cut out any stuff that interests you when you're reading the paper. Keep files."

"What? Does she live in a mansion? I've got boxes of clippings, in fact, they're moving me out." Roz said, spreading her hands wide. "I can never find a clipping when I want it. My kids keep playing with my stuff."

Richard Spain dropped in the chair next to me. At close range, his large features were beginning to coarsen. His long hair was back combed. He sprayed so hard that it stood high at the crown of his head. Tonight, he wore a leather jacket, with fringes.

"You're making yourself a real pain in the ass by trying to find Fulton," Spain whispered. "I know where he is."

"What? You said you didn't know." I said.

"Because I didn't want to talk in front of Nancy," said Richard. "I don't need another thing to piss her off. Fulton's a good lawyer, which means he knows the value of stalling. He's hiding out until this rape tape thing quiets down. The Delta would be a perfect place, and she's got a cabin up there. Then he'll come back and say, 'Hey, were you guys looking for me?'"

"I need to know where in the Delta," I said. "I need him to finish a novel we're working on together."

Spain said, "How can you justify that you can't finish your own novel? The story has to be in your head. Anyway, if he did go to the Delta, Nancy knows where he is. They're always talking about the Delta. Fulton used to have a real thing for her; I don't know why, that damn tough bitch."

"Oliver says Fulton might have left because of the rape tape," I said.

"I told Oliver the whole story about that rape tape thing just last week," Spain said. "I was with Fulton the day he first got notice of what was coming down from the Bar Association. He was really upset."

"Yeah, I heard," I said.

"Fulton wrote the Bar Association a letter. I don't know what they want from him. He said it was after a long hectic week. He said he was just trying to get some humor into an eye-glazing dull banquet." Spain said.

"See!" Emma said, smacking the table. I jumped. "It's just typical. Both Richard and Fulton think playing that rape tape was just bad taste, like scratching your crotch at the table. Never mind what it says about Fulton's attitude toward rape. The old lady, never mind about her."

"Emma, please, let's not start tonight." Spain said, rolling his eyes.

"You know why Fulton didn't understand what was wrong with playing that rape tape? Because rape is a control issue. Just like Fulton keeping me waiting for him all the time was a control issue," Emma said, slapping the writing book down on the table.

"Emma, I've had a bad day," Spain said, resting his head in one hand. "Let's not start the feminist crap."

"This is not feminist. This is human being. Are you capable of understanding that these legal jokers at dinner violated the old lady's right to privacy? She was raped twice!" Emma said.

"You're mad at Fulton because you two broke up," Richard said, poking a finger toward Emma.

"I am not. I have chosen to put that relationship behind me. I refuse to be angry. Anger requires energy, and I choose to direct that energy toward my writing." Emma said.

"Jesus! First Nancy and now you," Spain said, rubbing a forefinger back and forth across his bushy moustache. "Did you hear Nancy?" He turned to me. "I'm usually pretty good with women. No boasting, I just am. But I couldn't get her to lift a finger for me. Honest to God, I think she's a dyke. Not that I couldn't have brought her round to help me, because I could have, if you hadn't barged in and distracted her with all that Fulton crap. Then she got all upset and threw us both out."

"Didn't sound to me like she was going to help you," I said.

"Did Nancy say you published a couple of books?" Spain asked, taking a large stack of typed manuscript pages out of his canvas tote. "Maybe you could take a look at this manuscript. I'm stuck in a few places."

"Is Nancy Branscomb your editor?" an old man with a broken fingernail asked. Seated next to Josh, he grabbed me by the crook of the elbow. "I can never figure out how this guy got an editor and an agent. I can't get agents to read my stuff. The publishers won't read it unless it comes from an agent. So how are you supposed to start?"

"Because I'm a published author," Spain said. "My book won a prize for a first novel. That makes a difference."

"We have a lot of announcements tonight," Emma said, starting to hand out printed pages.

Several writers gave Emma grateful glances.

Roz muttered, "Here we go again."

I got the feeling Spain's successful first novel was a topic they felt had been sufficiently discussed.

"About Fulton," Spain whispered. "Why don't you come by the Kings Head Theater so we can talk? I've known him for years. I could give you some clues about him. We've got a new play in rehearsal, and I'm there almost every night."

He looped an arm on the back of my chair, immobilizing me.

He continued, "The critics called my first book a smashing debut. So you could give me some ideas on the new one. The first one even gave my acting career a lift."

"Your ass has an acting career," Josh muttered, "and it's falling. They can't put jeans on it anymore and zoom in for an ad."

"You son of a bitch!" said Richard.

"Josh, we are supportive of each other here. As writers, we face enough criticism." Emma scolded.

"Sorry," Josh said, grinning. "See, a chef has to keep growing, learning the craft, developing a signature of his own, a unique stamp that people know you for. But I don't see Spain developing in acting. Or writing, come to it. I just see him displaying his behind."

"Josh doesn't write. He just shuffles his index cards," Spain said.

"You should talk," Josh said.

"What's happening tonight? Stop this," Emma said.

Spain shot Josh a look of pure venom.

Emma picked up the book and continued to read with her index finger pointing, "The writer should choose one viewpoint character throughout the book. Don't be lured away from this single point of view. You vitiate the power of your writing if you keep switching points of view."

"Oh sure. Just like Ed McBain, right?" Josh put in.

"Oh, McBain," Roz said, moving her hand sidewise. "Like Chinese food. You finish one of his books, and an hour later you can't remember who did it or even who got done."

"Emma, is this the new *Writer's Digest*?" Josh asked, dragging the magazine across the table, "The library's copy is missing."

"What I want to tell you guys is that I pitched the concept of my new novel to one of the studios, and they loved it. Just loved it," Richard Spain said. "They told me to go back and flesh it out. I need you guys to brainstorm some plot turns."

"We spent the whole last meeting on your stuff," Josh objected. "Give somebody else a turn. I'm having trouble with the flow of some of my chef anecdotes."

"Josh, you have to know what you want from each anecdote," Emma said, pointing up. "If you're having trouble with a page it's probably because you haven't thought it through."

"How many books have you written?" I asked.

"Emma doesn't write," Josh said, thumbing through the *Writer's Digest*. "She talks."

"I don't want to hold you up," I said. I stood up and headed for the door.

"Wait," Josh said. He smacked the edges of his index cards on the table to align them in a pack and hurried out behind me. "I'm not staying. They're going to spend the whole time on Spain's writing again. You wanted to know about Fulton."

"You know something about Fulton? What's your full name?" I asked.

"Josh Baggins," he replied. He cast a glance back at the Club Room. "Not here. I live in Pacific Cliffs. It's not far. You can follow me."

I noticed that he was carrying the *Writer's Digest* under his arm.

CHAPTER SEVEN

Pacific Cliffs, Los Angeles, California

April 29, 2007

I followed Josh north on Pacific Coast Highway. He drove a dirty BMW. In the current drought, it was the badge of the ecologically aware rather than the simply slovenly.

Pacific Cliffs was a community of Craftsman houses behind neat lawns, but Josh braked at a two-story red farm house with a peaked roof. It looked like a house in a game of Monopoly. Stacks of lumber filled the parking pad. One of the garage doors was up, showing a work table fitted with a table saw, low hanging lights, and boxes of parts and tools hanging from pegboard nailed to the walls. The impression was of clutter. A van was parked in front of the other garage door. The trash barrels were overflowing with wood detritus and torn out plasterboard.

Josh negotiated the obstacle course of the two-foot-wide walkway. I was right behind him. Plants grew in ceramic containers above a sour patch of brown grass. A ceramic wind chime tinkled near the door. A large ceramic plaque on the outside wood wall said "Baggins." I noticed a cobalt blue under-glaze drawing of a hobbit, complete with furry feet. Tall grass filled with nettles plumed on the side of the walkway, where there wasn't any foot traffic. A wood box filled with children's Lego parts was near the door. Josh picked up some loose pieces of Lego and tossed them in the box. Somebody had been baking. The smell of muffins wafted outside the door.

"Hi, don't mind the mess," said a woman who joined us.

She was tall and wore glasses. Her mousy brown hair was cut in a no-nonsense short bob. She had wide-set eyes. Her good, even features were completely devoid of makeup. Her body looked athletic, but she must have been at least ten years older than her husband.

"This is my wife, Evelyn," Josh said.

She greeted him with a hug.

The real surprise inside the house was the kitchen, to the right of the garage. It was completely tiled; including floors, baseboards, and counters. A commercial stove was on the opposite wall. Two flanking Sub Zero refrigerators, all in stainless steel stood on either side of the stove. The sink had a stainless steel two-foot-high gooseneck faucet with a pullout spray.

"Nice, huh?" Josh said proudly. "This is the focal point of my life. I test a lot of my recipes here. I sometimes bring in a whole crew from L'Escargot and do catering. I'm setting up my own salumeria for hanging and curing Italian style meats, like salami, soppresata, and prosciutto."

He continued, "A whole bunch of chefs buy my salumeria because they can't get the good stuff anywhere else in Los Angeles. Did you know Mario Batali's new restaurant in New York City has a whole walk-in refrigerator devoted just to sausages?" He paused. "Excuse me. I didn't have time to eat all day. I'm starved."

He buttered two hot muffins and sprinkled feta cheese over a spinach salad. I hadn't eaten since breakfast. I was salivating over the smell of the muffins, but he didn't offer me any.

"Our neighbors are having meetings to decide the exact percentage by which we're depressing their property values, us with our lumber in the driveway and the open garage door all the time," Evelyn Baggins said, watching my appraising glance. "They're all into vinyl siding."

"Which replaced their aluminum siding," Josh put in.

"Which replaced their clapboard siding," Evelyn said.

They both laughed heartily. It gave the effect of a well-rehearsed routine. These two seemed to feed off each other, as if only close physical proximity allowed them to shine with their full wattage.

"And you built this kitchen?" I asked.

"You bet. I graduated from the Culinary Institute in San Francisco when I was only nineteen. I transferred there instead of high school. I knew I wanted to be a chef somewhere between sixteen and seventeen years old. When I was a kid, the other guys in the kitchen would give me the crap jobs, like cutting chickens. I'd come home and my hands would just be trashed, with cuts and gouges. Chickens can give you a nasty infection. But I'd rub oil on my hands and say, 'I learned more today.'"

"And now you're writing a book," I said.

"I'm just about finished with the book."

"He's so good in a kitchen," Evelyn said, smiling. "Really, he's an artist."

"I know kitchens. When I was still a teenager and earning under $20,000 a year at Mexican take-out places, I'd go to the top San Francisco restaurants and just order two courses. That's all I could afford. And I'd watch how the dining room was run. I'd always ask if I could see the kitchen. It's important to stay curious, and not get lazy, creatively speaking. You should get input but you shouldn't copy anything. We spent a lot of money on this kitchen, but I'll make the money back when I open my restaurant. I'm going to call it 'Chez Josh.'"

"He never calls it 'this place' or 'my place,'" Evelyn said, still beaming. "It's always 'Chez Josh'. He has a distinct, clear vision of what he wants."

"I might not make much money yet, but the richness of my work compensates for the lack of money. When I go to sleep at night, I lay in bed and think of recipes. I love it when things are clicking in a kitchen and the crew is firing and the waiters are running. There's an intensity. And the noise! I love that too. You have to feel it; it's like music. And I have plans. I'll have three fixed-price menus at Chez Josh. I'll serve local foods, stuff you can't get elsewhere. The menu will change with the seasons."

Evelyn said, "Fortunately, I make good money. I'm an emergency room nurse, and I work nights for extra money. I can get twelve-hour shifts. Of course, the higher paying night shifts mean I have to be away from my family for long stretches. I'm tired when I'm home with them."

"Evelyn has to have her whining time," Josh said, rolling his eyes.

"It's hard work, and messy," Evelyn said. "Come payday, everybody needs something, and it isn't just the kids. Even my patients have their hands out, saying, 'You got some money to lend me?' This old lady asked me last week. Her phone was disconnected. So she said, 'You get your check yet?'"

"I always knew I wanted a restaurant of my own, but Los Angeles was never an option," Josh said. "The rents are too high, and you have to keep turning the tables over. And it's harder to do cured meats in Los Angeles because the Health Department is stricter."

"You say you're opening up," I said.

"They're building this big waterfront project near Isleton in the Delta. It's called 'The Docklands in the Delta.' It's got condos, a marina, and a restaurant. And that restaurant, I saw its extraordinary potential right off."

"Wait. I heard about that somewhere, The Docklands at the Delta," I said.

"I worked up a proposal for the developer. They're worried I'm too young, but it's an amazing proposal. I think I have a great chance. Wait until you see the drawings I made of the restaurant," he said. "They'll blow you away."

He added spices to the spinach salad.

"They're going to have a wealthy resident base in the condos up there, of course," Josh said. "But they'll also need a destination restaurant where people will come up from San Francisco and down from Sacramento. That's exactly the kind of thing I'm great at. I'll feature crawdads and river fish. People will spend a couple of hours at the place. I'll have a garden for them to walk around. They can see the fresh herbs we grow."

"How did you two get engaged?" I asked. I tried not to swivel my head from one to the other, like a tennis match.

"It was the second marriage for both of us," Evelyn said. "We were at the Mexican restaurant down on Rose Avenue. Josh was the chef there then. I ordered a tostada, and he put the ring on top of the tostada." She laughed merrily.

"But we were with two other couples," she continued, "and I was so busy talking that I didn't start to eat. And I didn't see the ring."

I thought, why does it feel like everything these two said was a twice-told tale?

"Finally he just took my head and mushed it in the tostada," she said. "Then I saw the ring, and I cried. Everybody cried. And we ordered champagne."

"Evelyn has changed my life," Josh said, his slender chest puffing. "I'm less afraid, much more honest now."

I didn't mention the copy of *Writer's Digest* from the library.

"Maybe we could talk about why you asked me to come up here," I said.

"Maybe we could," he said, looking at me sideways. "And maybe we couldn't."

It had been a long day. I was exhausted. I was starving. I decided to level with him. He'd either tell me or he wouldn't; the sooner I found out, the better.

"In that case, I'm tired, and I'm leaving." I said, standing.

"Wait," he said, grabbing my arm. "I have to tell you about Richard Spain. Look, you know that book he's always talking about, the first one he won the prize for?"

He stopped. His eyes sought Evelyn's, and she nodded encouragement.

"The one where he carries the reviews," I said.

"Well, he didn't write it." Josh's said, his voice sinking to a whisper. "The guy wrote it, Edward Abelia, is dead. He shared an apartment with Richard Spain back then. Then Spain got a bigger apartment in Ocean Park and moved out. Anyway, Abelia didn't like computers. He wrote in a big spiral notebook. He had the notebook with him when he died."

"How did he die?" I asked.

"He was … uh … killed in an auto accident. I was driving, actually. Spain was in the car and he got hurt too."

I followed up, "So how did Spain get the notebook?"

"Uh … well—"

"Tell her," Evelyn urged.

"I'm trying to tell her, if you'd just shut up for one minute."

"Look, Josh," I said, "whether you tell me is up to you. But we'll all save a lot of time if you decide."

"I gave it to him," said Josh. "The paramedics took Spain and me to the hospital and I just picked up the notebook. I don't know why. I brought it to Spain's apartment a couple of hours later. After the accident, I mean. I was the driver, and I'd been drinking."

He picked up one of the milky glasses off the counter, rinsed it, and added it to the dishwasher.

"Understand, it was a bad time in my life," he said.

"And then?" I asked.

"And I accidentally left it on the table. I wasn't thinking about the damn notebook, was I? I mean, I was very, very, upset," he said.

He sat at the table and placed the spinach salad in front of himself. He took a large bite of the muffin.

"And Spain read the notebook because he was bedridden after the accident," Josh continued. "All I knew was that he kept his door locked for two weeks. When he came out, he said he had written a novel on his laptop. Well, nobody expected the damn thing to win a prize."

I stared and said, "But you knew who wrote it."

"Yeah, well," he said, taking a drink of water, "I have a firm feeling about the takers of the world, like Spain. You deal with them only if you have to. Then you make distance between you. But you save the talented people, and I'm talented."

I crossed my arms.

"Spain said I was going to need a really good defense lawyer. Me being drunk and all. He said he'd put me together with one, but—"

"But?"

"But I had to shut up about the notebook."

"Fulton. He was the lawyer," I said.

"Right," Josh said.

"So you just let Spain steal Abelia's work," I said.

His eyes swiveled to Evelyn. He said, "It was the rest of my life! I'm a chef, an artist, I do things for people. I did community service. I trained a whole crew of Latino kids to work a kitchen."

"This was your court-ordered community service?" I asked.

"Doesn't matter," he said. "I still helped people. I even taught those kids to make good sausage. Two of them were real hairnet heads. I got them jobs. I think you have to look at the whole picture of what a person does with his life, not just one incident. And remember, the book wasn't going to do Abelia any good. He was dead."

"All of this was a couple of years ago, right?" I asked.

"Yeah," he said, licking his lips. "But a few weeks ago—"

"What?" I asked.

"Well, I'm afraid," murmured Josh with shy regret, "that it was partly my fault."

"Josh went to Fulton's office and told him about the notebook," Evelyn interrupted. "Not that Josh thought Fulton would react the way he did."

"He's a criminal lawyer. Undentable. But he was Spain's friend, and I thought he ought to know."

"But it was as if something else was already bothering him," Evelyn said. "That's the only thing that could explain his reaction."

"And?" I said. I was tiring of both of them.

"I'm finished with probation for this DUI charge," Josh said. "Spain doesn't have anything to hold over me anymore."

"So?" I asked.

"Spain's always boasting about changing careers. He's crowing over everybody, about him being a full-time writer. He says all I do is play with index cards. Well, I take my book seriously. Just as seriously as he takes his. Lately he's been putting me down every chance he gets. Talking about his writing talent."

"So you got fed up," I said.

"He can't be a TV model much longer, which is how he's making most of his money," Josh said. "They don't pay him at that theater he hangs around. I mean, everything's starting to droop on him. He's forever in a gym. He tells people he's thirty-five, but he's actually forty-two. And I think he went to a plastic surgeon for his chin. So he's got to figure out something else to do for a living. He's decided he's a great writer. And he never shuts up about that damn first book! He carries around the review in his wallet, the one that said it was an impressive debut. People like Spain are always showing off, and they take over any conversation; they're disgusting."

"What did you do?" I asked.

"Most people realize that when you create wonderful food, you're a person who's a plus to the community. You're not just taking. You're an artist. You're giving back, and people respect that," he said.

Nice little air of meticulous fairness, I thought, the Josh point of view.

"What did you do a few weeks ago?" I repeated.

Josh squirmed and said, "Well, this part sounds bad, but that's when I got tired of Spain acting like such a big shot and talking about the prize and the novel all the time. So I told Fulton. About the book being Eddie Abelia's, and—"

"And what else?" I asked.

"No," he said. He curled the fingers into fists, looked from me to Evelyn, and said, "That's all I'm going to tell you."

"Look, friend, I don't know why you dragged me up here. Now you're giving me a bad time," I said.

"Stop snapping at him. This is very hard for him," Evelyn said.

"Because you're asking everybody about Fulton," Josh said. "I heard Spain tell you Fulton might have done a disappearing act because of the Bar Association inquiry. Well, let me tell you, Spain is paranoid about that book. It's all he's got. If Fulton started looking into whether Abelia was the one who wrote the book, I think Spain could have hurt him."

He wheeled on Evelyn and said, "Okay, you wanted me to tell somebody about what happened. Now I told somebody."

"There's more to it, Josh," I said. "You're not telling me everything."

"Now," he said to Evelyn. He walked out of the kitchen, salad in hand, "It's her problem."

I had had enough. I went home. And then the roof fell in.

CHAPTER EIGHT

Venice Beach, California

April 29, 2007

The telephone rang as I came in the door. The voice was an accusation.

"Where you been? This is Mrs. Caspia, your mother's neighbor. I've been calling you the whole day," she said.

"I was out—"

"Your mother fell."

"What?"

"On that step, you know that one step in front of the building? She says her feet somehow got tangled."

"Jesus, where is she?"

"At the Centinela Freeman Hospital, the one on Lincoln Boulevard, but you gotta come right now. I can't stay here anymore. My kids have been home for hours."

I grabbed my purse. The phone rang.

"You know what that son of a bitch Fulton did?" Florence shrieked.

"I'm on my way out the door—" I said.

"He burglarized my house!"

"Fulton? Fulton burglarized your house?" I asked.

"Goddamn right," she replied.

"That doesn't sound like Fulton," I said.

"It was Fulton," she said, "because all the drawers in his desk have been pulled out and dumped upside down. And the burglar didn't take the Mac computer that stood right there on the desk. That computer is cash, as any burglar knows."

"Florence, calm down—"

"I'm throwing out all his crap tonight. Everything! And I found a carton box full of stuff. Has a file with your name on it," she said.

"Thank God, it's got to be the outline," I said.

"You know what pisses me off?" asked Florence. "I brought home the people that were buying this place. For once in this lousy market, they had good credit. They took one look inside, with the place tossed. They told me it was a high crime area and they cancelled the escrow."

"The file with my name—" I said.

"You want it? You come over right now, because it's going out."

"Florence, please, I have a real emergency. I'll be there as soon as I can, I swear. Please don't throw it out, please."

She hung up. The phone rang as soon as I put it back on the receiver.

"You haven't called," Oliver brayed. "I've been calling you all day. Your tape's not on, and you certainly aren't home writing. Are you ducking me?"

"I got Fulton's file with my name," I said.

"Good," said Oliver. "You get the release signed?"

"I didn't find Fulton," I said. "Florence found a file in Fulton's stuff with my name on it. That's got to be the outline or the files he was working from."

"And you didn't beat it right over to Florence and get that outline?" he asked.

"Oliver, my mother fell. I've got to go to her right now," I said.

"You know the date today?" asked Oliver. "Today is April 29. I broke one of the metal wheels on my library ladder this morning, and it's an antique, so you know what kind of luck I'm going to have finding another wheel."

Oliver's office was in an old Spanish courtyard on Westwood Boulevard, south of Wilshire Boulevard. He'd owned the property for years. He had fought off developers' offers that had escalated every week. Currently, he rented out three of the four offices, delightfully tiny two-room units with dark oak floors and built-in bookcases with glass doors and lead glass windows. Four little buildings huddled around a central planting area filled with stands of dusty birds of paradise, as if for protection against the skyscrapers crowding them.

Oliver had painted his office pale yellow and lined it on three sides with book shelves. His oak library ladder rode a rail. It was the pride of his life. I remember when he got it. He talked about owning one ever since seeing Jimmy Stewart playing a publisher and cueballing around an office on a library ladder in the movie, *Bell, Book and Candle.* The ladder reached up twelve feet and bore a plate with the name of its old Los Angeles maker, now long gone. Oliver waxed it, and it smelled of lemon oil.

"Vera," Oliver said, "you're not writing."

"Yeah," I said. "You told me to stop writing and go and find Fulton."

"You're running around and being a nurse for your mother. You're doing everything else but writing. We're stretched out with these publishers. You're just not holding up your end," he said.

"If you can think back," I said, "we stood on my deck and had a conversation about Fulton signing the release. And me dropping everything and finding him."

"I'm taking on a new author, Mark Huntsinger. Do you know him?" he asked.

Oh yeah, I remembered him. Mark Huntsinger was an officious young man who wore black turtleneck shirts and taught at a local school. I'd been on a speakers panel with him.

"I am teaching children who are basically unteachable," Mark had announced in a nasal bray during that panel. "I am trying to teach them to write five coherent sentences. That would be a triumph."

"Do you really believe that?" I had asked him.

"Certainly," Mark had said. "These children will never pass the state exit test, so why are we penalizing them for their background? They come into school four years behind. In effect, there is nothing I can do that will teach these children on an acceptable level of skill."

"So why are you picking up a paycheck?" I asked.

The question didn't dent him. I met Huntsinger several hours later, at a tea for the participants, and he didn't recognize who I was. I had to repeat my name three or four times before he took it in. He was a man who didn't receive incoming messages.

"I have to protect myself with these publishers," Oliver said. His voice was weighty. "You aren't the only writer I represent, and I've got to keep my contacts open. It's how I make my living, so don't get mad at me."

I could hear the fear in his voice. He had bet everything he had by backing my novel, including his money and his future. And it was beginning to sound like it was not a winning bet.

So I knew what was going to happen. We had a few weeks left that Oliver could stall.

After that he'd be explaining how sorry he was that he had to sell me out.

"Oliver, tomorrow," I said. "I swear. Everything tomorrow."

"It's a small bone. Here, near the heel."

My mother's regular doctor had belatedly arrived at the hospital. He sucked his teeth as he pointed to the X-ray with his light pen. "But she'll have to have a light cast. I've called the orthopedic man, and he'll do the cast in an hour."

"I want to see her," I said, standing up.

"You know," he said, waving me back down in the chair. "You're going to have to make some plans. For your mother. Have you thought what you're going to do?"

"I just found out—" I said.

"I don't mean just this fall today. I mean the long term. Now she's afraid to live by herself," he said.

"Actually she's very independent," I said. "She's told me over and over she wants to stay in her own apartment."

"Well," he said, fiddling with the light pen, "you may have to start making decisions for her."

I sagged in the chair.

"You know," he said, "this is not going to get any better."

I went to find my mother, who was propped up on a gurney in the corridor.

"Oh, you're finally here," Mrs. Caspia said, standing up. I looked at her net of bad hair and her heavy arms protruding out of a house dress. "I'll go, then." She waved me into a nearby room.

I took out two twenty dollar bills and handed them to her. She made them disappear.

"Vera, I can't do this anymore," she said, lowering her voice. "My husband says I have to be home when the kids get home or God knows what they'll get into."

I alternated between appreciation and resentment of Mrs. Caspia. I appreciated her willingness to help and lessen my guilt at leaving my mother alone. I resented her because she had a lot of outspoken opinions. I didn't want to have to listen to her. She walked rapidly away. She took fast steps for a fat woman.

Tears slid down my mother's cheek, but her face wasn't contorted, as if her facial muscles didn't have the energy left to move. She had lost a lot of weight lately. Her arms had become spindly, and she slept much more. But she still kept her iron gray hair meticulously finger waved. A smell of pungent antiseptic permeated the hallway where her gurney was parked.

"Five hours," she whispered "Five hours! They took the X-rays, and they just left me sitting here five hours."

I took her hand. Papery skin and blue veins marked where the subcutaneous fat had disappeared with age. The pigmentation changes and liver spots had come from the Southern California sun.

"They don't see me," she said, grabbing me. "They walk by and look at the other wall. I should say 'Look, I'm here, you left me here and forgot me.'"

She was so weak, and she used to be so fierce. And she was leaving me. As sure as the sun was going to rise tomorrow, she was leaving me. She was dying. What, in the end, did I want? Did I have some fantasy of returning to my mother? The idea was pathetic. We had never gotten along.

"It'll be okay now, Mom," I said. "I'm here."

"What's wrong with me, Vera?" she said.

"Nothing's wrong with you—"

"They're going to put a cast on my foot. How will I manage? It's the last thing, Vera. The last thing."

"While you have the cast on, you'll come and stay with me," I said.

"No!" A voice shrieked inside me. "How will I write? How will I live?"

I don't work well with somebody in my house. For reasons I don't understand, my muse comes to me at four a.m., and I have to pad around the house, put on lights, boot up my computer. And my mother! Some people need to be in charge of every possible situation. My mother is one of them.

"I always took care of myself," she lamented. "I went out and worked. I did what I had to. I was shy when your father was alive. I don't know. Why was I so frightened?"

"For a while you'll just need some extra help." I said.

"I don't see how we'll manage. You live in that tiny place." She said.

She removed her hand. My house was the subject of a long and nonproductive argument between us.

"It's only temporary, Mom," I said. "Just while the cast's on your foot."

"It's not temporary," the voice inside me screamed. "It's not."

I could surely live a few weeks with her. I could live with her narrow ideas and her outbursts. Her life is so limited and now she needs me.

"Maybe just until I'm better," she said.

"Okay, missus, we're ready for you," the attendant said cheerily.

He lifted her by placing his arms under her armpits. Her hospital gown flopped open, and I saw her naked frail body, which weighed less than a hundred pounds.

Whoever said you can't be too thin should see my mother.

Thin is sick. Thin is old. Thin is dying.

CHAPTER NINE

VENICE BEACH, CALIFORNIA

May 1, 2007

Two days later, May 1, the doorbell rang. I dropped the pile of about thirty magazines I was moving. Barefoot, I was dressed in a T-shirt with prominent holes and my rattiest pair of jeans, and with a scarf tied round my hair.

I opened the door. Fred was standing there.

As I was standing next to him at the door, I noticed he had freckles, which I hadn't seen before. He was taller than I thought. Standing a gangly six feet tall, I put him at about one hundred seventy pounds. He was wearing neat tan chinos. He had ventured into a patterned white shirt, no tie. And a surprise, he was wearing tan and brown cowboy boots. He might have been in his forties but his thin hair, parted and combed 1950s style, held no gray.

"You called me," he said.

He carried a tan sports jacket, which he folded neatly, lining out, and hung on the back of one of my chairs. He had a beeper on his belt.

"Look, it's about this guy, Fulton Yee, that I'm looking for," I said, "I'm going to have to pay you for some help. I expected to have more time. It turns out I don't. That's why I called you and said I changed my mind about hiring you."

"Okay, for seventy-five dollars an hour, I'll find him," Fred said. "Plus expenses."

I did some silent mental division. Figuring a full forty-hour week, two weeks at that rate equaled $6,000. It would wipe out my savings, but I had to do it.

"Two weeks." I said. "That's all the money I have. That's the time frame. You have until May 15."

"I'll have a line on him long before that" Fred said. "Anything you can give me helps—like his full name, social security number, even something like his favorite magazine."

"I thought the idea of the course you taught at Bogie's Buddies was to train people to locate who they're looking for?" I asked.

"You're talking pro versus amateur," he said, shrugging. "There's no substitute for experience. I've also got somebody who works for Visa. I can see where they're sending his statements."

"I'll do a lot of the work," I said. "Give me a list. I'll do the deskwork. You do the footwork."

He liked the idea of cooperation. The longer we discussed it, the larger his participation grew. After a few minutes he was talking openly about taking a lead role.

"Also, I want a look at his current cases," he said. "He was a criminal lawyer. Maybe one of his clients turned out to be somebody nasty who he needs to hide from."

"I tried to find out. His office won't tell me—"

"I can find out who he represented. That's public record," he said. "What are you doing?"

His eyes fell on the boxes I was moving from my bedroom to my office. On top of one of them were my sleeping bag and my quilt.

"My mother's coming," I said. "I'm moving out of my bedroom and into the small room. The one I use as my office."

"Your mother's going to live here with you?"

"She's my mother," I said. "She fell, and she needs help for a short while. We don't get along, but I can't just leave her. Plus, she's already talking about going home, and she hasn't got here yet."

I picked up my quilt.

"Maybe she has things to do," he said.

That hadn't occurred to me. Adult children don't think their parents may have things to do. They know visits with parents interrupt their own lives. But they don't see it the other way, that their parents might have a schedule that can't be interrupted.

"You gave me a list of Fulton's women," he said. "Your name isn't on it."

"Fulton and I didn't have a sexual relationship. We had a writing relationship," I said.

"You married?" he asked.

"You're very direct."

He gave me a hawk stare beneath tan eyebrows as prominent as Cadillac tailfins.

"Saves time," he said.

"I once was. Not now. The marriage sort of dwindled."

"People do settle for that," he said.

"Not me," I said.

He followed me into the office. "I'm divorced," he said. "One kid; he's eight. His mom remarried and moved up to Northern California. Kid plays soccer. He seems to have a full life up there." He stopped. "I don't see him much any more. Sometimes when I'm with him, I don't think he remembers who I am."

"I'm sorry," I said.

"What the hell is this diagram doing here?" he asked.

His jaw dropped, and he pointed to my bulletin board.

"It's a bomb," I said.

"I know what it is. It's a nipple time bomb. Works great," he said. "The acid eats its way through the nipple in three to six hours, mixes with potassium chlorate and gunpowder, and detonates the dynamite. Boom! It's not the kind of thing that most people know about. It's certainly not what they stick up with thumb tacks on their office wall."

"Fulton drew it for me so I'd understand how it worked," I said. "It's for the book."

"And you just left it up there?"

"That bulletin board is sort of limbo," I said. "It has notes for projects long done. And never done. And ones never going to be done. I leave stuff there that I'm still thinking about."

He shook his head in disbelief and said, "People get nervous about diagrams of bombs these days. You ever hear of the Homeland Security Department? Those guys say they want to be proactive. They don't want to wait until a bomb goes off. They want to stop the plot before it matures. If somebody sees that diagram, you're going to be doing a lot of explaining to guys with cold eyes and square jaws and absolutely no sense of humor."

"The murderer in the novel has a vicious method," I said. I pulled an index card off the wall and handed it to him. "He finds out a person's birthday from public records. The day before the victim's birthday, he sends them the bomb in the bottom of a plant, with a card marked 'Don't open until your birthday.' While the victim is waiting, it kills him."

"The victims keep the bomb?" asked Fred.

"They usually put the plant right in the middle of a table, where they can see it," I said. "In the book, using that plant ruse, the murderer rigs an explosion at a real estate office, a car, and a school."

He picked another index card off the wall.

"The murderer is limited in thought," he read aloud, "capable of seeing only one move ahead. He's an opportunist, not a chess player."

"That's Fulton talking," I said. "He was really into chess."

"I read two of your books," he said, tacking back the card. "I never knew anybody before who published a book."

"Something changed. Fulton came here a few days before he vanished. Really fired up. Here," I said, picking up a spiral bound notebook. "He said, 'If you're playing a game of conspiracy chess, whatever piece you're using has to be of equal or greater power than your opponent's. If you use a pawn to block a queen, you're fucked.'" I put down the notebook. "I take very good notes."

"What did he say next?" Fred asked.

"Then he laughed a lot," I said.

"But he didn't tell you who he was talking about?"

"No, and I have no idea."

"The chess," said Fred, "did he ever talk about it again?"

"No," I replied. "I asked him, but he just said the murderer had a lack of continuity in his thinking. In the book, the murderer sets a bomb to go off on the Fourth of July, so the noise will be covered up.

Fulton said that was typical of the murderer. He grabbed opportunities rather than planning."

"Get that bomb diagram off your wall. That's my advice," said Fred, flicking a thumb at the diagram. "Right now. You got a locked file?"

"You're concerned for me?" I asked.

"I'm concerned for maintaining a client until I get paid," he said, leaning back. "I ran this guy, Fulton Yee, through our database. Only got basic information. And I asked around. I still know a couple guys on the force. They can't find much in their database either. I gotta tell you that I'm impressed. Most people don't know how to cover their tracks that well. He was probably a pretty good criminal lawyer."

He walked over to the bulletin board, moving with a rolling gait.

"All this about chess. What was he doing?" he asked.

"Structuring our book."

"No, I think he was bouncing ideas off your head," said Fred. "Real-life stuff. Trying ways of checkmating a real person."

"In the notes, it doesn't say who," I said.

"That's okay," said Fred. "The notes, and this stuff stuck all over your wall—that may be where he crossed himself. You kept them. He didn't know anybody else would see them."

We walked toward the front deck. My bedroom is past the bathroom. It is located in the back of the house near the street, which in the canals is called the court.

Venice Beach resembles the Delta because it's a somewhat laid-back state of mind. People comment that it doesn't feel like they're in Los Angeles. Venice has four parallel canals: Tabor, Abbott, Kinaloa, and Palms, and their courts, which are the streets that run behind them. Two more canals run at right angles: West Canal is parallel with the ocean, and East Canal, inland. So the canals form a grid.

When I moved here, the old Venice still existed. That old Venice had a deep distrust of the rest of Los Angeles, which held forth, in their minds, somewhere downtown. There was a shared viewpoint, a defiance of authority. The Peace and Freedom Party started in Venice. Many of the original radicals had moved on, but the distrust still existed.

A large artist community had left a benchmark. Many residents had huge portrait murals painted of themselves on an outside wall of their homes. They used these portraits for house identification instead of a street address. Nowadays the historical society organized Venice Mural Tours. Earnest people in flat shoes followed guides holding a tour group sign on a pole, right at the moment that most of the artists were being priced out.

That actually happens in California. Artists discover a cheap neighborhood. Trendy boutiques move in. Magazines do write-ups of the new coming area. Then developers hear of the action. Then the artists are priced out.

I led Fred through the door to the deck nearest the canal. It was hot in the sun. The gray paint was peeling off my clapboard wall. I always meant to put up an awning. Sammy was banging in his kitchen ten feet away. The spicy smell of the meat he was stir-frying with ginger wafted across the fence. The ducks swam up and began an immediate cacophony for food. Gulls swooped down. The female ducks circled their young, quacking. The deck had a social feel.

Fred said, "Ducks. They're ass end up."

"Ducks tip ass end up in shallow water and drill in the mud for plants and insects," I said. "Then they pick up sand and gravel and use it like grinders in their gizzards."

"I apologize for showing up unannounced," he said.

"That's fine," I said. "We said I'd try first, but I'm in a bad place now with time. I'm trying to find Fulton, but my mother fell."

"The ducks act like they're going to get fed," he remarked.

"I like to sit on my deck around six o'clock in he morning and have my coffee," I said. "We're mellow then, the ducks and me. But lately, by nightfall, the ducks and I have had it. We both start discordant quacking."

"How long you lived here?" he asked.

He selected one of the aluminum chairs and unfolded it. Then he unfolded his body in it.

"Ten years," I answered. "I walk down to the fishing pier in the evenings. It's great. Japanese families come down, put their children in sleeping bags, and fish all night. People come from all over Venice.

Lots of people down there are not even fishing. They're just watching the sunset and the waves."

"So you like a beach town?" he asked.

"I don't mind the disorder," I said. "Even the weekends that get crazy. It comes with the individualism. It suits me here. I could never live in a place where everything is mandated to look the same. I have a friend lives in a planned community in Irvine. They have rules about how high her geraniums can be. That would drive me crazy. Over here, I walk the canals in the early evenings, from the pier to my house. I see big houses, small houses, yards that are all deck, and yards with kids' swings. One guy has his whole yard in cactus. So you sometimes get somebody who lets his yard get covered with weeds. Or works on his car on his parking pad. That's the price."

"I think you should go to Florence right away," Fred said. "Tell her you really need that file she found. Say you'll get it out of her house, like now. She may get furious and pitch it out. I was going to just research data. But now I intend to get more directly involved."

He gave me a slow, rueful smile.

"Don't you have a gun?" I asked.

He was so thin; it was hard to see where he'd hide one. What would he be like in bed? Bony, I suddenly caught myself thinking. A bony packet of compressed energy.

Why was I thinking about men? My mother would be in my bedroom. Easy. I was thinking about men because I hadn't had sex for three months.

"Don't carry one," he said. "I spent enough time with a revolver. I did a tour as a military policeman. Besides, I like to show up unexpected on people's doorsteps. Like right now. I find out a lot that way. People get worried when you show up with a gun."

"So how do you get people to tell you things?" I asked.

"My main tool is me. I ask questions. Then I listen. Most people don't, you know, listen."

"How'd you get started?"

"At the bottom of the private eye food chain," he said. "I worked toward my license doing traffic accident investigation, witnesses, and stuff like that. Low man gets those. Nobody wants them. This okay?" He pointed to his cowboy boots before he put up his feet on an aluminum chair.

"There I was," he continued. "Skinny white dude with a tie. Walking around Watts at night."

"Well, you're still here," I said. "You've got some survival skills."

"People would rag on me, but I'd say, 'I'm really sorry to bother you with this, but you know, I've got a job to do too.' That worked. That's what I mean, my main tool is me."

"And now?" I asked.

"Now I bought into the agency," he said, grinning. "Saves a lot of arguing. I'm not real good working for other people."

I sensed that he was studying me.

A detective who owned part of the agency? I thought.

Now I was impressed.

This is not going to sound romantic, but let me tell you, a financially independent woman might talk about finding a soul mate, but when she meets a prospect her brain subconsciously sizes up his portfolio just as much as his other appendages. It has to do with whether he's successful in dealing with the world. And I respond better sexually to a man who could deal with the world.

One of the firm bases of my life has been to insist on having a way to support myself, not to need a man to support me. My mother's choices were limited because she was raised to be a wife, and a helpmate. She was married to a typical 1950s male. From my teenage years it was clear to me I had to find a different way. She must have recognized some of my feelings because she raised me and sustained me and educated me. I used the education to get out.

"Okay, tan man, we'll start the way you said—" I said.

"What?"

"Fred. I mean Fred," I said. "Okay, you start looking for Fulton."

There were probably a lot better ways of saying the next thing I said, but it came out.

"Do you dream in tan?" I asked.

"You mean the clothes?"

Ah, God, he was nimble. I hadn't expected him to get the reference.

"It's my work outfit," he said. "When I follow people, I need to fade into the background. Tan fades into the background."

He moved two fat files off my patio table. "What's with the newspaper clippings?" he asked.

"I read a lot of newspapers and magazines," I said. "I cut out pictures that give me ideas: a photo of a face with an interesting expression, sometimes a quote, sometimes a room setting. I have to cut out the photo right when I first see it because if I go back later looking I can never find it in the newspaper again. That's what's in those file cabinets in my office."

He picked up some magazines and let them drop to the top of the pile.

"*I.D.* and *Design Magazine*," he read the titles. "*Men's Health*?"

This relationship was going to be difficult. We weren't comfortable with each other.

"That's criticism of my reading?" I asked.

"I hear you have to write what you know," he said.

"What's in my imagination is what I know," I said. "I'm a mystery writer. I don't have to kill somebody to write it."

"But the guy who drew the diagram for you, or rather for your book," Fred said, jabbing a forefinger toward my office, "he did know about the bomb, right? So he didn't need his imagination."

"Fulton drew it. He was a criminal lawyer and I think it was in one of his cases."

"Fulton. The guy we're looking for."

"Right."

"So then, the real bomber," said Fred. "The guy who wanted to bring on annihilation. What's his name?"

"I don't know. I'm not even sure Fulton was taking it from a real case."

"I tell you," said Fred, "I think we should find out. Right now. Because I wonder how that guy feels about his lawyer writing a book about his bomb?"

CHAPTER TEN

Crenshaw District, Los Angeles, California

May 2, 2007

Florence's brittle edginess was getting to me, and I genuinely dreaded going to the house near Crenshaw again. I prepared for it. I had the feeling Florence knew a lot more than she was telling me. Whatever happened, I was not going to give the same lamentable show I had last time. Now I was back to Florence and I was going to get information out of her.

"I don't want to hear word one about that bastard, Fulton!" Florence said, banging open the front door.

I noticed one of her glossy blue fingernails was broken. I could faintly smell alcohol on her breath.

She whirled and I followed her back into the living room. Her back was rigid. It was the day after Fred's visit, Friday, May 2, and in the time since I'd been there, the interior walls of the Crenshaw house had been painted a soft butter yellow. The lighting had been changed, which made the place seem to exude warmth and coziness. A muscular young man of about twenty-five was draped on the couch in the living room. He was watching the big screen TV. He was barefoot and only wearing blue jeans speckled with the yellow paint of the walls. He was chewing something and wearing some kind of fragrance.

"Florence, you must know Fulton didn't burglarize your house," I said.

"You shut your mouth. I don't want to hear any story you two cooked up," she said.

I didn't mind her. She suddenly didn't frighten or even intimidate me.

"Florence, honey, now you don't want to get all worked up," the man said.

"Yeah," she looked pointedly at him. "He'll take quick care of Fulton if he has the balls to show his face here."

The man beamed proudly. The snob within me recoiled.

"Fulton didn't burglarize your house because he hasn't been near here," I said. "I'm still trying to find him."

"That sounds damn convenient. Then, when you find him, you tell him I'm not doing any more free work for him. Just because we're both Chinese he thinks I'm a goddamn coolie laborer. I spent hours looking up property ownership records on my computer he said he had to have."

"What? What ownership records?" I said, trying to sound nonchalant.

She sustained the suspense, minutely examining her broken fingernail.

"Half those old property records are incomplete. You wind up squinting and writing for more information. You end up with a thudding headache. He can take his Alien Land Law and jam it."

"His what law?" I asked. Could this be the liquor talking?

"Oh, you don't know about that law, right?" she said. She dropped on the sofa, moving her torso closer to the man. "You white bread people write the California histories, right? Somehow it didn't make the cut for the history books that the Chinese could only lease their land because the honorable State of California passed a law in 1913 that forbade the Chinese immigrants from purchasing land."

"I don't understand," I said. "Plenty of Chinese own property in California."

"Now," she said, "but the legislature didn't throw out that 1913 law until 1952. It took World War II to get rid of it. Believe me, the law was enforced. Except for merchants with an established business or students, see, all other Chinese were called unwanted laborers who 'endangered the good order of society.' One guy wrote that the Chinese workers were valued only because of their alleged 'passive obedience.'"

"How come I never heard of that law?" I asked.

"I didn't know about that Alien Land Law myself, because I'm from New York," she said. For the first time her voice betrayed a cold hard anger. "But it really made a difference up in the Delta, and Fulton grew up with it. Sort of snapped my head around for me, when I was reading about it. A big Chinese community was there. They were the last big group of Chinese agricultural workers, and all their houses were on leased land."

"Fulton was researching that law?" I asked.

"Fulton had a major interest in that law," Florence said. "He memorized all its history. You know the history books that talk about the rude, unbuttoned, animated spirit of California? They say California lacked the limitations of the East; and that the people here were charged with hope? Well, funny, somehow those books didn't mention the 1913 law!"

"He'd be too young," I said. "We'd be talking about the time of his grandfather."

"His family was there from way back," said Florence. "There was one prominent guy; I think his name was Maxwell or something. In 1922 he opposed Hoover Dam because—get this—he said the project was nothing but a scheme to allow Chinese to overrun California from an agricultural base in Mexico."

"But where did this guy, Maxwell, get his facts?" I asked.

"He didn't have any," said Florence. "He was a regular tin pot Hitler and very persuasive. He played right into the paranoia of the period."

"You found some of the stuff Maxwell wrote?" I asked.

"I sure did," she said. "His rallying cry was that there would be an Asian agricultural empire centered in the Delta, with an Asian seaport city connecting it with the world's markets, so guess what, that would be San Francisco."

"And Californians viewed that as a threat?" I asked.

"Maxwell said there'd be development 'done by Asians only for the benefit of Asians'. The result was Asians were forbidden to own land in California."

"But I don't get why Fulton asked you to research property records."

"He needed to trace the chain of property ownership for a big project up there," she said. "The Docklands at the Delta. He wanted to know who assembled the land for the new development. Where did that person get the land they sold to the developers? What happened to the original Chinese leaseholders in the area?"

"What the hell difference—"

"Because the old people tell stories they had a lease with an option to renew. And that they lost one copy of the lease in the flood of 1972. But they say there's one copy left, the one that belonged to the landowner. Nothing recorded, of course. And I went cross-eyed looking for it."

"I've looked through property records. It's hard to go through them," I said.

"When I started researching this Alien Land Law for Fulton, it whacked me in the head," she said. "Coming from the East Coast, I guess I got the idea I was white. I forgot what shape my eyes are, but I tell you, this opened my eyes up."

"Your eyes?" I asked. She was losing me.

"And my hair, of course," she said. "When I was a kid, I first learned that I had good hair, thick hair; I could keep my hair puffed out, and curled, to avoid the 1920s Lotus Blossom look. No page boy cuts. I could have my hair cut in layers to connote white; to connote success. It was up to me to mitigate my Asian face by having hair as mainstream as possible."

"Hey," the man said, sitting up straight, "you gotta watch the message of a woman's hairstyle. It can be a real relationship breaker. Guys have to pay attention."

"So you looked up stuff about the Alien Land Law?" I asked.

"I had this fury when I found out. I guess I always thought that when I was working I was American, not Chinese. People could relate to me as a person. In New York City, you can walk down the street in a sari or a burnoose, or even a diaper if you want. Nobody cares. So I didn't start out radical, but I decided Fulton was right. People needed to know California did this to the Chinese immigrants. And I was getting pretty radical. And then Fulton ripped off my house!" Her face tightened with anger.

"Fulton never spoke to me about that law," I said.

"You ever go to Locke?" she asked. "When the Chinatown in nearby Walnut Grove burned down in 1915, the local fire department wouldn't put out the fire. So the Chinese built their own town, on leased land. That was the first one. Swans Landing was the second."

"But how could they build with this Alien Land Law?" I asked.

"In Locke, a few Chinese families got permission from a rancher named George Locke to begin a new town on fourteen acres where one of his pear orchards stood. And they trusted him; they had to. They just had a verbal lease. The deal worked out and the town flourished: with bordellos, opium dens, and booze joints. The place was an honest to God Las Vegas in the 20s. Even today, Locke homeowners don't own the property their houses are on. It was the same with Swan's Landing, leased land. But the Swan's Landing Chinese had a written lease."

Something in Florence's voice crumbled my defenses. This was a side of the Golden State I didn't know.

"Maxwell didn't give up," said Florence, re-examining the broken fingernail. "The part I like best, he wrote something about how Asians were a menace and that any expedient necessary to eliminate the menace in advance would be justified as a military measure of national safety."

"Jesus, I can't believe that," I said.

"What that is, see," Florence said, "that's a call to genocide in case you don't recognize it."

"But Fulton never mentioned this Alien Land Law," I said.

"You're a fool," she said. "What on earth made you assume he would? Don't tell me you had the illusion that because you admire him and he is your collaborator, he would trust you sufficiently to show you an old ethnic wound?"

Her voice filled with a cold, hard hostility.

For a moment her eyes seemed to look through me. Her nose pinched tight in distaste. I realized she must be hard to cope with at her real estate office.

"Here's your damn file that you think is so important," she said. She reached in a cardboard box behind her and zoomed it across the floor at me. "Lucky you made it today. Garbage pickup is tomorrow."

She led me to the door and said, "I'm finished right now with this whole thing."

She didn't betray any emotion now. She was not interested in my feelings or anything else.

"Don't call me again," she said.

She stood in the door, a powerhouse Asian woman whose one regret seemed to be that she had only one life to fume over the racial indignities of California's past century.

Then she slammed the door.

CHAPTER ELEVEN

Venice Beach, California

May 2, 2007

"Phone's been ringing the whole morning," my mother said.

She was ensconced on the living room couch. The foot in the cast was propped up on a pillow on the coffee table. An aluminum walker was folded beside her.

I dashed across the living room and caught the phone on the fourth ring.

"Howard Patrick Willow," Fred said.

"Who?" I asked, dropping Fulton's file with my name on it on the floor. I cradled the phone on my ear.

"He was Fulton's client," he said. "The bomber. I'm coming over. I've got stuff you need to see."

"How did you—" I started.

"He was an A student. He made the bomb in the chemistry lab at Santa Monica College. Made a couple of them, as a matter of fact."

"I'd just about get to sleep, and that damn phone would ring," my mother said. Her hand trailed off the couch, holding a book.

"Started out making bombs as an intellectual exercise. Just to see if he could," Fred continued. "But then he needed money. A radical group on campus ordered some."

"Do you think he was the kid Florence said was talking to Fulton?" I asked.

"Don't know," Fred replied.

"And then?"

"Then he got in a fight with his girlfriend. She turned him in. The police stopped him and found the bomb sitting on the backseat of his car. I'll be there in five minutes. You need to see this."

"My mother lost her wedding ring yesterday afternoon," I said. I took the phone out on the deck. "I went in the bathroom. She was standing there in her slip, holding the sink stopper and weeping, 'Please! Please help me!' She said she was washing her hands. Then she dropped her ring down the sink. These days, that doesn't mean she did drop it down the sink, but I hired a plumber today."

"And?" Fred asked.

"And a large plumbing bill later, no ring. It was a keepsake, that ring. She might not remember to get dressed, but she wore her ring every day. It's gone now."

I hung up and walked back in the living room.

"Do you remember the lotto game?" my mother asked.

"What?" I asked, baffled.

"The wooden lotto game," she said. "You remember? It had round wooden counters with numbers."

"Wait, yeah, I do remember," I said. "Daddy covered a cigar box with wallpaper. He put in a bung hole with a cork. When the family came over, he'd play lotto with the kids. He'd shake the box. A wooden number would roll out. You'd cover the numbers on a card."

"That's right," she said, smiling.

"What happened to the lotto game?" I asked.

"Oh," she said. The smile slipped. "I don't know. It was in Daddy's closet. For years."

"Where did you get this?" I asked, taking the book from my mother's hand.

"It was yours," she said. "When you were a little girl. I found it in your office."

The book's dust jacket was torn, but the title was intact, *Fairy Tales of Many Lands*. Beneath the title was a color plate of a young woman with long trailing hair. She was seated on a riverbank. A man bent over her. His dark hair was cut in a page boy. A coronet and a jewel circled his brow.

I opened the book. The inside flap said, "The Children's Bookshelf." The pages were heavy stock that had yellowed with age near their brittle edges. My name was written in childish printing on the first page. The first page had a line drawing of a princess. Her face was hidden in her wimple. I had colored in her dress with a crayon.

"I haven't eaten a thing," my mother said, raising her head from the couch. "All day."

"Mom, you know the doctor said you have to eat."

"I don't have any appetite any more," she said. She pushed herself up from the back of the couch. "It's funny, I always dieted. I have diet books going back thirty years. Now I can't put on weight."

"I'll make you some soup tomorrow, Mom," I promised. "Chicken noodle, I'll make it fresh. You always liked that, chicken noodle."

"You? She asked. "You never cook."

My mother has the habit of using "never" and "always" in sentences to me. When I was a kid it drove me crazy and it still does. My attachment to that fiercely inconsistent woman remains strong but ambivalent.

"In the hospital, nobody could eat there," she said. "They insisted on feeding me. Try it some time. See if you don't pull back automatically when they come near your face. Then the stuff dribbles down your front."

"That'd sure make me stop eating," I said. "But you're here now."

"And they get the sizes of the bites wrong that they put in your mouth."

"So I'll cook tomorrow," I said.

"Read me a story," my mother said, sinking back in the pillows.

"Slow and steady often wins the race." I opened the book and began reading. "The hare once boasted of his speed before the other animals. 'I challenge anyone to race with me,' he said."

I had forgotten that the story was so short, no more than four pages. But she was asleep on the couch before I finished.

Would I want to plod steadily like the tortoise? I thought. Or would I trade the steadiness for the occasional flash of brilliance of the hare? Would I rather publish four good novels or one brilliant novel?

I knew the answer. Slow but steady wasn't going to make it for me.

"This kid used exactly the bomb Fulton diagrammed for you," Fred said, walking into the living room through the open canal side door. I hadn't realized he'd been standing there in the doorway, listening to me read to my mother.

"Where is he now?" I asked.

"He pleaded guilty to one count of conspiracy," he said. "He could have gotten fifteen years, but he agreed to cooperate with the district attorney's investigation. He was a sort of golden boy. Top student. He testified against every major figure in the scheme, including his girlfriend, who was a groupie for the radicals. He was a key witness against the guy who was the brains for the radicals, his former roommate. All the people he testified against were found guilty and went to jail."

"I don't understand. He didn't go to jail?" I asked.

"Seems Fulton worked a shrewd deal," Fred said. "Kid had a clean record. He testified against the group that hired him. The D.A. was more interested in the radical group, so the kid got five years suspended."

"Which means—" I said.

"Which means he's out," Fred said.

"Do you have a picture of him?" I asked.

"I'm going to call some old buddies I've got on the police. I could get a copy of his booking picture."

"You think Fulton disappeared because this kid threatened him?" I asked.

"I think it's a very real possibility," said Fred. "Get this, the bombs? This guy, Willow, used to send them in plants. He found out the person's birthday from public records and sent them the day before."

"So then Fulton was taking this stuff from his file," I said.

"I brought this," he said. "I couldn't decide if I should tell you, but now I think you better have a look."

The newspaper clipping was a small item. It was from the middle of the current *Santa Monica Register*. A bomb went off in a classroom at St. Andrew's School in Santa Monica during the weekend. Nobody had been hurt, but the damage to the school was placed at approximately

$5,000. Police commented that a plant had been delivered to a teacher late Friday. The plant bore a card in an envelope saying not to open it until her birthday, the following Monday.

"That's scary," I said.

"There's another thing," said Fred. "You said Fulton was researching a development named The Docklands at the Delta, up near where he was raised. I looked up the links to the corporate records. A company called Sandhill Crane Trust holds thousands of shares in The Docklands at the Delta project. And the owner of Sandhill Crane Trust is none other than Nancy Branscomb."

"Wait," I said. "Her father surely must have purchased the shares in her name. She might not even know she owns them, if his purpose was to try to hide his investments."

"I don't know. All I know is this certainly puts a new slant on Nancy," he said. He stood up. "That brings up the next thing. I think you should get out of your house for a while."

"What?" I asked.

"If this kid found out Fulton was writing a book about his bomb, you're the other author of the book. I think you should get scarce."

"Your paranoia is kicking in," I said.

"No, remember we're on my turf now. I know what I'm talking about," he said.

"It's impossible," I said, lowering my voice. "My mother is staying with me now. I haven't got a place we could both go."

"Then I want to give you a gun," he said.

"I've got no time to learn how to use a gun," I said.

"An automatic," Fred said. "A nine millimeter. It's got a short barrel, two, maybe three inches. It's not small, but it will fit in your purse."

"And I'd probably drop it and blow off my foot," I said.

"So don't drop it."

"And I don't know if I could shoot somebody anyway," I said.

"Okay," he said, frowning. "Stay here. But I'm going to stick around."

"I can't afford you," I said.

"Free," He replied

"Why?"

"Because you turn me on?" he asked.

His look held me a moment too long and I felt a jolt. Call it sexual pheromones. Call it recognition. I did not know this man, but there was some kind of connection.

Hoo boy, I thought.

He was intense. His body hummed with a pent-up energy. I'm a sucker for intense, a man who'd turn his total energy to me in bed and do nothing casually.

I could foresee difficulties. I wondered what was going to happen when my mother went home … when I got back up to speed … when I was snarling because I couldn't get a scene … when I was writing … or when I was walking around the house in the middle of the night because that's when I get writing ideas.

"Beats me then," he finished. "Maybe I'm just thinking. Do I want to piss off a woman spends serious time thinking up unusual ways to kill people?"

CHAPTER TWELVE

Venice Beach, California

May 3, 2007

"What the hell are you doing?" Sammy Chang asked. His jaw dropped when he poked his head through my kitchen door on Saturday, May 3.

"I bought a chicken. To make soup," I said.

I smacked down with a large cleaver and dismembered a thigh from a leg. It promptly skidded off the maple cutting board I had put on the countertop. It got lost in the dust bunnies on the floor at the end of the cabinets.

"Put that thing down before you lose a finger. I'll do it," Sammy said, taking the cleaver and examining the edge critically. "When was the last time you sharpened this? I mean, within the memory of man? Do you have a stone?"

"Sammy, right now I have a lot of things I'm responsible for doing," I said.

God, the true mark of motherhood, my mother's words, coming out of my mouth, as if etched in my brain.

Generations of mothers. The cleaver I was using was my maternal grandmother's. I could remember her cutting up chickens. We'd walk to a chicken store, the kind that had chickens alive in cages. I could smell that store a block away. When my grandmother bought a chicken, the man took it in the back and wrung its neck. That memory remained vivid from my childhood.

The cleaver was dull battleship gray. There were some rust spots from years of hard use. It had a round-shaped wooden handle. The blade was four inches wide, and it had a hole at the top right corner to hang it. It weighed about two pounds. I knew its weight because it was the same as one of my hand weights for aerobics.

I positioned the chicken carcass, less the one leg and thigh, back on the cutting board.

"I'll take this to my house to sharpen it," Sammy said, snatching the cleaver. "This cleaver is useless except for maybe mashing potatoes. You'll do a lot better with it when I bring it back."

I doubted it. But I almost shared Sammy's optimism. I needed to feel optimism this morning. The night with my mother hadn't been easy. She didn't sleep much. When she did sleep, she made little yelps. Each yelp lifted me off my sleeping bag to see if something was wrong.

She'd look up at me in surprise and ask, "What sound, darling? I didn't say anything."

"Sammy, did you ever have somebody die? An old person in your family?" I asked.

"Well, my parents. My grandpa raised me," he said

"And everybody they knew is dead," I said. "The only person who remembers things like an old wooden lotto game is you. It's a weird feeling because there's nobody you can talk to who remembers the same things you do. It's like erased memories."

"Vera, this has something to do with sharpening the cleaver?" asked Sammy.

"Because it's the same," I said. "I always wrote alone. Then with Fulton, I suddenly had somebody I could talk to in the middle of writing a story. He knew exactly what I was talking about. See, I've lost that. Now it's just like not having anybody else around who remembers."

"I'll make your dinner," Sammy said, starting to pack the leg and thigh of the chicken.

"Wait," I said. "Have some coffee. Sammy, did you ever hear of the Alien Land Law? Somebody told me it was passed in 1913 and prevented Chinese from owning land in California. They could only lease the land."

"Sure," Sammy said, wrapping the cleaver and the rest of the chicken in a dish towel. "My grandpa told me about it when I was little. My uncles had to be farm workers and tenant farmers because it was the law that Chinese immigrants couldn't own land. I used to speak Chinese, but I learned from him. My Chinese was archaic and people used to laugh at me because my language was old-fashioned. He told me to switch to English if they did that. That way, they'd be at a disadvantage."

"You had family in the Delta?" I asked.

"Some," he replied. "We're from Chicago. I had one uncle who was the manager in the old Bayside Cannery up there. It burned down in 1935."

"I hear there were a lot of fires in those wooden buildings in the Chinatowns," I said.

"Interesting story, this fire," he said. "Because the watchman swears he saw the ghost of the owner of the cannery standing on a flight of stairs. That's exactly where the fire stopped. So nobody would go near the foundation of the building after it burned down. They figured there were spirits there."

"You went up there a lot as a kid?" I asked.

"Every chance I got," said Sammy. "There were still lots of rural Chinese up there. See, they came from a part of China very much like the Delta. They knew how to build the levees."

"How did they wind up in the Delta?" I asked.

"This guy named Billy Sun brought them across the Pacific," said Sammy. "Then he had them picked up and sent up the Delta on a paddlewheel steamboat. There's a labyrinth of waterways up there, where the Sacramento, Mokelumne, and San Joaquin Rivers come together. When I was a kid, I used to think of those guys, standing on the deck of the *Delta King* or the *Delta Queen* with their eyes bugging out, while they watched the rear paddles whack the water. I hear sometimes the river current prevented the paddle wheelers from making a landing on the long wharf at Isleton. Then the men were given a signal to dive overboard. I think there were times when guys went overboard, either for reasons of their own or after some persuasion."

"And then they went to work for this Billy Sun?" I asked.

"He had a restaurant and these large wooden asparagus packing sheds," Sammy said. "You can still see the wooden buildings up there, along the Sacramento River. Asparagus became a real fashionable product in the 1920s, and Asians were 90 percent of the labor force in the prime area, between Courtland and Rio Vista. This guy, Billy Sun, he designed equipment to cut the asparagus shoots. Then he created a device sort of like a large guillotine for cutting off the ends. His packing crate label went all around the state. It had a big yellow sun, because of his name."

"And it was mostly Chinese who lived in the town?" I asked.

"Actually there were two groups of workers from Guangdong; one from the Sze Yap district and the other from the Chungshan district," said Sammy. "Believe me, these guys did not get along peacefully." Sammy's eyes took on a faraway look.

"An old guy told me Billy Sun bought a 1900 Chinese noodle making machine for the kitchen at his restaurant," Sammy continued. "None of the guys working for him had ever seen anything like it."

"Sounds like a real entrepreneur, this Billy Sun," I said.

"Yeah," said Sammy. "He also catered to the whites coming to Swanee to partake of the amusements, as they called it. That is, the gambling parlors, speakeasies, and opium dens that the Chinese all owned. Swanee wasn't incorporated. It didn't have any police, so it was wide open. But the prostitution business they ran in the fishing shacks along the river, that was all whites."

"But the Chinese all worked for Billy Sun," I said.

"Yeah, these guys stood on their feet twelve hours every day," said Sammy. "They lived in these cramped dormitories and had a daily life of … well … there's a phrase in Chinese that says, 'from the pillow to the stove.' So gambling was a magnet for them. It was their only recreation. The biggest draw was a gambling house in Locke called Dai Loy. That name meant 'big welcome.'"

Sammy leaned on the door and said, "I knew an old lady up there, Helen Louie. She had a cactus garden in the front of her house on Main Street. Each cactus was in a white ceramic toilet. Years before, when the Chinatown in Walnut Grove burned, the houses burned. But the toilets were left standing. None of the locals would take the toilets because they wouldn't use toilets the Chinese had used. So Helen took the toilets and made a cactus garden in front of her house. She's long gone, God rest her soul, but the cactus garden is still there."

"But you were a kid," I said. "What did you do up there?"

"It's paradise for a kid," said Sammy. "My grandpa would warn me to stay out of the river. As soon as his back was turned, I was in the river, swimming, fishing with my hands, and having mud fights. We lived in the two-story wooden houses where the workers lived. We'd get up really early, and we could see the river otter, beaver, and muskrats. The beaver are bad news. They make holes in the levees."

"All those years you stayed around the river?" I asked.

"After the cannery burned, my uncle farmed for a while. Did you know there's a street up near Ryde called Poverty Road? No kidding. The area was agricultural. It's rich Delta earth. The family story is he grew some opium, this uncle."

Sammy opened the canal door, and Fred loomed abruptly in the opening.

"Who are you?" Sammy asked. He stepped back, startled.

"A professional colleague," Fred said. He came through the door. "How'd you get in? I'm watching the canal door."

"Through the kitchen door. I'm her protector." Sammy put out his hand to shake.

"I see you've got a burn on the side of your hand," Fred said.

"What? Well, I'm a chef," Sammy said, pulling back his hand.

"When I look at someone's hand, I always look to see if there are any calluses and where on the hand they are, and how firm their handshake is and how sweaty," Fred observed.

"Just because you're into hands?" Sammy turned to me and asked, "Where do you find these people?"

"So then," Fred said, propping an elbow on a pine cabinet, "she rubbed a jar in the kitchen and you appeared in a puff of smoke?"

"Another smart ass," Sammy said, rolling his eyes. "At least this one doesn't park in my space."

"I guess that means we're not going to be lovers," Fred said.

"I have the cleaver," Sammy said, waving it.

They glared at each other. Sammy drew himself up to his full height of five foot seven inches. Fred drew himself up to his height, five inches taller than Sammy.

"My mother is sick," I complained. "I don't need rooster crap."

"Tell me about when you saw Florence yesterday," Fred said.

"I got the file from Florence. You were right; she said lucky I came, because she was going to pitch it," I said.

"Why?" Fred asked.

"She's selling the house," I said. "She said she had to come way down on the price because the house was on the market. Then it fell out of escrow because of the burglary. Now the property is stale, but she finally sold it."

"How could you have the file and not read it yet?" Fred demanded.

"I wanted to have a look, but did you ever try checking somebody out of a hospital?" I asked. "It took me almost a whole day. And it took the rest of the day to get her settled in my bedroom. This morning I went to the supermarket. After that, I was chopping a chicken, making chicken soup for my mother."

I was annoyed. I wondered why it was necessary to explain myself.

"We need to look right now—" Fred said.

"I have the file right here," I said. "VERA MOONACHIE" was written in block letters across the tab in Fulton's handwriting. "I told Florence to call me if she heard from Fulton," I said, "but she said the phone's disconnected."

"You're chopping up a chicken instead of reading the file?" Fred asked.

"No. I'm chopping up the chicken," Sammy said. "I'm the chef."

I started to thumb through the file and felt my hopes go into a tailspin. The file contained three loose leaf pages of columns of figures written in a crabbed handwriting.

"Wait," I said. I walked over to Fred to show him. "This isn't the outline. There's nothing here about the bomber or the bomb. Look, this is Fulton's handwriting on the side of the first page with the numbers. I think he copied this paragraph from some book: 'The Sacramento Delta is the second largest estuary in the United States. Through the California Aqueduct it provides two-thirds of the state's residents with drinking water. There are over a thousand miles of Delta levees right in the center of the state's most perilous water supply. The levee system is deteriorating, and in some places literally washing away. Many levees are nothing but piles of earth that were designed a century ago to protect cropland, not the housing communities that have now sprouted in the Delta. A major collapse in part of the Delta levees would drastically affect the entire state's water supply.' Then he wrote down all these numbers. Three lined pages of numbers. Long numbers. That's all."

"Then what was he doing?" Fred asked.

"Fulton hid this file, with my name on it," I said. "There must be a reason. He didn't do things casually."

"Could it be the numbers of the legal briefs he was working from?" asked Fred.

"Fred, a secret place, or a hiding place," I said. "Fulton didn't have a home. He was being thrown out of his office because of the rape tape, remember. He knew he was in danger. Where could he hide something?"

"Vera—" said Fred.

"In a file with my name on it, that's where," I said. "Anybody finding the file would assume it had to do with our book and skip right past it."

"Then there's something in that file worth hiding," said Fred.

I looked again at the three pages and said, "See, there are none of our character names."

"If your name was on it, that file has to connect with your book," Fred said.

"No," I said, turning pages. "I don't see any diagrams of the bomb in the book, like the one on my wall. If Fulton wanted Howard as a model for the murderer in our novel, he'd know what he wanted Howard to say. What he needed was to talk to Howard about exactly how Howard would put those thoughts into words."

"Then what made you think it was the outline?" Fred asked.

"There must be a reason my name is on this file," I said. "He must have left me a message buried in the damn file. I'll have to sit down and read every page. That's what I need. Another goddamn mystery."

That's when the phone rang.

After I picked it up, the first thing I heard was a loud crackling over the line, like cellophane being crushed in somebody's hand.

"This is a message from Fulton," a low male voice said.

"Fulton! Where—"

"Fulton says stop looking for him," the voice went on. "He doesn't want to be found."

Some suspicion was there, driving me nuts. It was a fear so terrible that I could only see glancing reflections of it.

My stomach lurched, and I detested the caller. I knew what that voice had done. In that pivotal moment he had inserted terror in my head. This was the kind of terror that would wake me up at two o'clock in the morning and keep me walking the house through a harrowing all-night session, until, exhausted, I'd fall asleep at dawn, the kind of terror that courage couldn't dent, leaving me adrift and tormented.

"I want to speak to Fulton," I demanded. "Right now."

"You get this message once," the voice said. "Only once."

With a click, the phone call ended.

I felt the back of my neck tingling. My breath came hard. It had quite simply never occurred to me that I would be stalked.

When I was a kid, there was a game called Blind Man's Bluff. They put a blindfold on you, and you had to guess which of the kids circled around and whacked you. There was a little retarded boy in the neighborhood named Robert. One day they put him in the middle. He was unable to guess which kid was hitting him.

They beat the hell out of him.

CHAPTER THIRTEEN

Venice Beach, California

May 5, 2007

It took some doing to get rid of Sammy and Fred. After the phone call, they were talking about splitting round-the-clock shifts sleeping on my couch. I don't do panic. You cannot function the way I live my life if you allow yourself to panic. But I was scared.

I need to be alone when I'm scared. I'm not at my best. Every fear has its own feeling. There's the fear when the wood in the house creaks in the middle of the night. There's the fear that I would have to provide long-term care for my mother. There's the fear that I'm developing a terrible disease. But the worst fear is a cloud, no face. I had been playing at finding Fulton. Now someone wasn't playing, and he was on the move.

And he knew where to find me.

Could Richard Spain have made the call? He was an actor. He'd know how to disguise his voice, to make the call sound threatening. He'd know about the cellophane trick. He had a motive. He wanted to block further inquiry into his first book.

"You better let me go with you to talk to Richard Spain," Fred said on the phone on Monday, May 5.

I gripped the phone and said, "No."

"Why not?"

"Because it's my job, not yours," I said.

"This visit might be dangerous," he replied.

"No," I repeated.

His exasperation was apparent. I fell silent. He'd called to check on me just as I had been on my way out to catch Spain at the theater. I needed to hear what Richard Spain had to tell me, and he had said he'd be at the theater every night.

The Kings Head Theater wasn't as grand as its name suggested. It consisted of a storefront on a corner that had been turned into a theater. The windows had been painted black and displayed blowups of favorable reviews of current shows. A computer-generated sign on the door said, 'Quiet Please, Performance in Progress!' Inside, half the space was a bare stage with two freestanding backdrops. The ceiling was crusted with stage lights on black horizontal pipes with loops of black electric wires showing. Heavy wires also looped near the stage. The other half of the storefront had tiers of unmatched drop front theater seats.

The actors were sprawled about on unmatched theater seats, drinking coffee. Richard Spain sat in a theater seat apart from the others. A script was in his lap. His feet were up on the back of the seat in front. Used paper coffee cups were strewn on the floor.

"Sit down anywhere, darling," he said, waving me toward one of the theater seats. I sat cautiously, not sure if it was attached to the floor.

"This is Vanessa," said Spain. "I'm running her lines with her. Vanessa, this is Vera."

Spain pulled on the arm of a slender woman. She was maybe in her early thirties. She was just getting that first ring on her neck. She wore jogging pants and a sleeveless tank top. I noticed her nipples were poking out. Her body was that of a dancer. It was firm enough so she must have worked at it. Her stomach was flat, and she didn't have any sag under her forearms. Her dark hair was cut short. She had used mousse to put it into spikes. Her eyes were open. They looked astonished under plucked brows. Her pupils were the peculiar dark green you sometimes see in Navajo jewelry. Her thin lips were lined in glossy red lipstick.

The glance she gave me was hostile, indicating she was possessive of Spain. She seated herself beside him and hung her black shoulder bag on the back of the chair.

She said, "I hope you're not going to be long. I mean, I don't know why you're here. We're getting ready to open, and we need this time to rehearse. I have the lead in the play. It's a bigger part than Richard's."

"But my part is critical," said Spain.

"Of course, Sam, he's the director," she said, stretching out long dancer's legs, "he has this rigid mind set. Every time I make a suggestion, even a tiny one about the lighting, he throws a temper tantrum."

"She has a wonderful scene in this play where she comes out with a long speech about being an artist," said Spain. "About never knowing when to stop. How you ruin the piece and end up with nothing if you go too far. I wrote that. I really wrote it for her. It's a good scene, but now it's become a battleground between her and Sam."

"It isn't my fault Sam is totally neurotic," Vanessa complained. "And I need a filtered spot on my face when I do the scene. You'd think I was asking Sam to reconstruct the theater."

"Well, you can't have an opinion," Spain expanded physically at the idea of the director's failings. "Sam is threatened by anybody creative. Now me, I don't give a goddamn what's in fashion; I have my own acting style."

"And I say in the play, 'Even when you sleep with some old guy, he still doesn't give you a fat scene, or crisp dialogue,'" Vanessa said. "I want to do it straight, a throwaway line. No big production. The line carries itself."

"It's my line, of course" Spain inserted. "I wrote that line."

"And there's zero help with wardrobe," she said, taking a cup of pineapple yogurt and a plastic spoon out of her bag. "I spotted a dress at the thrift shop on Sawtelle that would be perfect for the character. I think it was twenty dollars. You think they would buy it for me? They would not."

"It's not enough we work for free," said Spain.

She hooked a sneaker over the top of the seat in front of her and said, "We're here three nights a week for acting classes and rehearsals."

"How late were you here last night?" I asked.

I was conscious of Spain stirring restlessly in the chair beside me.

"After midnight," he said. "Sam thinks we should sleep here while we're getting a play together. He'd have us painting the sets if we gave him an inch."

"As long as we get reviewed," she said. "Any reviews, just so the world knows we exist."

"We'll get reviewed," Spain said. "I've been phoning the reviewers to come."

"Richard told me about you. He says you also shot down his time with Nancy Branscomb," Vanessa said and turned to me. "So, what? You've got the hots for him? He does bounce around from woman to woman, you know. But you seem to be following him. It mucks things up for us. We can't be open, rehearsing, if you're here."

"Which we don't have much time for, rehearsing," Spain said.

"Acting doesn't leave you much time for doing things," I said.

"Like what?" he asked.

"Like making phone calls," I said.

"But if we weren't getting acting jobs, what would we do for excitement in our lives?" Vanessa said. She looked at Spain, as if the question baffled her. "We'd be just like regular people. There would be nothing special about us."

He chimed in, "If I tell people I was on *Days of our Lives* or something, they say, 'You were?' and they look at you different."

"During the day," Vanessa said, "I work for the billing department at a cable TV company. They know I'm an actress. If I have to go for a reading, I just leave and then make up the time. Lately, we've been so busy here at the theater I've been working Saturdays, Sundays, any time I can make up the hours."

She stretched, reached high overhead, then bent from the hips. Still seated, she put palms on the floor.

"And my car is acting up. He uses my car all the time, because his is a clunker," she said, jabbing a thumb at Spain, "When it comes to having the rattle fixed on my car, he doesn't do it. He forgot about the rattle. He forgot to tell them about the broken mirror. I think he's going into some kind of pre-senility."

"Jesus," Spain muttered, "I don't know where she's going this week to take her bitch lessons, but it's really been something. And she had two drinks last night before I got her home. It was a real experience to be in the car while she's driving."

"I had one martini and one gin gimlet," Vanessa objected.

"And she's driving forty miles an hour in the fast lane on the freeway, weaving back and forth. And she's turning her head to talk to me," Spain said.

"And then I have my family, a real problem," Vanessa said, rolling her eyes.

"You said it," Richard said, nodding.

"My mother and sisters hate each other," said Vanessa. "I mean, they seriously hate each other. The only one who talks to everybody is me. And it's hard when your sisters hate each other. I got them to go to therapy. We went to this woman down in Redondo Beach. I keep trying to be the peacemaker, and the shrink said, 'Just let them fight.'"

"I told you that all along," Richard put in quickly. He seemed to wait for any break in the conversation. "And you didn't have to pay me."

"And it cost a fortune," said Vanessa. "The only one who got anything out of it was me. I'm real close to my sisters. I tell my mother the truth now. But they—they went to Europe together when they were about sixteen, and now they're thirty-eight and thirty-nine, and they're still mad about what happened in Europe."

"About your first novel," I said to Spain.

"A prize winner," Spain said. "I have a review—"

"I've been talking to Josh Baggins," I said.

"Oh Christ," Spain said, running a hand through his hair, "That's why I asked you to come here. We couldn't really talk at the writers meeting. That loser, Baggins, I helped him out once. He killed somebody, drunk driving. I got Fulton to defend him. Now he's got the idea I owe him care for the rest of his life, just because I helped him that once."

"He says you didn't write the novel," I said.

"Yeah, well, he's a liar. Lies, just all the time, lies."

"Why come up with this story?" I asked.

"Because he's a fucking little extortionist," said Spain. "He came to me and said I had to get money for him or he'd tell people I didn't write the novel. He needs money because he wants to start a restaurant—his great signature restaurant, he calls it—up in the Delta."

"You know he's been drinking again," Vanessa said. She uncoiled, took an emery board out of her purse, and started smoothing her nails.

"And he had to go join AA after the accident as a condition of parole," said Spain. "He can't handle the booze. So he drinks behind the back of mother Evelyn. She has the money, see. That's how they got that house up in Pacific Cliffs. That's a real upscale area. And she ain't gonna stand for him drinking."

"She supports him?" I asked.

"Forget about it," Spain said. "I kid you not. He doesn't even get to operate the TV. She has control of the clicker."

"Yeah, her first husband was rich. She gets primo support for all those kids. So old Josh lines up. Just one more on mom's tit," Vanessa pumped her hands obscenely, milking. She grinned, showing fluorescent teeth like white corn kernels.

"He said if I didn't get him money he was going to tell people I didn't write the novel." Spain said. "He picked a dead man, Eddie Abelia, to say wrote it. Very convenient. He's not here to deny it. Especially since Abelia is dead because Josh killed him drunk driving."

"He told that about the novel to Fulton?" I asked.

"Well, Christ knows what he told Fulton," said Spain, "but Fulton knew he was a liar. Josh gets in snits and makes up this crap. You can always tell. The stuff he spouts sounds like it came off some episode in a soap. Like he lied about my book. Fulton wouldn't have paid him any attention. He'd have said, 'Prove it.' And there is no proof."

"Josh is desperate for that restaurant," Vanessa chimed in, "Apparently mother Evelyn doesn't have quite that much money; not for the kind of restaurant he wants. So she works nights as an emergency room nurse for more money. Makes a pretty good buck. But it's still not enough. Must have been a surprise to Josh. Have you seen her? So now he's willing to step on anybody's face to get it. A real little shit."

"Why would Fulton go to the Delta?" I asked.

"Now, that was a surprise, when Emma said that." Spain said.

"I didn't know Fulton had an affair with Nancy," I said.

"Is that what it was?" Vanessa said, narrowing her eyes. "Did she tell you about having it off in strange places?"

"We went down to the boat show in Long Beach with them. A salesman was showing this yacht." Spain tumbled over himself, eager to be the one to tell before she could. These two seemed to wax fat, to feed off the spiteful gossip. "And Nancy made Fulton go in the front cabin, lock the door, and do it. The salesman was standing outside the door and knocking and yelling. When they came out there were about twenty people who wanted to see the boat. All had goddamn smirks on their faces."

"What about the restaurant?" Vanessa's eyes glittered, and her crimson lips worked with glee at the story. "They did it under the table in a restaurant. We were there."

"You mean while the restaurant was serving?" I asked.

"Sure, the tables had these long tablecloths that went down to the floor. She just gave him a sort of look. Then they left us sitting at the table alone and dropped down under the tablecloth," Vanessa said.

"We were really uncomfortable. I mean, what the hell was that?" Spain said.

Obviously Spain and Vanessa weren't really uncomfortable. Nothing gave the two of them more happiness than the vicious anecdote about another person. But they would never have been honest enough to say so. When somebody took their gossip amiss, nobody could be more surprised than they were.

"She was crazy for having a man in public places." Vanessa said. Her eyes were icy now with disdain. "I never could see it, myself."

"I think it was the only way a man could get her hot," Spain said. "Being in the theater, I've seen some weird stuff. But I put that scene in my novel. And I think that's why she's giving me such a bad time about my new book. It's just because I put that scene in there."

"She turned down your book?" I asked.

"She could help me. She could suggest a few changes, instead of just keep saying 'No, this isn't working.'" Spain said.

"Nancy said she hadn't seen Fulton in weeks. But Emma said Fulton went up to the Delta in Nancy's car," I said.

"So either Nancy's lying or Emma's lying," Vanessa said. She put the emery board back in her purse. "I have to go; my scene is coming up, and I have to get ready."

"Emma's got no reason to lie," Spain said.

I considered that statement, balancing Emma against Nancy. Of the two, I tended to believe Emma.

"But if Nancy drove up there with him," Spain finished, "she sure as hell knows where he went."

"Do you have a cell phone?" I asked.

"No, got rid of it. It went off in the middle of a scene once. Anyway I could never get it to work right. And what do I need it for?"

Stupid, I thought. Or just a good actor?

"I can tell you," Spain stood up to follow Vanessa backstage, "if that ball-breaking bitch, Nancy, drove up to the Delta with Fulton, what you need to do is stop farting around and bothering people with questions around here. Then go up to the Delta to Nancy's cabin and take a look."

CHAPTER FOURTEEN

SANTA MONICA, CALIFORNIA

May 7, 2007

"To the Delta?" Nancy Branscomb asked, lifting off the top piece of multigrain bread to inspect her grilled halibut sandwich. I could smell the toasted bread. "Of course I didn't go to the Delta with Fulton, and I certainly don't think he drove my car there. I told you, I lent him my green Subaru, but I certainly never thought he'd keep it this long. I told you, I don't see Fulton as much as I used to."

"But you do still own a place up there?" I asked.

It was Wednesday, May 7. My time was running out fast.

"It's the family's place," she said.

She frowned at the sandwich and opened a bottle of Perrier. We were eating at The Paddle, a bar on a corner of Main Street in Santa Monica. The table under my elbow had old movie posters stuck to it under a thick, glassy layer of polyurethane. Props from a movie studio hung from the bare wooden walls. Above us there was a full-sized, old-fashioned sled that hung from the ceiling. We were two blocks from the beach bike path. The clientele at this place wore cutting-edge jersey jogging clothes.

"The best times I remember, growing up as a kid, were there," she said, smiling in fond memory. "I'd wear torn jeans and T-shirts all summer. I'd walk my dog along the river banks and then float home.

Did you know the islands in the Delta are very different, one from the other? Some are private; some are public. For example Ryer Island raises grapes and cherries—expensive top-end crops. Grand Island raises corn and less expensive crops. There are tiny, old-style ferries between some of the islands. The ferries don't have any schedules. They cross whenever cars show up. I love that about the ferries. It gives you a real insight into the Delta."

"I'm glad you were able to have lunch with me," I said.

"The only reason I can give you this time is that I got my book list in yesterday," she said.

She was in locker room chic, green sweatpants and an ivory zippered top that said "Main Event" on one pocket. She wore Asics Gel Lyte running shoes and no socks. Today an elastic ponytail holder pulled up the long, dark hair at the crown.

She signaled the waitress and said, "Please take this back. The kitchen put mayo on it. I don't eat mayo." She sipped the Perrier and turned to me. "I hope you don't mind."

"Not at all. At nine bucks a sandwich, I want it to be right," I said.

"I'm a vegetarian" Nancy said, "but I eat chicken or fish twice a week for the protein. Anyway, Fulton used to come to the cabin when I was there, but he wouldn't be going there when I'm not. He certainly wouldn't go without telling me. It's just really a shack."

"Is there anybody up there I could call?" I asked.

"Nobody lives in the cabin," said Nancy. "Have you been to the Delta? It's flat, muddy farm land and rivers. It's deserted except in summer. Only the real river rats live there. Until recently, the roads didn't have names. Addresses are still hard to come by. People say, 'I live near road marker fifteen.'"

"Is there some way I'd recognize the cabin?" I asked.

"No, it's off Highway 160, the old levee road that runs along the Sacramento River. You don't mean to drive all the way up there, surely?" she asked.

"Try it now, honey," said the waitress cheerfully, returning with the new sandwich.

"I'm allergic to wheat," Nancy said. "I hope I'm not going to blow up because I'm eating this."

"Nancy, I learned you're a major owner in the Docklands project," I said.

She stiffened and said, "I can't believe you. Where do you get your nerve? How *dare* you go looking into my finances and violating my privacy?"

"Did you work with your father on the Docklands project?" I asked.

"It certainly is none of your business, but I'm the only thing holding back that disaster," she said.

"I just need to know—"

"My father and I have never been close," said Nancy. "But in his final years, that project became a major irritant between us. I joined an environmental group, Eco Delta, when I was at Davis. The Delta is a very delicate ecological balance. Do you know anything about it?"

"I've always liked to spend time up in the Delta," I said. "I go up there often, but I never thought much about the ecology. But I read about a growing problem with the levees in the newspaper."

"We're talking major ecological disaster," Nancy said. She almost had a tone of satisfaction. I heard the holier-than-thou ring of the ecological true believer contemplating the certain punishment of environmental sinners. She touched her lips with her napkin. "We're going to have a levee collapse the way the Delta is being overused. But the state has slashed levee maintenance money."

"The state wouldn't allow a levee breach—" I said.

She barked a laugh and said, "That's what everybody thinks, because there hasn't been a major levee breech since 1986. But let me tell you, since 1900, there have been levee breeches 157 times."

"Don't the farmers take care of the levees protecting their crops?" I asked.

"You really don't have any idea the size of the problems you're talking about," Nancy said. "And you're not alone in this state. There's this network of levees that was built to federal standards, but they aren't being maintained. There are also many hundreds of miles of locally owned and maintained levees that may be even more susceptible to collapse. Some of the adjacent farmers repair the levees, but many don't."

"I guess the state will wait for the disaster and then react," I said.

"Now new housing is being built right near the water in flat areas that are vulnerable to flooding," said Nancy. "Hundreds of houses! The state won't require flood insurance because it would discourage would-be homebuyers."

"Isn't there an environmental impact report?" I asked.

"Sure. It recommends bracing the levees. So they build highly engineered levees around the new housing. That just increases the chances of the older, weaker levees next door to the new ones failing."

She took another sip of the Perrier.

"The environmental impact report also says this Docklands project would generate hundreds of daily car trips on fragile levee roads, which are coming up on a hundred years old now," she said. "You should see some of the double trailer trucks going through there. Seventy feet of truck, and God knows what the weight is."

"Then what do you think is going to happen to the Docklands project?" I asked.

She leaned her head back against the booth and said, "The Dockland group cobbled together the financing from about twelve different lenders. Thank God their loan guarantee runs out next month. I hope the whole project will dry up and blow away when that happens. They're just the wrong kind of people for the Delta."

"They must know the money's close to running out," I said.

"A lovely group, they are," she said. Her voice turned bitter. "My father's partner, Stix Chimineas, is literally a felon. He pleaded guilty to felony theft in North Carolina. He stole $14,000 worth of tools from his own construction workers. The same construction workers whose paychecks he bounced. That's why he had to leave North Carolina at a dead run. One guy said if he found Chimineas he was going to crucify him to the outside wall of his own building with a nail gun. Chimineas thought I'd change my mind about the project if he showed me how much money I stood to make."

"So they've got to go forward with the development by next month or not at all," I said.

I looked at Nancy. She was an aggressive feminist vegan. I liked her ideas. I liked what she was doing about the Docklands project. I should like the woman. I didn't like her.

Well, the wall of manuscripts she was accumulating in her office, her own personal inside joke, didn't help. It also didn't help that she spoke at me, not to me, while telling me about the Delta. She was lecturing.

"As long as there have been levees and farmers in the Delta, there have been breaches and floods," she said. Her voice had the cadence of a memorized speech. "Some experts question whether farming should even continue on the land if it jeopardizes the state's water resources every time a levee breaks. Farmers, meanwhile, see some of the richest agricultural land in the state in the Delta mud."

"Could the state brace levees around the farms?" I asked.

"The problem is that many of the farms are below sea level and sinking more each year because farming compacts the soil," she said. "So some farms are now twenty-five feet below sea level. They're not islands anymore. They're holes. The Department of Water Resources has been nattering for years about who should repair the levees. Now they're asking for fees levied on all Central Valley property owners, the whole area, to pay for levee improvements. Guess how that's going to fly."

She continued, "There's a bond up for vote that would include repairing the levees. And then there's the water quality problem. Southern California wants to suck water out of the Delta. The Sacramento and San Joaquin Rivers drain into San Francisco Bay. If fresh water is drained from the rivers, the vacuum will draw in saltwater upstream from San Francisco Bay, which will upset the water balance."

"Sure," I said, "the dreaded Peripheral Canal. I heard about it, but I thought that got voted down."

"It did," she said, nodding vigorously. "But that doesn't mean the people who want it, the water barons, have stopped trying. If they succeed, the saltwater will contaminate the drinking water supply. It will also wreck the fishing. And the agriculture. It will wreck everything."

"Nancy, this is interesting, but what has it got to do with Fulton?" I asked.

She sighed, as if at a painful memory. She said, "Fulton came to me a year ago with this wild idea that I should agree to vote my shares to go forward with the Docklands project … on the one condition that the developer would pay the original Chinese leaseholders."

"And you said no," I said.

"Fulton and I had a violent argument, and I sent him packing, I can tell you," she said. "I told him I didn't care about the Chinese leaseholders. We're talking about something that happened almost a hundred years ago. I didn't want the developers to build, under any conditions. I hated the whole project."

"And you've held out," I said.

"Now I'm finally getting to where I may be able to get rid of it, because their financing dries up next month," she said. "I told you I haven't seen Fulton for a while. That was because of the fight we had. If you were listening, of course. My experience is that many people simply don't listen."

I managed to keep my mouth shut. What an incredible talent the woman had for pissing me off.

"When he called and asked to borrow my car, I thought he'd gotten over the fight and wanted to make it up with me," she said. "Lending him my car for a few days seemed a cheap enough price. But I certainly didn't know he'd have it this long or anything about driving to the Delta."

She turned away from the remains of the sandwich. Her mouth was pursed, as if the thought of food in the face of disaster turned her off. She pushed the plate away and stood up to leave.

She said, "I need to get back to my workout."

"One other thing," I said quickly. "Did Fulton ever talk to you about a kid he represented, a bomb suspect named Howard Willow?"

She cocked her head and said, "That was one of several interesting things from his law files that he discussed with me in terms of using parts in a mystery. Why else would I bother to be here? It's all about the novel you're doing with Fulton."

At least I can't kid myself, I thought. She's not enjoying the food or my company.

"There's something you should know about Howard Willow," she said as she gathered her fanny pack and armband, attaching her heart rate monitor. "Fulton told me he's out of jail now. If he went after Fulton for writing the novel, I assume he'll be coming after you.

"And Fulton said the vicious little bastard blows people up," Nancy finished.

CHAPTER FIFTEEN

The Sacramento Delta, California

May 10, 2007

Highway 160, the levee road through the Sacramento Delta, mounds up fifteen feet above the surrounding flat farmland. Behind the levee, facing the river, stand the occasional two-story farm houses. The levee road is parallel with their second-story windows.

The Sacramento Delta area of California stretches at the convergence of the Sacramento and San Joaquin Rivers. Roughly from Sacramento on the north to Antioch on the south, it's a thousand miles of waterways. The farms, small towns, and sloughs were built after the levees were put in to reclaim the marshland and its rich earth.

I had enlisted Mrs. Caspia's services to take care of my mother for the day. Now Fred and I were driving at the level of the top blossoms of the pear trees. There were white blossoms as far as the eye could see, trees planted in geometric rows in the rich Delta earth.

Fred was driving his battered Honda Accord. We'd left Highway 4 at Antioch and gone over the great arch of the John A. Nejedly Bridge and plopped down on Sherman Island on Saturday, May 10. Then we passed the tiny somnolent Delta towns riding the levee road. This early in the spring, traffic disappears on the winding, two-lane blacktop. We matched our pace to the occasional piece of slow farm equipment on the road. We were crossing the river on the bridges, from the levee road on one side of the Sacramento River to the other, like a shoe being laced.

Delta mud follows the Delta road. It was late in the year for a rainstorm, but the heavy ashen clouds pushed low to the ground, and the pear blossoms were flapping in a cutting wind. A great blue heron beat its wings as it took off from the opposite riverbank.

"How many more of these bridges?" Fred asked.

He leaned forward to peer through the wind-whipped rain as he navigated his car across the Walnut Grove Bridge near Locke. The old black cast-iron bridge had a massive presence. It looked like a bridge made from a child's erector set.

"And what the hell is that thing?" he asked. He jerked a finger up at the massive concrete counterweight, which made the Bascule bridge look like a poised praying mantis.

"Relax," I said. I wiped the condensation off the inside of the windshield with my sleeve. The rain had started gently enough. It had been a soft drizzle, but then it had increased steadily. The river began to roil. "This is a Bascule bridge. It opens like a castle drawbridge."

"A what bridge?" asked Fred.

"Bascule," I said. "It means 'seesaw' in French. That's pretty much how it works. It's an engineering feat. This bridge replaces the first cantilevered counterweight drawbridge west of the Mississippi. So enjoy it."

He looked at me dubiously.

"Works pretty well most of the time," I said. "There was a big flood in 1986. A wall of cold brown water carved a hole in the levee and washed out the crane on the bridge. Then it crushed the boats trying to get under."

"Great," he said. "That's very comforting. Weather's getting worse."

"Too bad it's raining," I said. "You could see where the windsurfers fly. In the summer it's like entering another world. They're everywhere. They look like flying fish. They have favorite beaches, with names like 'Refrigerator Beach.' And they're a joy to look at. No fat on these people. They're fit."

"Getting hard to see with this rain," Fred said.

"Does the defogger in this car work?" I asked.

"How would I know?" Fred asked. "I live in Los Angeles. I don't use a defogger. Tell me again what in hell are we doing here."

"Because Richard Spain thinks Fulton is in the Delta. Fulton grew up here near Isleton; it's just south of us now. Wait'll you see it. Isleton has the feeling of a place time passed by. It's a sleepy town, with big old trees. It's a great place to see on foot, but you have to ratchet down the pace to about half speed. If you walk at a Los Angeles pace, you'll run into people. You'll smash your nose on one of the swinging doors of the restaurants. Isleton used to be an important riverboat stop, but now it has only the one commercial street, left over from prohibition days."

"Why would he come here?" Fred asked.

"Fulton told me it was the best time of his life," I said. "He'd come home from elementary school. This was a segregated school, mind you. Asians only. The schools stayed segregated until World War II. But he'd come home and go in the river and catch a fish. His mother would fry the fish for him for dinner. I just thought if he was going to hide, this is the place he'd go. Where he felt safe."

For a long time I'd had no idea how to find Fulton. Now I could imagine that Fulton would make a run for the cabin. My thinking wasn't active or purposeful; I simply thought about the place. The cabin took on a presence. It was distant, exotic, remote. Then there was the climate. Cool and quiet, mysterious, with its dreaming fogs and chill. I really thought Fulton was there.

"He's still playing Huckleberry Finn?" Fred said. "You said he was a weird dude. This is a weird place for a kid."

"The Delta was real open country when he grew up," I said. "Bartlett pear farmland. The river towns that sprang up during the Gold Rush were still here. They still had ferryboats that picked up people at all the little towns. Then they ran down to San Francisco. You know that building on the marina that's a marine museum now? That was the ferry terminal. Fulton said they had steamboat races until 1936. That year, one steamboat whipped the other so bad they stopped the races."

"And all these iron bridges—"

"I like them, the bridges," I said. "Sacramento feels a world away, but it's just thirty miles."

"I get lost on these Delta roads," he said. "The city could put up a sign. Maybe it's not a city. California or Sacramento; somebody could put up a sign."

"People here figure if you don't know your way, you don't belong here," I said. "Plus there are five different counties in the Delta. Each has its own rules. You see new buildings in some places and no new buildings in others. Some counties allow growth. Some counties, Solano County for example, are hell-bent against it."

"With this rain," Fred said, "we're going to have trouble finding that cabin."

"I've got a pretty good idea where it is," I lied. "I know exactly what it looks like. Don't worry about rain. This time of year, worry about fog. You won't be able to find the front of the car."

I looked across a field of mustard plants that were blazing citron yellow on an island farm. I saw a passing rust bucket freighter heading toward the Stockton Deepwater Channel. It looked so close, I felt like I could touch its huge bulk. It looked like it was swimming across the meadow. On the right side of the bridge, I could see an angler in a small rowboat, fishing for the lurking shad. The river is wide here, and I felt the silence and the silver light reflected off the surface of the water. The water that goes in channels with names like Hog and Little Potato and Lost Whisky.

There wasn't much traffic today. An occasional pickup truck was exiting one of the little old ratty RV parks. These trucks appeared ghostly coming toward us, lights on through the blowing rain, even at high noon. It was raining sideways now. I could see the drops running off the rim around the passenger side window.

"Explain to me again why we're driving all the way up here to look for Fulton," Fred said.

"Fulton is missing. Without him I can't finish the novel, because I don't know who the murderer is," I said.

"I got that part. If we find Fulton and he signs off on this novel, could you finish it?" Fred asked.

"You have to understand the way we worked," I said. "He did the structure; I did the writing. But he'd only give me the story three chapters at a time as he worked out the outline. He wanted to outline every chapter. That's what we did for six of the eight months we worked together. Sort of like walking with your feet tied in hobble step. By the time I wrote those chapters and he was satisfied, I was ready to kill him."

"But he must have given you the main idea," Fred said. "The plot."

"Fulton was into puzzle novels. You remember I told you he's a chess player? He kept saying, 'It's got to be tight. Everything working its way toward the ending from different angles. I'll line out what has to happen in each chapter. You write the chapter. Then we'll boil it down.' I told him it was a crazy way to work, but with Fulton, you worked his way or no way."

"Can't you decide how to finish the book?" Fred asked.

"The murder solution is supposed to come from the clues Fulton put in the novel. He didn't tell me who the murderer is. That way, he insisted, I'd make all the characters fully rounded rather than dropping unconscious hints about the murderer. I could pick a murderer, but then it wouldn't be the same novel."

"I could read it," Fred said. "The novel."

"What?"

"I spend a lot of my life at the criminal courts. I could probably come up with suggestions. I sometimes read mysteries. A lot of my job is waiting—when I'm following somebody, or waiting for a court case," he said, waving an arm toward the back seat of the car.

I saw paperback novels on the floor in the rear. There were two shiny ones and an old one. I'm a closet voyeur about other people's reading. I can be seen in houses, when my host goes for coffee, making a quick check of the bookshelf. I'm always surprised by what people read.

I ran my eye over Fred's books.

Two Donald Westlake novels, so he liked caper novels. And the old paperback was A.B.Guthrie's *The Way West.* So he liked history.

"Scam ain't been worked that I don't know," Fred said. "Lunch?"

We went to Al the Wop's, right after it opened at eleven thirty in the morning. It was an unlikely spaghetti and steak emporium on the main street of the Chinese town of Locke. The restaurant serves open jars of peanut butter on the table. It's a head snapper to come off the empty levee road and step into the crowds waiting for service at Al's. The twenty-foot high ceiling is crusted with business cards thrown up with dollar bills and stuck with thumbtacks. For a dollar the bartender would teach someone the trick to get a card to stick up there. Once a year they take down the bills and have a liver and onions feast. The money goes for charity. The fog doesn't affect business at Al's, which thrives by serving large portions of meat at moderate prices. Their clientele is hefty. In bad fogs, patrons simply sleep on the floor under the billiard table.

"That's a waste," Fred said, nodding toward my choice of salad. "Steak's really good here." He drank a mug of steaming tea to wash down a New York steak that looked raw. It covered half his plate.

"How come you get a girl to yourself?" the bartender asked. As he came out from the bar, I noticed that his muscles stretched the arms of his black T-shirt. He wiped the table and served my mug of tea. "Me and my buddies, we have to share one girl," he rolled on. "She wants to eat out twice a week. It's okay. Don't get mad. If you have a fight, you don't lose your girlfriend. You just lose your turn. You should have some minestrone in this weather." He gestured to a basin of minestrone going by.

I felt like warming my hands on him. Instead I warmed my fingers around the mug. The tea smelled of lemon. I let the steam bathe my face. Then I sucked up one searing sip and felt the warmth radiate through my chest. Unlike the bar, the dining room had a low ceiling. The wooden walls were warped with age. At the next rectangular table a quartet of fishermen had decided the day was too wet and blowing to get in a boat. They had switched their attention to a mountain of pasta piled between them on large white crockery plates. I could smell the tomatoes and the pungent garlic. I salivated over my damn salad. Fred attacked a plate of thick cottage fries with his fingers.

When we left, we sidled up the concrete sidewalk. The lay of the land resulted in buildings that were peculiar to Locke. Two-story structures were banked into the levee. They had entrances from both River Street, which was on top of the levee, and one story down on the narrow Main Street, which was one block inland at the levee's base. One side of the only street in town clung to the inside of the levee.

Covered staircases were built in the narrow, steep alleys in between these buildings. Even in the rain, I could see numerous little rear and side gardens with fruit trees and vegetables, providing islands of green. Now rain was beading on the planks of the long flights of stairs. Overhanging balconies protected us from the rain. We avoided the quick little rivulets in the street and on the cracked brown door frames.

We found the car and ducked into it. As we drove up the hill to the highway, Fred looked back at the ramshackle town, the two-story, weathered clapboard buildings of Locke, leaning on one another, like dominoes.

"The only town left that was built exclusively for the Chinese," I explained. "Sammy told me that after a fire in 1915 burned the Walnut Grove Chinatown, the Chinese built their own town. But they had to build it on leased land because of a law back then, which said Chinese couldn't own land. And they built these levees you're driving on, which was terrible work. Locke still has a Chinese museum in an old gambling house, but the state government closed all the gambling businesses in town. Merchants moved out in the 1950s. Now there are only about eighty people living in Locke."

"How come you know about the Delta?" Fred asked.

"I've always loved it. Ever since I first saw it years ago. I think it's the emptiness that gets me, after Los Angeles. So I drive up here, along Highway 160. Every chance I get. I just sit and think and let my pace slow down. This road is the most beautiful back road in California."

"Looks deserted," Fred said.

"Remote," I said. "Like the fog. The feeling of remoteness comes quickly to the Delta. Weddings are the big moneymaker here in the Delta now. Big crowds. These places, the Ryde Hotel, and the Grand Island Mansion, they rent themselves out for weddings and receptions. Lots of people, parking problems. People park on the road and you can't get by. Then these places are empty the rest of the week."

"Signs," he said. "Me, I like places with street signs."

Walnut Grove Avenue had a sign. Five miles south of Locke, it was a road covered with potholes and pebbles. It was lined on the riverside with small wooden shacks that were unpainted and shuttered. The land looked flat and dead. The sere brown of dead grass still covered the pushy chartreuse of spring sprouts. Crows cawed and flew up in brief loops. A few scrub oaks clung to the riverbank, where bowing tree branches dipped in the water. Across the river a chorus of dogs let loose with barks, high yelps, low yelps, off-key yelps.

The river was wide at this point. Spatters of drops whipped by the wind broke the surface. I looked at the Bay and River area map. I was aware that I was getting cold.

We slalomed through the potholes of the dirt road another mile. The treetops started snagging the low clouds. There weren't any other cars, not even parked. There weren't any signs of habitation at any of the wood shacks. Fred jerked the wheel as the road took an abrupt turn to the right. I could now hear the ripple of the current against the rocks lining the river. The land between the road and the river was narrower. The houses hugged the bank.

Further up the dirt road, the houses became widely spaced. There were some vacant lots. Trees and bushes obscured many houses. Beyond a curve in the road, I saw a wooden fence with no name on it. The gate was open.

"This is it," I said, putting my hand on Fred's arm. "This is the picture in Nancy's office."

"Let me turn the car around," he said. "This road is going to be a swamp with this rain."

I waited while he moved the car back and forth, but I drummed with my fingertips. Then I jumped out to approach the house.

"Nancy said she wasn't here since Christmas?" Fred asked. He was beside me. "Somebody was here. Look."

He pointed to grass that car tracks had pushed down. The tracks headed for a clearing. I knocked aside the trailing branches of a bougainvillea that covered part of the fence and walked up a rutted driveway to the house.

The small house was neglected. It hadn't been painted in years. It was maybe twenty feet deep by thirty feet along the river, but situated right, at the outer edge of a bend of the river. A small dock jutted out over the water. It was built over a four-foot-high concrete block foundation that must have lifted it above the periodic flooding.

I walked up a short flight of stairs to a modest deck on the yard side. I used my sleeve to smear the dirt off a window and looked at the murky interior. Ample plates and cutlery suggested somebody had once lived here full-time. I could see a group of appliances along one wall, forming a kitchen. I also saw upholstered furniture grouped around a coffee table in front of a TV set, and books in a low bookcase. Beyond that, a wall separated what might be a bedroom or a bathroom.

Fred said, "Why would a rich guy want to stay in a place like this? There's nothing here. You can look in any direction. There's nobody. Seems like a helluva place for a vacation. That river isn't pretty. It's all brown, and it looks like there's a bad current. The river stinks here real bad. The ocean in Los Angeles smells at low tide, but it's a cleaner smell. This river smells like rotting vegetation."

"You either love it here in the Delta or hate it," I said. "There's no middle ground."

I followed Fred around to the side facing the water. A smell of the mud bottom came up on the wind from the now-roiled river. Years back, some owner had built a porch swing. The chains still hung from a cross-beam, now clicking in the wind gusts.

"I don't think it's ugly," I said. "It's the kind of house where I start dreaming about remodeling. A skylight over the living room. Maybe a wall of windows along the river. A long deck on the water side. You'd be able to see one of the old iron bridges to the south."

"Lock's broken," Fred said, turning the handle. "Ain't worth a shit."

With each step my senses warned of danger.

We walked in silently, with our breaths held. The house smelled of fish, but it wasn't unpleasant. It was like an old creel. I stopped. I could feel a presence in this house. I felt I was even more of an intrusion in the bedroom. There was a small mahogany drop front desk. All its drawers were turned upside down. The contents were flung across the bedspread. Someone had scarred it with a knife, trying to pry up the baize writing surface. The dust on the floor, black with silt, had been disturbed by someone who had left a pattern of sneakers.

"Somebody tossed the place. Doesn't seem to be anything of value," Fred said, filtering through the items on the bed. "Fishing licenses, old letters, some photos."

There was an album page with empty photo corners where some photos had been ripped out. Fred lifted a man's wristwatch with a large round face and an expansion band. He dropped it back on the bedspread.

We heard a sound. A man was watching us from the doorway. I jumped back and stood closer to Fred. The man was medium sized, perhaps fifty-five years old. Muscular, he had thinning brown hair that was turning gray. He had the kind of strong bony face you earn. His leathery complexion indicated a person who works outdoors. He lounged in the doorframe, but he was not relaxed. More like coiled. He wore Carhartt jeans and a blue rain jacket and the kind of brown leather construction boots that lace up to the ankle. Only his eyes were unusual. The heavy brow ridge protected them so they were inset. They stared at us with sharp, unblinking, cold alertness.

"Who the hell are you?" he asked.

A good hater, I thought. Maybe a little crazy.

His expression made it clear that we were on his turf, invading his space uninvited.

"Nancy Branscomb gave me permission to be here," I lied. "I could ask you the same question. Who are you and what are you doing here?"

"My name is Stix Chimeneas," he said. "This is my partner's place. I was looking for some paperwork. I saw the car and thought Nancy might be here."

"Stix?" Fred asked.

"From my days as a carpenter," he said. "Like stick construction of a house."

"Partner," I said. "You're the other developer. The Docklands at the Delta."

"Going to be a wonderful project," he said, nodding. "It will revive this area and bring in jobs, bring in investment. It has to be done with taste, of course."

"I hear there are serious environmental questions," I said.

"Big projects make big targets," he said. "People have this fear of a development that is going to pave over everything. But you'd be surprised what a good developer could do for this area. For starters, make it available for a lot more people to enjoy."

"Didn't you just apply for a permit for more retail space in the project?" I asked.

"We're trying to place an enormous amount of recreational space on a mud riverbank. We've found we need to do extensive rebuilding. The retail space is going to have to subsidize the remediation work," he said, stepping closer to us.

"So the environmental questions—" I asked.

"We'll work through the environmental questions," he said. "How did you get in?"

"The door by the river was open," Fred said.

"You need to leave now," Stix said. "I'll get a padlock on that door."

"Did you search this place?" Fred asked, waving a hand.

"Not me. Probably kids," he said, shaking his head. "We get cars full of them joy riding up on the weekends."

"Why would kids have removed some photos from the photo album?" Fred asked.

"Who knows why kids would do anything?" Stix said.

The wind was blowing off the river now, rattling the loose windows on the river side. I shivered as we left the house. I looked south on the river. I saw the boat houses and docks of the small shacks we had passed coming in. Chimeneas busied himself with the door nearest the river.

I was surprised when, instead of abating, my sense of uneasiness increased as I was moving away from the cabin.

In the yard a large white Chevy Explorer was parked next to Fred's car, with a license plate that said "STIX 1." Stix came out and gave us a long, hostile look before he got in the Explorer. He kicked dirt at us as he pulled up to the road. As Fred opened his car door, I turned and walked up the ruts to the clearing. The ruts followed a path covered with dead leaves that meandered off. On the side of the path, knots of shrubs rose and fell in waves of different colors of green. Dense mosses clung to the base of the trees. The grass waved in the wind. A clearing hadn't been there long. It had been made by a parked green Subaru, which had scratched some of the nearby trees and flattened the tall grass.

"A green Subaru," I called to Fred. "Nancy said her car is a green Subaru. Fulton has been here."

"Beats me how he could have gone anywhere from here," Fred said, swiveling his head. "Without a car."

"Somebody else was here," I said. "That's how Fulton got out."

"Somebody who had a car."

"Not Nancy. She'd have taken her car," I said.

"Then who?" asked Fred.

"How about Mr. Stix-like-stick-construction-of-a-house? He spotted us. Maybe he spotted Fulton," I said.

"No," Fred said, shaking his head dubiously. "Concentrate on Howard Willow. With him, we know he's a murderer."

CHAPTER SIXTEEN

The Sacramento Delta, California

May 10, 2007

I heard the buzzing of the flies first, big iridescent bottle flies, flies that would show up in my nightmares for years. Heavy buzzing, like you hear in hot August. Except that now it was a freezing day in May.

"The people here live behind a network of earthen dikes built to hold back the water, a fifteen-foot-high fortress of mud and gravel." I was chattering and nervous. I was lecturing like Nancy. "The levees have held for decades, but they're one hundred years old now. The state government keeps trying to get money for redoing them."

"Why are we riding on these levee roads if they're dangerous?" Fred asked.

"They're the only roads. We've got to circle back to get Highway 4," I said. "No way I want to drive on these Delta roads after dark. We can take the J-Mack ferry across Steamboat Slough. That will save some time."

"In this rain?" Fred asked.

"The ferries operate round the clock, and in any weather. And they're free. I don't know how come they're free, because they're owned by Caltrans," I said.

Fred was driving fast to get to the ferry before dark. I pulled my parka over my lap and started to drift off to sleep. Unscheduled naps can produce vivid dreams, but I skimmed along on the thin surface of sleep. The Delta settlements we passed felt peacefully timeless and good for naps.

I jerked awake. Fred swore as the front passenger side wheel fell into a pothole, covering the windshield with spume.

The J-Mack ferry leaves at the bottom of two short hills that descend like a Y-shaped staircase to a platform. The platform is where you drive a car on the ferry. The ferry is little more than a twenty-five foot by fifty foot flat, steel barge with an operators cabin on the left side and a handy rear ramp that drops flat to let a maximum six cars ride at a time. The flat platform stays down for the four-hundred-foot trip across the slough. A sign on the flat platform said, "Wait Here For Ferry. Drive On In Low Gear. Lights Out." Large signs facing the river traffic read "Do Not Pass Ferry When Light Is Flashing."

"Why's that light flashing?" Fred asked, looking unhappy.

The rain was blowing across the top of the slough now, making patterns.

"It's dangerous here," I said. "If you're in a speedboat, you can't see the cable pulling the ferry until it comes up out of the water. A red greased cable is just below the water surface. If you try to speed past the J-Mack ferry in your boat when the lights are flashing, you could hit that cable and flip your boat."

"Jesus," Fred said.

"For me, the free ferries are the best part of the Delta," I said. "But one guy was speeding in a boat. He hit the cable and was decapitated. I hear three boaters were killed in the past decade. The signs warn boaters that the cable will surface as the ferry crosses and rise at the ends to pull the ferry to the other shore. Boaters sometimes don't pay attention."

"You sure we want to do this?" Fred said. A smell of the mud bottom filled my nose, mixed with the smell of grease.

"Sure," I said. We drove over the flat metal platform and got on the ferry. "You'll get to go on a boat ride. Relax." I wished I felt as positive as I was trying to sound. "This J-Mack ferry is actually one of the newer ones. This one was built in 1966. There used to be a lot more ferries, from the 1920s to about the 1970s. A cable ferry is a lot cheaper than a bridge. Now the ferries are disappearing. Only five are left, and three of those go only to private property."

"Caltrans owning this ferry doesn't make me feel better," Fred said.

The yellow and black traffic arm dropped behind us. With a massive clanking, the ferry, guided by its cable, started to move across the slough. The water was brown with the rain. The cable, which was under the water when we started, started to rise out of the water to guide the ferry to the other side.

"River is muddy," Fred said, looking out the car window.

"That's what the word 'slough' means," I said. "It's Old English for a place full of soft deep mud."

"What, you got bit by a dictionary?" Fred asked.

"I get off on words, and the sound of words. I'm a writer; it's what I do," I said.

Most of my friends were too used to my obsessive interest in vocabulary to pay attention.

The movement of the ferry and the gas fumes from the car were making me nauseous.

"I've got to get out of the car for a while," I said.

I put on my hooded Gore-Tex parka. My blue jeans were wet from walking in the grass at the cabin. Clammy and cold, I caught the full force of the wind. I couldn't stop shaking. I could feel the toes of my shoes turning up in the damp river air.

That's when my eye caught it. A rope had wrapped itself under the water around the red cable.

"What's that?" I asked, pointing it out to the woman ferry operator.

"Beats me," she said, looking. "Shouldn't be there. It won't stop us. This ferry will run right over anything except maybe a big old log with branches. Wait a minute." She stepped back to the operator's cabin to grab a grappling hook on a long pole. She pulled on the rope as we passed it, but it evaded her.

"Fred," I said, knocking on the car window. "Help us."

All three of us pulled on the grappling hook. We hauled in about ten feet of rope, which seemed to be attached to something.

Fred leaned way over the back deck. He was parallel with the water and grabbed for the rope. The rope skittered away from the boat, and he reached out for it. Just then a wave hit the ferry. Suddenly Fred lost his balance. With his legs wheeling and his hands snatching at the air, he tumbled into the river with a massive splash.

I started to giggle with nervousness. He looked so drowned as he came up choking.

"Jesus Christ," he gurgled. He swam back to the end of the ferry. "There's something down here. Wait! This shouldn't be here."

"Get him out!" The operator said.

"If you'd stop laughing like a nut, you could help me," Fred said accusingly. "Pull this damn thing up on the ferry."

He pushed up the top of a zippered garment bag that was slimy with mud.

I fought down the waves of shock and urgency to get him out of the water.

That's when I heard the buzzing of the flies. They were coming from inside the zippered garment bag. As the bag rose out of the water, it tore. The flies swarmed around the top of the zipper.

None of Fred's or the operator's words registered with me. The scene simply dropped into my velvet-lined shock pocket.

"Here," Fred said.

He put his arms around the garment bag and pushed it up out of the water. Then Fred scrambled, and we pulled on his arms. His arms were muddy and slippery. He fell back twice, but we finally got him out of the water. He knelt on the deck. He was dripping puddles of water. The soaked cuffs of his pants were flapping around his bony ankles. He was shivering uncontrollably. We all pulled. The garment bag came up onto the flat platform of the ferry.

"I'll get a blanket," said the operator. "This guy is going to freeze."

The side of the garment bag was ripped. I could see that something was inside. It looked like a bundle of clothes covered with mud and twigs and leaves. The cold air made a wave in front of my eyes. I doubled over the pipe railings and vomited the salad from lunch.

"Wait," Fred said, putting a hand on my arm.

"No," I said, shaking it off. "I have to see this with my own two eyes, even if it's bad."

I tugged through the rip. The bag turned, and my stomach lurched. A body was inside. Its face was bloated, and some kind of fish had been eating it. One ear was gone. A knife was stuck under its breastbone. Yet I recognized the pattern of male baldness.

That's when I screamed and screamed. I was looking at Fulton.

CHAPTER SEVENTEEN

The Sacramento Delta, California

May 10, 2007

Fred called the police on his cell phone, which he had left in the car. It took an hour for them to come. Five different County Sheriff's Departments have responsibility for parts of the Delta. San Joaquin County has responsibility for water patrol, and they had to sort out the jurisdiction, figuring out who should respond to our location. Some county borders run along the middle of waterways. In an emergency, boats from one county will go into another county.

The police finally arrived in the form of a short, no-nonsense San Joaquin sheriff named Ted Saunders. He came on a boat that did routine law enforcement, like a patrol car. He had a muscular body that stood about five-foot-nine in his dark green uniform. His belly was just starting to protrude over his belt. He looked to be about forty-five years old. When he took off his cap, his scraggly brown hair was thinning. I could see his freckled scalp. He seemed more interested in what we were doing in the Delta than in Fulton's body.

"So tell me again how it was you came to be here?" he asked. From the measurements he had taken, he started to sketch the scene in a spiral notebook.

"It's all in the statements," Fred said. "She was writing a novel with the dead man. We drove up from Los Angeles to look for him."

"But you say you didn't know he was here," Saunders said.

"Ms. Moonachie wanted to have a look," said Fred.

"And you were headed for a cabin up here to look. This here cabin is your place? You own it?" Saunders asked.

"No," I said. "It belongs to a woman named Nancy Branscomb."

"And she gave you the key?" Saunders asked.

"No," I seemed to be repeating myself. A litany of nos. "She didn't know I was coming here today."

I looked at the clearing where the ferry landed. Fulton had been strange, but he and I had shared a mental life while writing the book. I felt acutely bereft. I didn't have anybody to bounce a story back and forth anymore.

Back to solitary confinement in my head.

"Just tell me why you're here," said Saunders, turning to me. "I don't want to get information in little pieces."

"Who put him in a garment bag?" I asked. My mouth was rancid with the loss of the salad. "Fulton's dead and you're talking about why I'm here. Why aren't you finding out what happened to him?"

"We won't know that until the coroner's team gets here. They have to drive from the County Crime Lab in Sacramento. We don't get much in the way of murders here," he said, folding the notebook.

I nodded at the implied rebuke. We had infected his pristine Delta with our Los Angeles ways. The result was a body.

"I'm assigned to the police boat," he said. "I've had to dive in this slough for bodies from boating accidents. I've never had a ferry cable present one to me."

He picked his next words carefully. "You're sure you can identify the victim, Ms. Moonachie? It must be difficult to tell."

"The victim was Asian," I said. "And I recognized his hairline."

"His hairline?" Saunders said, looking up.

"He had a receding hairline." I said. An impulse seized me. I bent and placed a folded piece of paper on the cable track to the clearing. It was a goodbye momento for Fulton, instead of flowers.

"What are you doing?" Saunders asked, looking incredulous.

"It's a page from a novel we were working on. I'm leaving it for him." I said.

Saunders boomed, "This is a sealed crime scene. All the way up to the yellow tape out there near the road." He pointed. "Get that paper out of there. Put your hands in your pockets when you walk out. Don't put anything here!"

"You know the piece of paper isn't part of the crime scene. Just pick it up after we leave," Fred protested.

"I still don't understand what you're doing here," he said, whirling on Fred, who looked like a homeless man, wrapped in a gray blanket, with his mud-streaked face. He held Fred's soaked business card with two fingers, away from his body. "A private detective. From Los Angeles."

"I drove Ms. Moonachie—" Fred started.

"And you think you're one of the boys," said Saunders. "You can tell me what to do at a crime scene?"

"I don't think anything—" Fred said.

Saunders said, "Let me tell you something about this place. The Delta is my place. These are simple people, country people. They don't think much of murder. They don't think much of fancy Los Angeles '*private* detectives.' How did you come to pull up the garment bag?" He was on me again. "You couldn't see it in the water."

He was not stupid, this sheriff.

"She saw the rope on the cable," Fred said. "It was tied to the garment bag. Look, you can see she's shook up—"

"Don't interrupt again," Saunders' voice was low, but there was no mistaking him. "We don't like unsolved murders here. And we don't tend to trust people who come four hundred miles to find a body."

"Can we leave now?" I asked. "He's chilled to the bone, and we have to drive back to Los Angeles. I have to care for an aged mother." Even to me, it sounded witless.

He gave us a long stare and said, "All right. Get your ID back from my officer. We are to be kept informed of your whereabouts. Both of you. Do you understand?"

"Clearly," we said.

I didn't care to trifle with this sheriff. And I was already on his shit list.

We drove in silence. We were almost back to Highway 4.

"You carried that page of the novel with you," Fred said. He hadn't spoken. Now he accused me. "You knew you'd be leaving it."

"I felt it," I said. "The page was part of our novel. It was a connection between us."

"I'm jealous," said Fred.

"Don't be," I said. "Writing is a part of me that always worked alone. I just went crazy because I suddenly had somebody to talk to about what was in my head."

It took us six hours to drive back home. We had left Los Angeles to drive north to the Delta at six o'clock in the morning. It was after midnight when Fred dropped me off. I stood in the paved court at the rear of my house. I was unable to go in. I was beyond exhausted. I didn't think I could face inside yet. The day had been too much. Truthfully, I didn't have any choice.

"How's she doing?" I asked. I stretched out my hand with five twenty dollar bills as I came through the door.

"Fine," Mrs. Caspia whisked the twenties into her capacious purse. "I had no idea you were going to be so late. Good thing my husband's on disability this month. He's home with the kids."

"Right," I said. My voice sounded hollow. I was dizzy. I only had the salad at lunch today, and I'd lost that.

"She's so sweet, really, you know," Mrs. Caspia said. "I feel like she's my own mother."

"Thanks," I said.

"To tell you the truth, I'm glad to get out of the house," she said. "My husband hurt his knee on the job. He's driving me crazy."

"How's my mother?" I asked.

"He follows me in the kitchen," she said. "All of a sudden I don't know how to cook. If I throw out a slice of bread that got moldy, he says, 'Don't throw that out. I'm not bringing in a regular salary, remember.' Now he has to come shopping with me every time I go to Costco. First of all, it takes him so long to get ready that I lose half the day. Then he walks around the whole store complaining about prices!"

"So my mother is all right?" I tried again.

"Today wasn't a good day," Mrs. Caspia said. What was unspoken was that maybe, please God, tomorrow would be less bad. Not good. Less bad.

"She's in bed?" I asked.

"She's fine now. Just fine," Mrs. Caspia said. She was halfway out the door. "But she got upset because she couldn't think of olive."

"What?"

"You know, olives," she said. "You have a jar of them in the fridge, and she wanted some. She couldn't think of the word, and I couldn't understand what she was talking about. She really threw a tantrum and said I was stupid. She finally said, 'You know, the things with the nut in the middle.'"

"Oh."

"Don't worry about it," she said, waving a hand.

"This is very recent," I said. "She never used to have trouble with words."

She said, "I read a magazine article that said there's two kinds of memory: short-term memory and long-term memory. Both are different." She opened the door of her car. "I tell my kids, that's why they don't remember anything after a day when they cram for a test. You have to make the connection with your permanent memory. You have to say out loud, 'I am putting my glasses on top of the refrigerator.' Then you'll remember."

"I have to write myself a note," I said. "I don't ever look at the note, but it sets the idea in my memory."

"That article said what we lose is our short-term memory when we're older. It's like you can only put so much in your head. When you're old and you put in something new, there's no room, so the new stuff falls out," she said.

She settled behind the wheel with a series of grunts.

"It was a great article. Next time I come, I'll bring it to you," she promised.

She ground her gears and drove off.

CHAPTER EIGHTEEN

Culver City, California

May 19, 2007

Fulton's funeral was held more than a week later, after the autopsy was done and the police finally released the body. I had been numb, unable to write, as I took things day by day. It was Monday, May 19. In the foggy cold of a West Los Angeles morning, I got several surprises.

First, Fulton was buried with a full requiem mass at a Catholic church. A bell tolled once, then again, then again, as I walked with the other mourners through massive doors with the coffin leading the way. I clutched my purse in front of me as I headed into the dank Gothic austerity of St. Mallachy's Church, stepping inside from the gray, early morning coastal fog. As we entered, each mourner was given a printed program of the order of the mass. A separate piece of folded paper inside the program said that after the mass there would be a reception in the church hall. Then Fulton's body would be driven north for burial in the family plot in the Delta.

The church was located on a corner on Washington Boulevard in Culver City, a busy street with four lanes of traffic, a cacophony of honks and motor noises. Entering the church was entering another world. The interior was dark, except for the light filtering through the stained glass windows three stories up in the vaulted nave, and the guttering candles in front of the white marble statues of saints. The pews were dark oak. Generations of pious knees had split the leather of the kneeling risers. St. Mallachy's had that unmistakable odor of a Catholic church, a combination of candles and incense. The smell of dry air and dust stuffed my nose.

Second, Florence was at the service, dressed in a dark purple pantsuit and a pink blouse and a swooping pink felt hat. Somebody knew how to get hold of Fulton's parents, because they were at the mass. His mother hid under a dark straw hat, weeping in the first row, beside the closed coffin. Periodically his father, a small Asian man in a dark suit and a white shirt buttoned tightly to his neck, would put his head on his hand on the back of the railing in front of him and whisper, "My son." His eyes were closed.

Nancy Branscomb sat several rows behind Fulton's parents. She clutched the top of the pew in front of her so tightly that the veins stood out on the back of her hand. Oliver was there, sleek and well-dressed in a dark suit and vest. On the right side of the aisle, Emma Sawtooth sat with Richard Spain and Vanessa halfway down the church. Emma wore a dark jacket instead of her poncho. I sat halfway back on the left side of the aisle. Josh and Evelyn were near me.

I saw most of the members of the writers group, including the man with the broken fingernails. Roz was there, and a young Latina I didn't know. She bowed her head as she sat alone. She wore a black lace head scarf and a cheap gray wool suit. She was the only person who whispered soft responses to the litany of the service for the dead.

The other surprise was Sheriff Ted Saunders, who loomed with his deputy in the vestibule of the church. Next to him was a uniformed Los Angeles police officer. Saunders put my name on a list the deputy was writing.

"I need to speak with people after the service," he told me. "Save me time rounding everyone up."

"I didn't know Fulton was Catholic," I said, sliding in next to Nancy.

"He didn't practice," she said. Her face looked drained, a contrast because she had looked so healthy. "But he was educated at a Catholic high school."

"He never used Catholic words," I said.

She looked at me blankly.

"You know, Catholic words, like 'occasion of sin,' or 'plenary indulgence,' or 'genuflect,'" I suggested.

She shrugged and faced forward.

"That San Joaquin sheriff in the vestibule wants to speak to us after the service," I said.

"Where do you come off giving him my name, talking about me," she said bitterly. "Telling him about my cabin? I gather you broke in. I had no idea you were even going up there."

"You think you'd rather have found Fulton yourself?" I asked.

"You didn't ask my permission to go there. You certainly had no right to involve me in this investigation!" she said.

"Shush," Fred said, as people glared at us.

The priest circled the coffin swinging a censer. Then he climbed a small circular set of stairs to the pulpit.

As I heard the ancient prayers and pleas for the repose of Fulton's soul, I tried to prevent the image of his body in that coffin, looking like I had last seen it, from coming into my mind.

This gray Gothic pile of a church with its huge altar didn't extend comfort. It didn't seem to belong in West Los Angeles, nor did it seem to be the antechamber to a welcoming heaven. This Gothic fortress looked like a repository for all the rules that Fulton broke. And I broke.

And then the priest served Communion. About a third of the congregation filed to the altar to receive the host. Then the pallbearers escorted the coffin out of the church. Fulton's parents followed. His father held the arm of his mother to support her faltering steps. The rest of the congregation followed. We shivered on the sidewalk and waited silently while the coffin was loaded into the hearse.

Saunders was waiting outside the church, waving a beefy arm to beckon the people he wanted into a huddled group.

"I didn't interrupt the service, but I need a word with all of you," he said. He was wearing a black baseball cap that said "Sheriff" on front.

"I've never been to a Catholic funeral before," Fred whispered.

"I can't pray," I said." I feel like jumping up and yelling, 'Fulton, you didn't tell me the rest of the story. Now what am I going to do?'"

"He didn't have a choice about being killed," Fred said.

"I'm not allowed to be mad at the dead?" I asked. "Where was God when Fulton died? God's got rules against being mad at the dead?"

"You are getting very angry," Fred said, using his hands to gesture to me to lower my voice.

Was it true? I thought. Was I getting to be an angry crone? The third stage in the cycle of women?

Aging women are devalued in Southern California. There is a thriving business in cosmetic surgery, but I knew the fairy godmothers in the fairy tale book I was reading to my mother were sweetened versions of the mythic, wise, old woman, the woman who knew things other people didn't. I knew the three phases of women; maiden, wife, and crone. Maybe I was becoming the crone. I should start concentrating now if I wanted the cognitive power of the crone and start being more intuitive. I wanted to know a lot of things. Specifically, I wanted to know who stabbed Fulton. I wanted to know who stuffed him in a garment bag and put him in the slough.

I turned to Fred and said, "It's a bad way to kill a man, leaving him zipped in a garment bag, in the mud and water. Unburied. I keep thinking maybe there are other chunks of Fulton eaten by fish, or stuck in the levees somewhere. It's indecent."

Florence stalked out of the church.

"Ask me your questions," she snapped at Saunders, "because I'm finished. And Fulton was dead when I was burglarized, so now I know he wasn't the burglar at my house," she said to me.

"I'm dealing with the dead body in the Delta," Saunders said. "The LAPD can have any burglary here. I need to know what Fulton Yee was doing up on the Sacramento River. And I want a look at this lady's cabin." He pointed to Nancy Branscomb.

I needed to know how I could get the rag-wrapped bundle I remembered flushed out of my mind. I wanted to wash out the area behind my eyes and return to seeing Fulton as he had been—alive, creative, and enthusiastic. I would have to make my excuses to Fulton's parents to remain at the church as Saunders demanded, and not go to the reception.

"I want to know if any of you were up there with him," Saunders said. "And I want to know how you knew he was up in the Delta." He looked at me.

"She knew because I told her," Emma said. She loomed up behind me. "Fulton went up there in Nancy Branscomb's car." She pointed an accusing finger at Nancy.

"Will you two just shut your mouths? You don't know what you're talking about," Nancy said. "He borrowed my car, and I still don't have it back. But I didn't know a goddamn thing about Fulton going to the Delta."

"But why did he go?" Emma asked.

"We all know why," Vanessa said. Her eyes flicked from one of us to the other. "Richard won't let me say, because he wants to suck up to Nancy so she'll help him get his new book published. But that bitch drove Fulton up to her cabin and then killed him. I think he got tired of her weird sex games."

"I didn't kill anybody," Nancy screamed. "How dare you? Check my office; I've been there every day."

"Vanessa! For Christ's sake," Richard Spain took her arm, moving her away.

"Quiet down," Saunders boomed. "All of you. I'll talk to you one at a time. The rest of you are going to wait right here. We'll start with you." He pointed to Emma.

They walked to where the uniformed Los Angeles police officer lounged against the door of a large white SUV. His expression showed boredom. On the door of the SUV was an emblem with the state capitol building in gold inside a seven-pointed star. The image was surrounded by a green circle that said "Sheriff, San Joaquin County", with six more stars. Near us, Saunders's deputy took up a stance, rocking slightly on his heels. Hands behind his back, he kept his eyes on us. I had the feeling he'd deck us if we tried a break for freedom.

"I haven't seen him in weeks," I could hear Emma saying to Saunders, "but he told me he was going to the Delta with Nancy Branscomb."

Oliver came out of the church and walked me apart from the group.

"What was in that file Fulton left for you?" he asked.

"Nothing to do with the novel we were writing. Even worse luck, it was just some lists of numbers." I said.

Fleshy bags hung under Oliver's eyes. All the healthy people were looking bad today. When I shook hands, his were warm and sweaty, despite the cold fog.

"I hear there wasn't much left of Fulton. Poor guy," Oliver said.

Josh Baggins abruptly materialized next to Oliver.

"You're Richard Spain's agent, right?" he asked. "I just finished an incredible book of chef's recipes and anecdotes. I'm shopping for an agent."

"Doesn't sound like my type of thing," Oliver said. "I do mostly fiction."

"Just take a look," Josh urged. "The recipes will blow you away. Once I taste a dish, I can duplicate it. I can taste what they hide in there, cumin, whatever. I have an incredible palate. That's a gift. They can't teach you that. You have it or you don't. You want to get in on this. Because I'm going to open a restaurant up in the new Docklands project. The book will be my signature book."

"Oh, you're the one who put in a proposal for the new restaurant up in Isleton," Nancy said.

"Project's held up right now. There's talk about bracing the mud bank. There's also some crap about the waterfront up there now, the parking issues, and the environment," Josh said. "But it will get itself sorted out. Going to be a great project. Bring that Delta area into modern times."

"Seems like you'd have to be round the bend to want to open another restaurant. There are hundreds of them in San Francisco and probably hundreds more in Sacramento," Oliver said dubiously.

I screwed my eyes tight shut.

"This isn't the time, here at a funeral." Oliver said to Josh. "Just drop the manuscript off at my office." He turned to me. "Let's grab a coffee, Vera."

"I've got to stay and talk to this sheriff," I said.

He ran a hand through his hair and said, "I didn't come just for the funeral. I've been talking to the publisher. We only have less than two weeks."

Oliver was smiling, but his eyes were telegraphing something else too. Maybe it was because I was sick. Maybe I was sensitive due to the funeral. But I couldn't shake the vague sense of uneasiness about Oliver. Miserable day, miserable mood.

"Oliver, please, it's enough for today," I said.

"Okay. Then I need to see you at my office, Vera. Let's say Tuesday at three. Be there."

I watched his retreating back. He didn't say why he needed to see me, but that wasn't unusual. I took deep breaths. These summonses without explanation were Oliver's method of keeping the writers frightened and in their place. I tried to ignore the sensation of things gone badly wrong.

"Ridiculous ceremony," Nancy said. I realized with surprise that she had been crying. "I would have preferred to say good-bye by having him cremated. But his parents insisted on this dreadful mass."

"Cremation," Emma said. She had returned from the SUV. "Let me tell you about the mechanics of cremation. Cremation sounds great—everybody has this idea: 'we'll stand on a shoreline and say a prayer and let the ashes blow off our hands into the sea.' Everybody thinks it's like cigarette ashes. Well, it's not just ashes. There are lots of big pieces of bone, which holds down the ashes."

"I don't want to hear this," Nancy said, pulling her coat tighter.

"And the wind comes off the water and blows the ashes back in your mouth. It's a mess," said Emma.

"Enough," Nancy said, holding up a hand. "I can't stand these people. If you want me," she said to Saunders, "walk with me to my car."

"Nancy, if you're leaving, it's important we talk." Richard Spain said, grabbing her forearm. "About my book."

"Not now," she said, shaking him off.

My ears were ringing from the cremation discussion. I hadn't had breakfast, and the dry heaves I'd been fighting during the mass came again. I didn't feel like talking to Saunders. I closed my eyes, but I couldn't shut out his voice.

He had more questions for me. Why had I driven all the way to the Delta? Why had I gone to the cabin? The answers seemed obvious to me. Because I was looking for Fulton. Saunders' face started to go in and out of focus.

"That's enough," Fred said, taking my arm.

"I don't need you taking care of me," I said.

We argued. It was an uneasy sparring, a marking of turf for a relationship that didn't yet exist.

"You again," Saunders said, swiveling to Fred. "I told you to stop interrupting. I get the feeling you two know more than you're telling me. Or you wouldn't have found that body."

"Nobody cares about my burglary, right?" Florence said. "That's just not important enough for any police to pay any attention. Real estate business is going through a bad cycle right now, and I've got a tough enough time without a burglary."

She put her ID back in her purse and snapped it shut.

"We don't know a damn thing about your burglary," Fred said. "And she's had enough for today."

"I came here today to say good-bye to Fulton," Florence said. "I figured we were together for a year, what the hell. Now I'm leaving. And I want you all to stay away from me."

The ground felt like it was rolling under my feet. It was like the beginning of an earthquake.

"This doesn't sound like just collecting information," I said to Saunders. "You sound like you think I killed Fulton."

"I don't know what the legal status is," Nancy said to Saunders, "I don't even know if you have jurisdiction down here. You're bothering us when there's a genuine killer loose, and you're not talking to him. He killed several people with a bomb. Fulton defended him, and he was writing a novel about him. With her." She pointed to me.

"It keeps coming back to you, doesn't it," Saunders said, swiveling to me. "The page you were so hot to leave, was from that novel? He was taking parts of the novel from the court case with this bomber?"

"I think so," I said.

"But you didn't think it was necessary to tell me that when we found the body. I said you two weren't telling me all you knew. Did I say that?" Saunders said, his question directed at his deputy.

"You said that, sir," said the deputy.

"So what's the name of this killer?" asked Saunders.

"Howard Patrick Willow," Fred said.

"You got an address?" Saunders said, writing the name.

"No. And this guy isn't easy to find. I ran him through my database, and I can't find him. Believe me, that is unusual."

"I remember what Fulton said," Nancy added. "He said this guy was an icy-eyed little killer. So, go find him. I'm leaving."

"We think Fulton was taking the information, including the diagram of the bomb, from his actual criminal file. He defended Willow," Fred said.

"And I'm leaving too," I said. "I feel sick."

The Latina I had noticed left the church, dropping a rosary into a worn leather handbag. She wasn't as young as I thought she was, maybe thirty.

Saunders deputy was taking her name and address as I walked to Fred's car.

"Clarita Valdez," she said as she gave him her driver's license.

"Clarita Valdez?" I said, stopping. "Wait. Your name was on Fulton's telephone log. I've been trying for days to find you. No phone is listed for you. Could I talk to you?"

"Are you butting in again?" asked the deputy.

"Sure, but I don't know anything about Fulton's murder," she said. "I was returning Fulton's phone calls, but we kept missing each other. I think he wanted to talk to me about my brother."

"Your brother?" Fred asked.

"He's dead, my brother Edward," she said. "My full name is Clarita Abelia Valdez."

CHAPTER NINETEEN

West Los Angeles, California

May 20, 2007

I stood in the interior hallway of the two-story stucco building and rang the bell of Clarita Valdez's apartment. Most apartments in Los Angeles have outside walkways, even on the second story. I had forgotten how an inside hallway becomes ripe with pungent cooking smells. This one had a strong smell of frying onions and beans. And something else, cut cilantro, maybe.

Clarita lived in the Mar Vista section, which means "sea view" in Spanish, but there was no sea view from her apartment near Washington Place and Coolidge Avenue in West Lost Angeles. The view out of her living room window was across a scraggly patch of grass to the mirror image apartment twenty feet away. Downstairs, bicycles were propped against the stucco wall of the building. Their frames were locked to trees. Two women, seated in plastic folding chairs, gossiped on the grass.

The small living room had cream colored walls and the kind of window shades that roll up with a snap. The room was filled with large matching furniture, including a couch with a heavy maple coffee table in front of it. Opposite the couch stood an entertainment center that took up most of the far wall, with a twenty-seven inch TV currently playing *Gilligan's Island*. In this episode the humor was that Bob

Denver, the actor playing Gilligan, had inexplicably lost all his hair and was cue-ball bald. The TV image had the black shadows behind the figures that occur when film has been restored. On top of the TV was a vase with an arrangement of flowers made of feathers.

"There's only tea," Clarita said. "I work nights as a nurse's assistant in a convalescent home. My husband works days in the meat department of a supermarket. I have too much food to lug home from the market to also get coffee."

"Tea is great," I said.

"You kids left a mess," she called into the single bedroom. She moved a Barbie doll and swept an armful of Barbie clothing off the couch to make room for me. "Go downstairs and play."

A gaggle of five little girls left the bedroom, ran past us through the living room, paused to stare at me, and ran out the door.

On the TV the Captain had discovered Gilligan's baldness. He was going through a series of head jerks and double takes.

"I got my three little sisters with me right now, plus my own two. My father has a heart condition. Since Eddie died, my parents can't handle the little kids."

"You took on raising three extra children?" I said, astonished. "How can you do that?"

"We were nine when I was growing up," she said, shrugging. "Now we're seven here, with my sisters. Doesn't seem so much to me."

"And you've got all five children living with you in this apartment?" I asked.

"Things are going to get a lot better soon," she said. Her voice was firm. "You know that woman, Florence, who was at the funeral? I got to talking to her when I kept telephoning her house, trying to reach Fulton. She owns a real estate business. She's going to sell us a house she owns herself. It's over by Crenshaw. It's her own property, so she can give us a really good deal on it."

"Oh," I said, imagining a vision of the polished floors of Florence's house after five little girls had been running on them.

"The kids will have their own yard to play in. It won't be like here where people tell them no all the time," Clarita said, nodding to the window. "We'll buy a plastic pool and fill it with a hose. All the kids can all play in it."

"So you'll be moving," I said.

"The house is small, but it has a large yard. My husband and his brothers, they will build a barbecue. He will bring meat home on the weekends and we will have barbecues. There's a separate garage. My husband will make two rooms in the garage for my parents to live in. My mother will have a small garden. She grew up in the country, and she has always wanted that."

"Tell me about your brother, Eddie," I said.

"He was killed in a car accident, Eddie," Clarita said. "Fulton was the lawyer for the guy driving, Josh Baggins. I saw him, the driver, today at Fulton's funeral. Guy was drunk, but Fulton got him off with just community service and counseling."

She carefully carried in a tray with two mugs, the kind with cartoon characters on the sides. She poured hot water into the mugs. Steam rose above them.

"Yet you went to Fulton's funeral," I said.

"It's part of my religion," she said, handing me a cup, "I was raised Catholic, but now I belong to the Foursquare church. It was very hard for me to forgive. So I talked to my pastor. That's why I went to the funeral. It's a Christian testimonial of forgiveness. My pastor says hate will rot out the pocket you carry it around in."

"Me, I tend to have a long memory when people have hurt me," I said.

"That's exactly it," she said, nodding. "Forgiving is not about the other person. It's about you. All that energy you're using up in hate, you could take that energy and be doing something useful."

She dealt out the tea bags from a Lipton's box into the mugs.

"And you prayed for the repose of Fulton's soul?" I asked.

Like an obedient child, Clarita interlaced her fingers in her lap. "I took time off from work. I went to the trial of that miserable little drunk. Do you understand what it means when the man who caused the crash didn't get any punishment? It's as if it was decided that Eddie's life had no value. And the anger was inside me."

"Clarita—"

"My pastor showed me," she said. "St. John writes, 'This saying is hard.' And it is hard to live fully as Christ did. It took hard work, but I have come to see that we are as God made us, including the man who was driving."

Wow. I thought. I never knew a truly spiritual person before.

On the TV somebody asked the actress playing the society wife what she wanted to eat. She said, "A hard boiled egg." Then she clapped her hand over her mouth, horrified. The soundtrack screamed with laughter.

"Was your brother a member of the Foursquare Church?"

"No, I joined after Eddie's death," said Clarita. "To help me. Do you know anything about Eddie?"

"No, that's why I'm here."

"Sugar?" she asked.

"Yes, please."

She used a spoon to remove a cube from a covered sugar bowl and put it in my cup. We listened as the children outside chased each other through the grass. Then they knocked over a plastic folding chair with a crash. One of the women seated downstairs gave a sharp command in Spanish.

"Eddie, he was always the smartest of us kids," said Clarita. "But, you know, different. Never any trouble. Always with his nose in a book. My mother would always yell at him to go outside and play with the other kids."

"He was younger than you?" I asked.

"Eleven years," she said. "I looked after him because my mom had to work in a restaurant. When she came home, she was so tired she could barely lift up her arms. So, you know how it is with Latino parents. They don't want their kids leaving the house. But Eddie got into a college that had some special program to bring in more Latinos, so the college paid for everything, even tutoring. And he went."

"He got your parents to agree?" I asked.

"No, Pop didn't agree, but Eddie went anyway. It was hard on him, because Pop was already sick with heart trouble then, and he said Eddie's place was at home, working and helping the family."

"Did you see much of Eddie while he was at college?"

"No," said Clarita. "Beside the age difference, there was always the argument with Pop. But I know Eddie didn't like it at the college. He didn't like the other students much. He was used to being part of a big family, with everybody yelling. He liked the life back where we lived."

"So, you don't know if he was writing a book at college?" I asked.

"No," she said. "When he died it was a really bad scene, with my parents praying and crying and putting up pictures of him. That's when I found my way to the Lord." She raised her eyes.

"I think Eddie wrote a novel, in one of those notebooks, the kind with the metal spiral."

"That's what Fulton wanted, something about seeing if I had a notebook that came to me with Eddie's things. Of course I have notebooks from before. Eddie was forever scribbling stuff."

She had spoken in a soft voice. Now it trailed off. She looked down at the mugs, wiped her eyes, and took in a deep breath.

"Thanks for the tea," I said. The mug was now half empty. The tea was tepid. "Could I see the notebooks you do have?"

"Sure," she said, walking into the bedroom. I heard a closet being opened. She returned with five notebooks, tied together with white butcher's twine. Clarita slipped the string off the notebooks and she touched them lovingly with her fingertips before handing them to me.

And there it was. The top notebook. The cover was dirty and said "360 Sheets Narrow Ruled." Sticking out like a prong, the metal spiral had worked loose at the bottom. The writing was untitled. The handwriting inside was very small, with words crossed out. I recognized the text. It was the first chapter of the book Richard Spain had published.

"Clarita, how did you get this notebook?" I asked, standing up.

"It was with a whole bunch of Eddie's things. Richard Spain was Eddie's roommate, and I guess he left the notebook with Eddie's things when he moved to his own place. The manager at his apartment house was surprised. I don't think he expected me to come for Eddie's stuff. But I loved him, Eddie. No way I would let them put his stuff out on the curb to be picked up by a garbage truck."

"Clarita, Richard Spain may have copied this book and published it, and said it was his," I said.

"He stole Eddie's book?" Clarita said, speaking too calmly. She selected her words with care. "He took the book, the last thing of him?"

"Spain claimed he wrote the book," I said.

A sudden ingrained caution made my stomach tense.

"He was at the church today, Spain. I saw him. He was also in the court. He helped his friend, Josh Baggins, him and Fulton. They helped the drunk who killed Eddie," she said.

"Clarita—"

"Spain published Eddie's book?" Clarita said. Her voice sounded strangled. She was having trouble speaking. "Is there any money for us?"

"I don't know exactly how the money works," I said.

"And the people around Eddie knew this secret? They held Eddie's family away from his book. I need to know about the money," Clarita said. "Things have been hard for my parents now, since my father is not working."

"Clarita, I'll call the publisher for you," I said. "But you're going to have to prove Eddie wrote Spain's book."

"No," she said, setting down her mug. "I don't want you to call. I don't want you to do anything. I'll go tomorrow to the Legal Aid on Venice Boulevard."

"It will be easier if I call," I said. "I'll be glad to help, but I'll need the notebook."

I looked at Clarita. Her eyes were wary.

"No. You cannot have it. One of those people told you something," she said, jabbing a finger at me. "You knew about the notebook as soon as you saw Eddie's handwriting. You stick together, you people."

"I didn't know—" I said.

Her chin came up and her lips pursed. She said, "You try to push us out, people like Eddie and me and our family. Fulton didn't tell me about Edward's book being published. Fulton, the man who called me."

"Fulton didn't have any proof," I said. "He was calling people looking for the notebook."

"You know, I have been dreaming, about Eddie," said Clarita. "And it scares me, because he's dead more than a year. Why should I keep dreaming about him? But they say the dead person comes back for unfinished business. I think that book is why Eddie keeps making me dream about him."

"Clarita, will you listen—" I said.

"Shut up! Shut up!" she said. She glared at me over the mugs. "You couldn't have figured this out so quickly, to have connected the notebook with those who rob the dead."

Her voice was a lament, a litany. She wasn't talking to me anymore; she was crooning.

"I'm sorry—" I said.

"You don't care about those who stole from Eddie. And that man who called me, that Fulton. He didn't care either."

"I don't know, Clarita," I said. "I don't know the answers about the money."

"But about my brother you know, right?" she said. "You know they stole from him when he was dead? I think you should go now. This is my house. Please leave."

She put the mugs neatly on the tray. She shut off the TV. With immense dignity and her back straight, she went through to the kitchen. She had total conviction we were all in a conspiracy against her.

CHAPTER TWENTY

West Los Angeles, California

May 22, 2007

"Oh, for Christ's sake, that's all I need now, this goddamn woman suing me!" Oliver said, slapping his hand on his desk.

"I wanted to find out about the notebook," I said.

"Who told you to go bother this woman?" Oliver asked. "You didn't ask me first, and now you have her all upset."

"She was one of Fulton's last calls—" Fred said.

"Well we're no longer looking for Fulton," Oliver said. "That's one thing we don't have to do. We know where Fulton is. And we're just about out of time. So why were you bothering this woman?"

"Look, the notebook has pages from Eddie Abelia's book," I said.

"I'm delighted you solved your curiosity. Now I'm going to get sued," Oliver said.

I worked to keep the exasperation out of my voice.

"Okay," I said, "tell me if the bomber, this Howard Willow, could have had any connection with Richard Spain's book. Or Eddie Abelia's book. Or even my book."

"I know a connection," Fred said. "You told me that in the book the murderer blew up a real estate office, a car, and a school. Well the bombings now are a school and a real estate office."

"That's backwards," I said, stopping. "Why would he do it backwards?"

"Because he hasn't got the ending," Fred said. "You and Fulton didn't end the book."

"Vera, I have something important to discuss with you. The matter is personal. Naturally I assumed we'd be speaking privately," Oliver said, looking around his office.

"Considering what I hired Fred for," I said. "I can't see we're going to shock him. He stays."

"Could Howard Willow have seen a copy of your book so far?" Oliver said, leaning back. "That's how he'd know his bomb is in your novel. Think. How did he get it? You and Fulton had copies of what you were working on, and Fulton's dead, so I think he's got Fulton's copy."

"But Fulton wouldn't give him a copy. Fulton was claiming the book wasn't based on Willow," Fred said.

"Maybe that's why Florence's house was searched," I said.

"I enjoy conspiracy theories as much as the next guy, folks," Oliver said, making a tent of his hands, "but it's reality time."

"You've got another explanation for the order of the bombings?" Fred asked.

"You never have been able to handle ambiguity, Vera," said Oliver. "Fred, I must say, you are no better. You can't see these are two parallel but unconnected situations."

The longer this meeting went on, the more my sense of disquiet grew. Something was going on with Oliver.

"You don't think the bomber's working from the book?" I asked.

I knew Oliver had his own agenda, but I couldn't believe he didn't see a connection.

"I think the suggestion is ludicrous," Oliver said. His voice was beginning to sound more confident. "You say the numbers you found in the file Fulton left with your name on it have nothing to do with your novel. They're just a series of long numbers. Well, this current bombing has nothing to do with your novel either. I repeat, we have two parallel but unconnected situations."

"Oliver, you said at the church we had to meet. Why am I here today?" I asked.

"As you know, I have been speaking to the publishers. There's a matter we need to discuss," he said.

"He does this to me," I said, turning to Fred. "He summons me over and then farts around before he gets to what he wants to say. Makes me wait for it."

"I have arrived at a tentative compromise," Oliver said.

"You're not yelling," I said, looking closely at him. "Why aren't you yelling, Oliver?" I asked. "The first of June kill date is in just over a week."

"With no small amount of effort on my part I have managed to extricate us from this mess you got us into," Oliver said.

"I didn't get us into any mess."

"Mark Huntsinger," he said. "You know I told you I took him on, Vera. He just finished a wonderful crime novel. Deals with autoerotic asphyxiation. When people hang themselves for a sexual thrill."

"What has Mark got to do with anything?" I asked.

"Amazing first chapter," said Oliver. "It starts off with a young man found hanging in a closet, wearing women's underwear. The police call it 'suicide caused by orgasmic enhancement.' Don't you love that phrase? Now, there's a mental image. Book's going to be a smash."

"What about Mark?" I asked. My paranoia was kicking in.

"I have persuaded the publisher to take Marks novel in lieu of yours. Let me tell you, it took some doing." Oliver said.

I sat, stunned. I couldn't speak. I wasn't even sure Oliver was saying what it sounded like he was saying. Oliver was an agent, with an agent's survival instincts. But I had not thought him capable of this.

"Oliver, you can't do that," I finally said.

"Your problem, Vera, is that you don't read carefully," said Oliver. "You didn't read our contract, which has a cancellation clause by either party with two months notice. Not reading carefully probably accounts for your casual lifestyle. I have sent you a written notice in the mail. I might say, I had to throw in my commission as a binder for Mark." He swiveled in his chair and hooked his thumbs on the armholes of his vest. "Because the publisher had already given an advance to your goddamn Fulton."

"You're dropping my novel?" I said, feeling the blood drain from my face.

Oliver paused, looking thoughtful. He said, "Just listen for a minute, Vera. Simply listen. This will give you time to finish the novel at your own pace, which we can both agree now you certainly seem to need."

The barb stung, as Oliver had intended it to.

"And stop you from alienating the publisher, Oliver," I said.

"We decided this was best," he said.

The pronoun stopped me. We. Not as in me and Oliver. As in Oliver and Mark Huntsinger.

"Oliver, can we discuss this over lunch?" I asked.

"I'm very busy, Vera," he replied.

I actually managed to keep my temper. I said, "We're all busy. This collaboration with Fulton was your idea, and I'm trying to deal with the problem that resulted."

He flipped through his desk calendar and said, "I'm booked solid. And frankly, there's nothing further to discuss. And your abrasive attitude is not helping."

I looked at Oliver. I couldn't seem to hear him. I could see him, and he seemed to be moving in slow motion. Oliver had sold me out and given my deal to another writer. He had dropped me.

There would be no lunch.

"Do you realize what you put me through?" I asked. "It was your idea I should go find Fulton. I finally found Abelia's notebook."

"I have no idea why Fulton was trying to find Abelia's notebook," Oliver said.

"I can think of a reason," Fred said, dusting off his hands.

"What?" asked Oliver.

"Let's say Fulton found out that Spain's book was written by Eddie Abelia. And he saw certain, well, advantages in proving it," Fred said.

"Speak in plain English," Oliver barked.

"He could have gone to some of the people involved who were at risk, like Richard Spain or Nancy Branscomb, and told them he could be persuaded to keep quiet."

"For what?" asked Oliver.

"Money is a good start," Fred said.

"Spain doesn't have any money," Oliver said triumphantly.

"But you see, you do," Fred said, stretching out. He swiveled his head to look around the office. "This is a valuable piece of property. You represented Spain on the novel. You're asshole deep in a bad done deal, and you'll do anything to avoid being sued."

"How dare you!" Oliver said, leaping to his feet behind his large oak desk, his face red with fury.

"Hey, don't go ballistic," Fred said. He held up his hands as if to ward off a blow.

"That's ridiculous," Oliver fumed. "If that's your standard, we were all involved with Spain's book. Nancy Branscomb was his editor; Fulton did his legal work; Emma Sawtooth did a lot of rewrites."

"Then each of you has a better motive than this kid bomber being mad about his bomb being in Vera's book. I believe Fulton knew about the original notebook. He was using that knowledge to blackmail somebody," Fred said.

"Brilliant! You think you're smart, don't you?" Oliver said, glaring at Fred.

"Moderately smart," said Fred. "Smarter than you."

"Except Fulton didn't have any money," I said. "He didn't even have money to rent a decent car, remember? He tried to borrow Emma's."

"Maybe he hadn't got paid yet," Fred said.

"It's not Fulton's style," I said, shaking my head. "Fulton could be nasty, but he wasn't stupid. How about Josh Baggins? Now he might have tried a little blackmail."

"I have to leave; I have an appointment," Oliver said. "This has been very unpleasant, and I'd like you to leave my office. Now."

"Golly, Ollie, we sure wouldn't want to be unpleasant," Fred drawled.

"I have to check in at my house before we leave," I said. I grabbed Oliver's cell phone off his desk.

The phone rang six times before my mother picked it up.

"There's a surprise here for you," she said gaily.

I looked at Fred, and then at Oliver. "Did one of you send me something?"

They both looked blank.

"What surprise?" I asked.

"Well, I don't want to tell you and spoil it," she said.

"Mom, would you please tell me," I said.

"I couldn't get you anything for your birthday," she said. "I couldn't get out. Maybe tomorrow, if Mrs. Caspia comes over."

"Mom," I said. An icy feeling descended on me. "I want you to tell me what's there. Now!"

"A beautiful plant," she said. "For your birthday this week."

I began to shake. "Mom," I said, "I want you to put the plant in the yard. Do you understand? In the yard."

"Oh no, honey. It's so pretty, with a big ribbon bow," she said. "I put it on the table in the living room. Right near the window."

"Mom, I'll call you right back," I said, hanging up.

I looked at Fred and said, "Somebody sent me a plant. For my birthday."

"Jesus." He shot out of the chair. "Let's go!"

"It'll take too long," I said.

I dialed rapidly. "Mrs. Caspia, this is Vera Moonachie. I need you to go over to my mother, right away."

"I don't know," she said. "I've got nobody for my kids."

"Please. Somebody sent me a bomb," I said. "It's in a plant. Just get it out of the house."

Silence.

"A bomb?" she asked finally.

"You just need to get it in the yard," I said.

"No," she said. "I'm not fiddling with no bomb."

"There's no danger. There's a timer—" I said.

"I don't know what you think, but I don't think it's fair. I raise my kids. My husband works hard and gets disabled. Now you ask me to do something like this."

"It takes three hours—" I said.

"No," she said. "No! I have kids."

She hung up.

"How long did you say it takes? The nipple bomb?" I asked Fred.

"Three to six hours," he said.

I dialed rapidly.

"Mom," I said, "listen carefully. How long ago did they deliver the plant?"

"Oh," she sang, "I've been really careful with it. It's been a couple of hours."

CHAPTER TWENTY-ONE

▼

Venice Beach, California

May 22, 2007

The rush hour traffic crawled west from Westwood toward the ocean on the Santa Monica Freeway under a visible layer of gray brown fumes.

Fred honked, weaved, and drove the Honda like a madman. After a few miles we passed a stalled car in the fast lane, the cause of the problem. It took us an additional five minutes while we tried to make a lane change.

Fred swore, "Cocksuckers will not let you in! They will not! They see you signal. They see you have to get in their lane!"

"Hurry," I whispered.

"We'll do better on surface streets," he said. He pulled off the freeway and took Bundy south to Venice Boulevard. The needle on his speedometer rose.

I traveled Venice Boulevard daily. When you live two blocks from the ocean, driving west to return home was the only way. But every east-west street becomes gridlocked in the late afternoon. Today the route seemed to have attracted every incompetent driver in Los Angeles. It took us four lights to make the turn off Venice Boulevard onto Ocean Avenue. We only made it then because Fred swerved around the woman in the car in front of us, who was sitting, petrified by the cross traffic on Ocean Avenue, apparently for the rest of the afternoon.

I moved abruptly and ripped my hand on the rusted window frame of Fred's Honda and started to bleed all over the good skirt I had worn to go to Oliver's office.

"Let me see that," Fred said, grabbing my hand.

"No," I said. "Just drive."

I made a fist of my other hand and dug my fingernails in my palm. My breath was short and I started to choke.

"The theory about Howie killing Fulton, because of the novel you were writing, may be right," Fred said.

"Howie planned this," I said. "He planned it. How else could he know my birthday and where I live? The bomb was conceived months ago, to force me and Fulton to pay him. He terrorizes people; terror turns him on. He had this plan that we'd be a continuing source of income for him."

"He's made a mistake," Fred said. "Up until now he stayed hidden. We didn't even know if he was still in this area. Now he's broken radio silence, because we know he's around."

I looked down at our clasped hands. They were smeared with blood. I pulled mine away and wiped my forehead. More blood came off on my face.

How could it be taking so long to get to my house? I thought.

It was like one of those nightmares, where you have to get someplace in a hurry but your feet are stuck to the pavement and the road is a ribbon lengthening in front of you.

"What if the nipple bomb kills my mother?" I asked. "What if she dies because of me?"

I thought of our lives together, our frequent crises, and our continuing arguments.

Could this be the last thing I did to my mother? I thought. She had always looked with a dim view at my way of life. I wondered if it was actually going to kill her.

"I'm going to cut through 28th Avenue," Fred said.

I shivered, but it was from panic, not the air temperature.

Through the rest of the ride I thought about my new feeling for my mother. I felt a responsibility for what was happening to her. Against this threat, my arguments with her took on less importance.

Fred made the right hand turn onto Dell Avenue and came to a stop. The sign for Kinaloa Canal loomed up. The one moon bridge we had to cross to get over the canal to my house was blocked. A sedan with the logo of a local realtor on its door was parked at the crest of the arch. The driver was gesturing with a real estate flyer and explaining to a car full of prospects the glories of owning property in the canals.

Fred leaned on the horn, which produced only an irritated backward glance from the realtor. Fred stamped on the gas to try to swerve around the realtor. The Honda promptly stalled. Fred shouted imprecations.

The late afternoon sunshine slanted off the canals as I jerked open the car door, leaving Fred screaming. I ran the one block to the court outside my house. I was still grappling keys out of my purse when Fred screeched toward my parking pad.

"Wait!" he yelled. "The bomb takes three to six hours, but there's something else he could do. If it's got a mercury switch, you'll set it off if you move it!"

I didn't wait. I knew what this bomb was about, now. It was about Howie's rage. It was about hatred. And I had decided I valued human life above everything.

How dare he send a bomb disguised as a plant to my house, endanger my mother, just as sane, normal life went on just outside my walls? I thought.

I knew what had changed me. The pain and disillusionment with Oliver fell away from me, but they would return. Meanwhile I had to do something. It was as if my feeling for Fred had an extra dimension, a tangential power, which had revived love for my mother.

How could the love my mother and I must have felt when I was a child have changed to a relationship where she and I could barely stand to be in the same room without stomach cramps? I thought.

When elderly people die, people like to say, "Well, they lived a good life." I didn't know how much life she had left, or how much she might have relished it, but this plant bomb was trying to steal the end of my mother's life.

I hadn't reckoned with my trudge through a group of my neighbors, who were out in the warm sunny afternoon and wanted to socialize. Several neighborhood yapping dogs thought I was playing since they had seen me running. These final obstacles pushed me to my wit's end. I weaved through them, gasping and crying, and ran to my house. Then I felt the rough kitchen door with my right foot. I kicked open the door, ran to the living room, picked up the plant, and hurled it through the open deck door. It flew across six feet of wooden deck and went into the canal.

"Vera! For heaven's sake!" my mother said. She climbed out of her chair, but that seemed to be the limit of her strength.

The next thing I knew, I couldn't hear. I was spread-eagled on my back on the floor of my living room, knocked there by a massive explosion.

CHAPTER TWENTY-TWO

Venice Beach, California

May 22, 2007

My shoulder felt twisted. I felt like somebody had knocked me down with a sledgehammer. I could see Fred's lips moving furiously, but I couldn't hear anything he was saying. I tried to answer, but I couldn't hear myself either.

After a few minutes my hearing came back with a rushing sound and what I heard was Fred bellowing.

"Woman," he raged, "you take stubborn to a whole new level."

"Umpf," I replied.

"What is with you?" he said, "You didn't hear me say, 'don't move it?'"

I groaned. From Fred's furious expression, I suspected I wasn't about to get any tenderness.

"Check my mother," I said.

"I think she's just shocked," Fred said. "Howie's branching out. A mercury switch as a backup. Clever. Uses mercury to make the electrical connection when the thing moves. If you tilt the plant, the mercury slides and the thing goes off."

"Mother," I croaked as I tried to roll over.

"You realize that you could have been killed. You could have been horribly crippled," Fred raged.

I started gingerly moving my body to check.

Arms, legs, two of each, functioning, I thought. Fingers, toes, working.

The wood floor pushed against my hip. My shoulder and neck hurt.

"Vera," my mother whimpered. "Vera, something knocked me down."

A cloud of plaster dust rose to my nose. My mother had been knocked back into the chair. She was covered with small pieces of white plasterboard. Her mouth was agape. Fred started picking plasterboard off her.

I got up and moved like a crab. I examined my knee where a shard of glass had cut it. My deck was gone, as was the living room window, and the railing I'd spent last summer building on the deck along the canal. I looked toward my parking pad. Sammy was running over.

"What the hell was that?" Sammy asked, his mouth hanging open.

"Somebody bombed me," I said.

"Jesus, whatever you're doing, you've got to stop it!" Sammy said. He stared openmouthed at the debris. "This is getting out of hand. And you." He jabbed a finger at Fred, "You said you were watching out for her. So where the hell were you?"

The next day Fred picked glass out of the frame of my broken living room window.

"Look at the positive side," Fred said. "You're a mystery writer. Look at all the different kinds of cops who were here yesterday. You couldn't pay for that kind of information."

"Yeah, they were all in my living room yesterday. I couldn't believe how fast they got here," I said.

"LAPD bomb squad—" he said, ticking them off on his fingers.

"And the guys with green plastic covers over their shoes," I said.

"I heard them say they'd bring in a dive team to recover the device, since you threw it in the canal," Fred said.

"I'm still pissed off," I said. "One detective pointedly said he'd already had an inquiry about me."

"Yeah, an inquiry from Ted Saunders," Fred said.

"And Saunders said that I was a person of interest to them in a murder up in the Delta," I said. I started for the door.

"Where are you going?" Fred asked.

"I have to go get fresh clothes for my mother from her apartment," I replied.

"What are you talking about?" Fred said, astonished. "You were just bombed yesterday!"

"I can't handle the whole shock at once," I said. "I need to take time now. I have to do other things. That's the way I am. I can handle problems, but I have to take them in small bites. Beside, the clothes my mother was wearing are full of plaster dust." I went in the bedroom for the car keys in my purse and noticed the picture frame that had a wedding photo of my parents was empty. It was just the empty frame, standing. The mat was still intact, a square hole in the middle.

"Could the bomb have knocked the wedding photo out of this frame?" I asked after I brought it to Fred.

"No, I tore it up yesterday morning," my mother said. "I let the pieces fly into the canal." I walked her to the TV, clucking over her and soothing her. She settled down to her programs. She didn't have any expression.

"Mom, I won't be long. Try to stay in the chair," I said. "There's still glass all around on the carpet. You could get cut."

Fred drove me. My mother lived in a large complex of two-story buildings just east of Lincoln Boulevard. Each building was painted a peculiar anemic tan. We walked past a long line of windows in my mother's building to her apartment. Each apartment had security bars. Most of the residents were seniors. The place had a sour old-people smell. It was strange being here in the heart of the city but so removed from its life.

Her apartment smelled closed up and stale. I threw the food in her refrigerator out, containers and all, into a big black trash bag.

I think everybody has a capacity for shock, and mine was now overloaded, because when I went to her closet to get her clothes, I was stunned to see plastic boxes full of junk jewelry on the floor of her closet. There was box after box. Many of them still had the original price tags.

"Could she have been shoplifting?" I asked myself.

The chill spreading through me had to be a late reaction to the bomb. I brought a handful of the boxes out to Fred.

"Why do you think that?" Fred asked, looking at the boxes.

"It's a thought that would never have occurred to me before," I said. "But she never had anything she wanted in her life. She always wanted to travel. My father hated the idea. He knew she wouldn't go alone. So she stayed home and ran errands."

"She made her own decisions, Vera, about how she wanted to live. Life is about the decisions we make," he said.

"And she always wanted a house of her own. She had decorating ideas," I continued. "When I was sick as a little girl, she'd let me sleep in her bed and look through her manila folder of room settings she liked. Her 'inspiration file,' she called it. It was bulging at the seams with dog-eared magazine clippings of window treatments and room arrangements and wall arrangements and paint colors she liked. One day, the file was gone. But she never got her house."

"Why would she be shoplifting?" Fred asked.

"All her life she gave up what she wanted immediately," I said. "She thought she'd be rewarded in the future. Now it's the end of her life, but there's no reward. She never threw a fit and demanded stuff. She never got anything she wanted. Maybe now she just started taking stuff."

I looked around the apartment. I looked at the same linoleum floor that was there when she moved in sixteen years ago. I looked around the stove at the dropped food gunk.

Should I wash it? I thought. If I washed her kitchen floor, would it mean she'd be safe?

"And she's so bitter," I said, "that I expect her to taste bitter on my lips when I kiss her."

I walked through her living room and went past the couch that was too large for the room. I picked up two skirts and two pairs of flat shoes that I had put on the couch. And the pink sweater! It had been in her closet all the time. I locked the door. A distinct sadness crept into my mind. I was ready to cry over her tattered living room throw rugs.

I was going to have to fight off acute depression. I could usually corral the sadness that I've harbored on and off throughout my life. I replace it with a low-level anxiety that was fixated on disconnected fears, like whether or not my car would start. Now I thought of my mother's life, and the melancholy washed over me.

We stopped by a lumber yard. Later I sat in my bean bag chair while Fred nailed up a four by eight foot sheet of plywood over my shattered living room window. I never realized how much difference that window made in my house. Now the living room, instead of looking out on the canal, was a closed box. For the first time, I realized how small the room was.

The deck was buried under mounds of broken glass, burned chair cushions, and shredded wall board. Inside, there was the stench of explosive material and the damp of the water-soaked carpet. From the outside my house looked blinded, the victim of a madman's attack.

I hate tiny, miserable, dark, tight rooms. Now I was living in one. I finally got my mother soothed and into the bedroom and down for a nap. Fred and I were sitting in the darkness of my living room.

"Vera," Fred said, putting down the hammer. "The bomb. We have to talk about it. You've got to focus."

"I'm too tired," I said. Tears started in my eyes.

"Shush, shush," he said.

He picked up my hairbrush off the nearest pile of debris and started brushing my hair. That's a nonsexual act. Then he began gently brushing the skin on my shoulders.

This might sound strange, but I guess my shoulders are my erogenous zone. It was the most erotic thing. Then, still behind me, he kissed the nape of my neck. It's as if he could read my body, this strange tan man. I'm a sucker for a kiss in the hollow of the neck. I had been on an emotional roller coaster for the day. Now he was making my body as hot as an oven.

"Vera, I want you," he whispered. "So decide."

I had been avoiding that decision. He was definitely adept, I'll say that. We dropped on the couch, which I had cleared of glass that morning for my mother. He reached around me from behind and began to stroke me. He cradled me and I leaned back into him.

My hands ached to touch his body. It was not enough to run my hands all over him. I moistened and I ached for first sex with him.

Well, first sex, not young sex. Because I remember young sex. It would be really bad news to start that kind of desperation again. Who would want to go through young sex again, walking around singing Puccini and going through all those ridiculous heats and fights? But first sex, new sex with a new man, was something different.

I thought he'd be an intense and intuitive lover. I hadn't expected the joyful carnality we shared. We laughed and touched each other's bodies. It had been a while for me.

I always reserve a piece of myself, a little piece of ice in my heart. I try to sit beside myself during sex, to be an observer, not to give everything. If necessary, I mentally add up my possible Visa bill to prevent going off a cliff. Now the ice melted.

He slipped his hands around my waist and put them under my breasts. He lifted me and set me on him. His body felt flat and hard against me. I ran my hand over the tendons in his back. I could feel my nipples hardening. He had brushed my hair all around my head. When I revolved to straddle him, I had to look at him through strands of hair. The man with blue jeans at Florence's house was right. What a woman does to her hair is a barometer of her emotions.

I could feel him against my belly, hard, demanding. I heard the sound of his zipper.

"Do you want me to stop?" he asked.

"Oh no," I said. "Oh no."

After Fred left, I was in a sweaty state. Then I had a dream about a shadowy man, and I followed the man into a basement room.

He turned to me and said, "This is where I make the bombs."

It was the time of day when the gray evening mist off the canal creates a barrier between houses as well as between sleeping and waking. I got up, disoriented. I couldn't tell at first if it was a dream or real.

When I write, I have a theory that I dream more vividly. Not about what I'm writing about. Just more vivid dreams in general.

One older woman writer I knew lived in an assisted living residence for the elderly. She was writing every day. A dream made her scream so loud one night that the staff came crashing into her apartment. They monitored the residents with a microphone. They thought she was in difficulty.

It's like you take a cap off some psychic well.

That night I was in a puddle of sweat. The sleeping bag was too hot. The floor hurt where I had been bruised. I put on the light and looked at the watch I was wearing. Three o'clock in the morning. I wore my mother's watch. I would wear it for a while. Maybe it would connect us.

Why do I need a connection with her? I thought.

Her watch was a Timex. Like all her stuff, it was cheap. She was paranoid about spending money. So how did she get the junk jewelry unless she shoplifted?

I knew my mother wouldn't discuss the shoplifting. If I brought it up, she'd say, "Well, we don't have to talk about unpleasant things." If I persisted, she'd accuse me of being tough.

I'm not tough. I'm tough minded.

Maybe it's a reaction to her that I go through so much cash. I'm a seminar junkie, and I can easily spend $300 on a seminar on writing, or investing, or self-improvement. I'd also buy the texts they peddle; cheaply printed books with spiral binders that I stored and never read. I didn't mind spending the money. It was the lack of value that got to me. But one of the points of having disposable income is that I could waste it.

One of the seminars asked, "When was the last time you dealt with the wild woman inside yourself?"

The teacher said that I need to touch the wild woman to write well. I am so out of touch with myself that at first I couldn't even remember a wild woman. Do I know any women that deal with their wild woman inside? I want to know when I ran wild. Was it trained out of me so young that I never got to be wild at all? My mother called me a rude girl. Now I felt different because I was wild during sex with Fred.

Did I learn to be passive from my mother, who spent her life reading women's magazines and then became fierce at the end? She had an odd standard of what was important. She saw herself as one of the suburban ladies in articles in *The Ladies Home Journal.* It wasn't until now, when she knew she wasn't going to get any of that life, that she didn't give a damn anymore. At least now we could talk instead of chatter. She was honest. And she tore up her wedding picture.

God, I prayed fervently, I've done my best. Keep her safe. I can't face a month of lying awake nights feeling guilty about her. Okay, God. You sent me a man, God, I won't get too specific; I won't get too impossible. Call it pleasure. Call it recognition. I know what my faults are when I am with a man. But I was trembling.

Would I have to clear out her apartment? Would I have to put out sixteen years of her life in plastic supermarket bags for pickup at the curb? Her Tupperware?

Maybe I'd find out she had a hidden life, a lover, or some guilty vice like shoplifting that gave her pleasure.

I kept hearing the blast of the bomb. There was one shred of ceiling plasterboard that hung down, like a big piece of sandwich bread.

And I was awake, so I tried to write some. My printer went down. I didn't know whether it was due to the explosion or what.

There is a relationship between my guilt and my printer going down. Every time my guilt rises, my printer goes down. It bullies me, that goddamn electronic doppelganger, because it knows I don't feel competent about computer hardware. Or software, come to that. All I want a computer to do is make writing easier. This printer possesses a vindictive spirit that watches me stealthily and strikes when I am weak.

I am trying to put my finger on exactly why this printer defeats me.

This business of 'I can't put my finger on it,' that also disturbs me. It's a writer's business to put her finger on exactly the words that reflect an emotion. About a printer, about a person.

About Howie.

I looked at the index cards that were still taped to the wall of my office; I never got time to take them down.

"The murderer was competent, and confident," Fulton scribbled on one card, "with a thirst for knowledge. He sought to come in just under the professional level on any subject that interested him. His approach to anything new that interested him was to study."

Another card read, "Not likeable. He's moody, but he keeps coming up with these pockets of obscure knowledge—like native plant dyes, or military maneuvers, or chemistry, for example."

I had no solution for my mystery novel. That was a structure problem. Oliver said structure was my weak point. He said that I was better at dialog and lovely little embellishments. That was one of Oliver's better skills, the way he made you feel so good about your insecurities. I had abdicated my responsibility. I had offloaded the structure problem of my novel to Fulton. Now I was paying for it.

First Oliver dropped me. Then there was the bomb. Then first sex with Fred. Images rushed in on me. I turned the light back out.

Extensive reading. Howie. It was my last thought before I finally fell back asleep.

I was going to find that little prick, Howie.

CHAPTER TWENTY-THREE

San Fernando Valley, California

May 25, 2007

"What do you mean you found him?" Fred said two days later.

"I found him," I said.

"All the stuff I got on the data banks I couldn't find him—"

"I got lucky."

"Don't patronize me—" Fred warned.

"Are you coming with me or not?" I asked. "Because now I could use some muscle."

"But how?" he asked.

"I put myself in Howie's head," I said. "It's what you do when you're writing a character. You think like the character and speak like the character. Then you listen. You check to see if that's what the character would have done."

"You're gonna become intellectual on me—" Fred said.

"Somebody had to get into Howie's mind. Here's this guy who makes bombs and kills people. His tortured or Looney Tunes mind, whatever. That's what I did last night, in the middle of the night," I said.

"I don't really get how you can do that," he said.

"I did it, but I got physically sick," I said. "I had to get up and leave the computer, because I nearly threw up. You know, like when you can feel the throw up in your chest."

"Jesus," he said after a pause, "I gotta tell you, it makes me uncomfortable that you can do that. Like you're two people. It's schizoid."

"I figured his thing is to be around books," I said. "Schools are the pond where he's a big fish, a star. School is the only place he's successful. That meant he'd need a copy of his transcript, even if he carried it by hand, even if he waited a year to make sure the coast was clear. So I had a friend who works in the office of Santa Monica College check all the transcripts sent to local colleges. He's at Cal State Northridge. I got his class schedule. Yesterday I went there after his classes and followed him home. So now I know where he lives. I need to talk to him."

An hour later we were standing in front of an eight-foot-high wooden wall off Vanowen Boulevard in the San Fernando Valley. A small muscular woman opened the gate when we rang. Her face was as brown as a walnut, and her hands, which slid the bolt on the gate, were covered with mud.

"We'd like to see Howard Willow." Fred said, handing her his card.

"I'll have to ask," she said, looking startled. "Can I see some ID?"

We showed her our driver's licenses. She left us standing outside the fence, but we could see through the gate while she walked to a small rear building that was nearly hidden by bamboo.

The property consisted of two lots. Two small houses sat on one of them, one behind the other. From the front wall to the rear fence, a garden entirely occupied the second. Vegetables grew in raised banks corralled by redwood header boards and separated by gravel paths. Rows of tomatoes were supported by woven twig trellises, backed up by a tall hedge that blocked out the wind. I could smell basil. A wooden bowl near the kitchen door held young zucchini, with their orange blossoms still attached. On one wall of the house was what looked like controls for a complex drip watering system. Between the two houses was a small meditation pool with a deer scare fountain. The bamboo spout would tip when full and strike a smooth round rock, making a click.

When she came back, she was talking about her plants, which struck me as bizarre.

"Howard made a plan for my garden," she said. "He arranged my plants in natural pairs. The plants protect each other, so I don't have to use pesticides."

"What?" I asked.

"My plants," said the woman. "Howard's very good with plants."

"We know that," Fred said grimly.

"The fennel growing next to the roses," she said, pointing a finger that had the fingernail rimmed with mud, "keeps away ants. They don't like the smell of the fennel. Howard wants to know what you want with him. He has to be careful."

"We're sorry to disturb him. I'm a private detective," Fred said.

"A private detective?" a voice asked.

Howie had heard us. He spoke from the rear of the front building, not the rear building where she had walked. She must have phoned him from the rear building. He had been watching us through the screen.

"All right, come in," he said. "I need you to tell me how you found me."

My eyes tried to adjust from the dazzling sun of the garden to the dark interior of the kitchen, which the adjacent porch shaded. At first, I could only see an outline of a pudgy man, about five foot six inches tall.

We followed him through the messy kitchen and headed toward a small side room where a computer screen glowed with a chess board. The room was ten by twelve feet, small enough so that all three of us couldn't move around the furniture at the same time. It was furnished with what looked like family castoffs. Across from the door was a small attractive drop front desk made of mahogany. Next to it was a high wooden table holding a computer screen, towers, a printer, and a fax machine. In front of the table were two rolling stenographer chairs. Adjacent to the door where we stood were two gray, metal, four-drawer filing cabinets. The window wasn't open, and the room smelled stale. Computer paper covered every piece of furniture. Three stacks of paper were on the floor. One pile was organized cross hatched by subject. The door of the room was cleverly made like a baffle. If it was slid closed on its inside tracks no one would know the room existed. A hand lettered sign on his computer said "Cypherstuds."

"What's Cypherstuds?" Fred asked.

I could see Howard Willow's face now. He was a round man, with a round head and a round body. He looked like a figure made when a child sets one round stone on another. His features were small for his head. His face was ovoid. I caught the glitter of glasses. He wore some kind of embroidered Mexican shirt cut in a deep "V" at his chest, blue denim pants, and sandals. Hairy toes protruded.

"I organized a group of privacy advocates. They're encryption specialists," he said.

"Encryption?" Fred continued, as if this were a normal conversation instead of a dialogue with a murderer.

My throat ached, my eyes stung, and I fought back tears. I didn't trust myself to speak. I was afraid my voice would crack. This loser had attacked my lair, my sanctuary. I only wanted to scramble my fingers around his fat neck.

"Hiding information with a code." Howie continued from his chair, "Primarily from the Feds."

"You mean from the IRS?" Fred asked.

"Not just them. Anybody with the Feds. For centuries people have been defending privacy with closed doors and secret writing," he brayed. Spittle sprayed from the wet lips. "That doesn't work anymore, so we defend what's in a computer with cryptography."

He swiveled toward us and said, "My mother has to screen visitors before I see them"

Fred stepped into the room. It was a nicely timed move. Because I was behind Fred, Howie would have had to run over both of us to escape. If he came toward me, I was ready to do serious damage.

There was a flicker of surliness as he crossed one leather sandal over the other blue denim knee. Willow was the wrong name for him. Prominent love handles bulged out his loose shirt at the waist. His hair behind a high-domed forehead hung like a helmet, brown, lank and straight. His jaw line displayed wispy hairs, the beginning of a beard over a double chin.

"You're playing chess against the computer?" Fred said, looking at the screen.

"No. That's not much fun. I'm playing against a person," Howie said.

"Fulton played chess," I managed to say.

"Fulton did a lot of things, none of them in an outstanding fashion, including chess. He and I had a number of games. I won every one." he replied.

"Fulton was your lawyer when you were charged with making a bomb?" Fred asked.

"He and I had a number of arguments about legal strategy," said Howie.

"You studied law?" Fred asked. He slid me one of the chairs in the room and leaned casually against the doorjamb. Nobody would be leaving.

"I read the standard texts on courtroom defense," Howie said, rocking his head, side to side. "How did you find me?"

"At your trial, Fulton still got you a reasonably good deal." Fred said.

"Fulton got me shit. I was never charged with killing anybody, remember," said Howie. "I'm not responsible for what other people did. The case didn't really involve me, and I only pleaded guilty because the police were helping to keep me out of prison. I'll tell you right off the bat, I don't think he was a good lawyer. He didn't understand people."

"So you came up with the idea of the deal?" Fred asked.

"Right," said Howie. "The deal was my suggestion. The others went to prison, but I made a deal by agreeing to act as a police informant. The police knew I made the bomb, but they wanted my information more. In return I received credit for one hundred fifty days of time served. I was released on probation. Since then, I've had to hide, to keep those maniacs I turned in, people who have IQs about one point higher than a rock, from killing me. Hence my widowed mother as a gate guard."

"You're worried the radicals will find you?" Fred asked.

"And I don't think it's fair," said Howie. "I kept my end of the police bargain. I do everything legally. I do all the right stuff, follow all the rules. Then there are these people hunting me. I'm using a different name and social security number. So I need to know how you found me."

"Can't be," Fred said. "The wrong social security number pops up immediately on my screen. I either get the wrong number plus the right one or I get the person the number really belongs to."

"You think you're so smart," Howie brayed. "It never occurs to you somebody could outthink you. Do you know what my SAT scores were? I got a 779 math and a perfect 800 verbal. I was just an incredibly bright kid academically. I had the highest test scores in my school system. I had a 180 IQ. I took an IQ test online last week, and I still got a 170-plus. I've kept my ability to problem solve as well as my conceptual ability and sophisticated logic."

"Probably the only bomber in America who tells people his SAT scores," I muttered.

"What if I do this, Ms. Brilliant," said Howie. "It's easy for me to get the social security number of some male my age. Then I write Social Security and tell them I've lost my card, and ask for a duplicate card mailed to me at a post office box. After a month, I drop the box. Then I use that card and name. Now what do you get on your screen?"

"The social matches the name you're using," Fred admitted.

"And neither says Howard Patrick Willow. So much for your database," he crowed.

But not to get into your advanced college courses, I thought. You needed your real name and transcript to get into those.

"So your sealed guilty plea deal paid off handsomely," said Fred.

"They were murderers!" said Howie. "The prosecution was talking about giving me a fairly long sentence. I turned in the lunatics; I wanted them off the street."

"So you got out on probation—" said Fred.

"But my cooperation put me in great danger," said Howie. "There's a code of being accepted with these people. That's why they trusted me, because they thought I wouldn't—"

"Squeal," Fred put in smoothly.

"Now I spend my time hiding," said Howie. "I have to communicate only through my modem, in order to avoid a bunch of people who are flat-out crazy."

"Is there a reason you don't move to another part of the country?" Fred said. He seemed to keep him talking.

"My mother refuses, absolutely refuses, to sell this place so we can move out of this damn city," he replied. "Go someplace where I can leave the house!"

"But you know these radical students by sight, right?" asked Fred.

"There's one guy in particular, a hateful person. He was my roommate. He hated everybody, for no reason. But I just wrote him off as another political nut. Nobody thought he'd actually bomb people. Well, he did, and he's the guy looking for me. I've already covered this with other people. I've testified to this."

"Maybe not enough," Fred said.

"You snake! You liar! You bombed my house!" I yelled. I couldn't keep quiet another second.

"Only when there was nobody there," he explained calmly. "It was to get your attention. Look at the pattern. Nobody gets hurt. A bomb on the weekend at the school. Nobody there. A bomb in the middle of the night at the real estate office. Nobody there. I knew you'd recognize the pattern from your book. Your house, when you were away at a meeting with your agent. Nobody there. I'm very careful."

"My mother was there!" I said.

I had shaken him. "What mother?"

"Why would you take such a dangerous chance?" I yelled. "You could have killed her!"

"Because he's an arrogant little twerp?" Fred suggested.

"You need witness protection," I said.

"I need to know how you found me. That's the only reason you're inside here. So tell me how you did it," Howie said.

"Good," I said. "Then we have information you need. You have information we want."

"A swap. That's what you're suggesting." He said. He was comfortable with bargaining. He'd been successful with the police.

"Did you play chess with Nancy Branscomb?" Fred asked.

"Christ, no. A difficult, difficult woman," he said. He put his hands flat on his desk. He had bitten off the hard skin around his thumbnail to the point where it had bled recently. "Fulton had something going with her."

"You found out Fulton was writing a novel," I said.

Behind the round glasses, the blue eyes appraised me. He said, "I know where you live, Vera Moonachie. I'll tell you what I told Fulton. If you're going to use my bomb as the basis of your novel, I should get paid."

"You argued with Fulton about that," I said. "Outside Florence's house."

"My, my, you have been busy finding things out," he said. "He denied using my file. He claimed he was working from a number of files and denied the novel was based on my case. Some bunch of bullshit."

"But you still pressed Fulton for a cut," I said.

"Well, that only seems fair. It's not as if I don't need the money," he said. He waved a hand around his surroundings.

"Tell them what he said to you," his mother said as she worked her fingers up the doorjamb.

"Get out of here!" he screamed, and slammed the door, almost catching her fingers. "I told you never to come in here when I'm talking to people!"

He turned to us. His small mouth was tight. "Just because I had to come back to live with her, she thinks she can take over my life. It's hell on my nerves. Dealing with her bugging me and a pack of morons trying to kill me."

"What did your mother mean about what Fulton said to you?" Fred bore in.

"You tried to kill me, you bastard. Like you did Fulton!" I said. I fought the urge to wipe the smug look off his face with a smack to the side of his head.

"That's ridiculous. Think about it. You'll see it makes no sense," Howard Willow said. He leaned away from me. "I needed Fulton to get cash out of the book because he was the one taking my information out of his file. I certainly didn't try to kill him."

"Vera, hold it," Fred said, reaching across to immobilize me. He then turned to Howie. "So you're complaining people are hunting you, but you were out threatening people?"

"I don't know where you're coming from," Howard said, shaking his head. "But you really believe I offed Fulton? Well, I didn't."

"You just sit there and deny everything!" I said.

"You just don't get it, do you?" he said, rolling his eyes. "It's easy to check. I'm still on probation. I can't leave town without getting my probation officer's permission, and I didn't. The newspaper said Fulton's body was found in a river in the Delta. So I certainly wasn't in the Delta murdering Fulton."

"I know you know something about Fulton's death," I said.

"I'll give you a freebie, just to show you I'm kindly. Richard Spain and Josh Baggins. Now there's a pair. I call them the ventriloquist and his dummy."

"What about them?" I asked.

"Spain is hyper about getting another book published. He turns out reams of stuff, but it's all crap. He had some kind of hold on Baggins. I think it was about that accident Baggins had," said Howie.

"What has that got to do with Fulton's death?" I asked.

"Because it's Josh's fault Fulton died," he said, smirking. "You two really are slow-witted. Josh was responsible for the deaths of two men: Eddie Abelia and Fulton."

"All right," Fred said. He guided me back in the chair and moved his hand down, a calming motion. "You wanted our attention. You've got it. Explain."

"Josh got Fulton killed. Now I can't get money," said Howie.

"What are you talking about?" I asked.

"Josh is the one who gave Fulton the photocopy of pages from Eddie Abelia's notebook. Josh had photocopied some pages. That way it was safe to kiss Spain off," Howie said.

"What?" I asked.

"You didn't know that, did you, you two geniuses?" asked Howie. "You didn't want to believe me about Josh and Richard, but, you see, I was right." He was enjoying the effect. "See, Spain dumped the original notebook back in with Eddie Abelia's stuff. He thought he was safe. He never thought anybody would take that stuff."

"Why didn't he just get rid of it?" I asked.

"You have to understand Spain," said Howie. "Because he never thought anybody would find it. He figured nothing could ever be proved about his novel. This way he wasn't connected to the notebook. He didn't know that Josh, the original no-balls Josh, his good buddy, photocopied some pages before giving it to him. Fulton told me the night I went to his house."

He stretched out luxuriously. He was delighted to be center stage.

"You can't cover up for Spain," he said smoothly, "Or Josh. The word is already out. I think Josh was going to use the photocopy of the novel pages if Spain kept pushing him, making his life shit. But the meddling little bastard, he got in a snit. And he gave the photocopy to Fulton."

Howie's mouth worked around the gossip, tasting it. Then in the very next breath, with complete sincerity, he said, "Give Josh my regards."

"So what did Fulton do with it?" Fred asked.

"Fulton had an ego," said Howie. "He thought of himself as some kind of master chess player. Pathetic. I couldn't persuade him otherwise. With some people you can say, 'Look, friend, you're never going to be able to pull this off.' And with other people, well, it would just invoke wrath."

"What. Did. He. Do," Fred said in separate words.

"Fulton said he needed to control his queen. Naturally I assumed he was talking about using the notebook pages," Howie said.

"No, no," I said, "it's déjà vu. That's what he said in the index cards. He needed something strong enough to control his queen."

"What queen?" Fred said, looking from one of us to the other.

"The queen," Howie said, "Nancy Branscomb. I'd assume that's obvious. Now that's quite enough. I've given you valuable information. I hope you'll be more reasonable about paying for my story than Fulton was."

"I'm not paying you a goddamn cent," I said. I wouldn't give Howie the satisfaction of knowing how much he had shaken me.

"We're finished here," Fred said, standing up.

"You said you'd tell me how you found me," Howie whined. "I told you all this. You promised."

"I lied." I said.

Howie looked from Fred to me. "Bear in mind I do have my little methods. You're a real charmer." He gave me the finger.

"Let's be honest here. You thought you had a method of extorting money from Fulton," Fred said. "You figured he was a meal ticket.

Because Fulton was using material that was attorney-client privileged from your defense. But he disguised that material by having Vera listed as the author of the book."

"You're the man who always has the answers," Howie sneered.

Fred didn't see it coming because his head was turned to me. When Fred and I stood up to leave, Howie suddenly clasped his hands and whirled them around his head like a mallet and brought them down on Fred's neck. Fred tripped over one of the stenographer's chairs and wound up, legs spread, sitting on the floor with a surprised expression. Howie clasped his hands again and moved toward Fred to deliver a second blow.

Until then he had been pathetic. But in his eyes, I saw something that suggested a quick feral intelligence. I saw the killer Fulton had seen.

I fight verbally, not physically, but even I could recognize a crisis. I yanked the fax machine out of its socket and off the wooden table. I raised it above my head and brought it crashing down on Howie. He must have heard something because he whirled toward me and brought up his hand, deflecting the blow. But the move gave Fred time to get on his feet.

"Let go of it," Fred said, pulling the fax machine away from Howie.

Fred grabbed Howie's hand and started to squeeze, hard. Howie started to whimper. He was afraid of pain, this cool young man who made bombs.

"I don't know why people go back on their word with me like this," he whined.

"You're out of the bomb business," Fred said. "Because I know where to find you. I'll tag you and put you in my database and put you in with some interesting company. And I know exactly who to tell, certain people, where to find you."

"You'd expose me—" said Howie.

"Oh, you betcha," said Fred.

Fred backhanded Howie, and he landed in a heap. From some pocket Fred removed a pair of handcuffs and cuffed Howie to one leg of the wooden table.

"Figure out how to get out of those cuffs," Fred said, dropping the key in his pocket. "Think of it as an SAT question."

On our way out, Fred stopped to pull the tag off one of the sacks of fertilizer leaning against the wall.

"Fifty pounds of urea," he read. He put the tag in his pocket.

"What's urea?" I asked.

"Common ingredient in fertilizer," he said. "People put it on lawns, makes them grow green."

"So? Why are we taking the tag?" I asked.

"Also what some people use to make bombs," he replied.

CHAPTER TWENTY-FOUR

Venice Beach, California

May 27, 2007

The sun peeked around my boarded living room window on the fresh and wonderful morning of my birthday, May 27. It was the kind of day Los Angeles occasionally springs on its inhabitants to keep them hopeful.

"Happy birthday," Fred said.

He was bearing two large grocery bags. He reached in one and handed me a package wrapped with birthday paper and a lot of cellophane tape. With his hands, he made little denigrating movements toward the package.

"It's no biggie," he said.

I opened it and found a purple fanny pack with two compartments and four black zipper pulls with tassels. For my birthday I was wearing a cotton skirt that came down to my shins, with a full-sleeved peasant blouse. I clipped on the fanny pack and strutted joyfully around.

"You said you liked to run," he said, clearing his throat. "So I figured."

"It's great," I said.

"You're not going into some goddamn fit about being forty, I hope," he said.

"Not me," I said. "I can run 10Ks now in a different age group. I've been running against women who are thirty to thirty-nine. Now I'll be running against women forty to fifty. I should take a medal. If Howie doesn't blow me up."

"I'm making lunch for your birthday," Fred said. "I brought everything."

In the kitchen, Fred reached for fresh rosemary to sprinkle over the lamb chops he was putting in the oven. He rattled the oven racks a little more than was necessary. I think he wanted to be sure my mom and I were aware how hard he was working to make lunch.

"Lamb? Pretty fancy for a single gentleman," I said.

I breathed in the wonderful smell of the roasting lamb.

"I'm a good cook," he said. "Simple stuff. I took a couple of cooking classes at The Learning Warehouse. I don't have to pay. They comp me, since I teach there."

What was happening? I thought.

It had been a while since I'd been involved with a man. I had simplified my life and cut back on social life, so I could write. When I woke up in the middle of the night, I wasn't thinking of a man. I was thinking of how I could express something in a novel in the most felicitous manner. A relationship would be impossible, with this rail-thin tan man who was so politically incorrect and who thought I was an intellectual because I read the *New York Times.* But I realized that being almost killed and having a bomb nearly destroy my house had sharply reorganized my priorities.

"Finish the story you were reading," my mother urged from the couch.

I picked up the book of fairy tales. I said, "So the princess picked up the frog with her finger and thumb and carried him upstairs, where she put him in a corner. When she got into bed, he crept over and said, 'I am tired and want to sleep as well as you do. Lift me up, or I will tell your mother.' Then she became very angry. She picked him up and threw him with all her might against the wall, saying, 'Now you may rest, you horrid frog!' But when he fell to the ground, he had changed from a frog into a handsome prince."

"What?" Fred asked, walking in from the kitchen. "Wait a minute, I thought the Princess kissed the frog and he turned into a prince."

"So did I," I said, looking at the book cover. "But it's right here. This book is the original version, as collected by the Brothers Grimm."

"Why does everybody telling the story say that she kissed the frog?" asked Fred.

"Story got hijacked," I said. "Somebody decided he didn't want to train little girls to throw their boyfriends against the wall. The kiss story was more acceptable training for little girls."

"I like lamb chops," my mother said. She dragged her foot with the cast to a stool near the kitchen doorway and took up a position. "Lamb chops are my favorite. Such a nice young man, and he can cook. That's good, Vera, because you certainly can't."

"You said you believe Howie's alibi now, because he couldn't leave town," I said. I wanted to stay on the bomb subject. "But then who killed Fulton?"

Fred started chopping lettuce for a salad. He said, "I have to go on my gut reaction. Howie has an unswerving eye on what he wants. His needing Fulton alive to pay him makes sense."

"But why bomb me?" I asked.

"Who knows?" he asked. "Hey, it's easy to learn how to make a nipple bomb. I know some people keep diagrams up on their wall. Uh, I brought a bottle of merlot. I could open it."

"Why not? It's my birthday," I said.

"Just for you and your mother," he said. "Iced tea for me."

A little warning bell went off in my head. He didn't drink. That sounded like AA. Alcoholism in a mate is another thing I went through once. I didn't want another round.

He looked at me, unwavering.

"But I still don't know who's the murderer," I said.

"Fulton said the murderer in the novel planned only one move ahead. Is that Howie?" Fred asked.

"No," I admitted. "Howie plans. Howie schemes."

"Howie said Josh started this whole thing," Fred started putting food on the table. "Josh didn't tell you about giving Fulton the photocopies of pages from Abelia's novel. I think it's time we have another talk with Josh."

"We scare him?" I asked.

"We create a little tension in his brain, anxiety, worry, thoughts of self-preservation. Ah, I love it. My stock in trade," he replied.

He drizzled oil on the salad and threw in a handful of croutons. Then he spread his hands palms up and awaited admiration.

My mother was happy during lunch, chewing the bone of her lamb chop. As if by right, she took the head of the table, chattering to Fred about when I was a little girl.

She got on the subject of my hair, which was too long and not curled. Across the table came the clear perception that, though I was loved, she wasn't responsible for my casual appearance.

"You should wear a skirt like that more often, dear," my mother said. "You've got my slender waist."

"I'm wearing it for my birthday."

"Of course, I always had more on top," she said.

"Mother, for God's sake—" I said.

"I'm a waist man," Fred put in hastily. "Always been a waist man."

"You wear such dark clothes," she said. "You should wear a light dress. For an appointment with a gentleman."

What, I thought, she considered Fred a suitor?

But being almost blown up had raised my threshold for what bothered me. Her comment didn't get to me.

"It's nice that you have a young man," she said.

"Mother, do not start," I said. "Just please do not start."

"You want to be alone when you're old," she said. "Like me?"

This conversation was going nowhere. We'd had it before. She desperately wanted me to be a wife, and I had been a wife. But I was younger then. Since then, I'd matured and found my way to writing. I knew I'd never again be able to subjugate myself to the demands of a relationship, the way she had adapted to my father. My priorities were different now.

"She's smart as a whip. She knows she can't rely on looks," my mother caroled with merry laughter. "Contact lenses aren't going to help her much."

She could still occasionally come up with the old savage wit.

"Of course, her looks don't matter anyway," she said, pouring herself more wine. "She spends her life writing like some hermit in a monastic cave."

We had a strained relationship. I had spent a lot of therapeutic hours trying to pull away from this game of hug and slap.

These moments were almost harder when she was being sociable, compared to when we fought the way we used to do. They led me to false hope for returning to a closeness to her that never existed.

"Since you have to fix the living room anyway, you should change around the furniture," my mother chatted. "If you put the sofa where the new window is going in, you'd have more light for reading, which is what you're always doing. Why do you have all those boxes of books in your office? Give them to the library book sale. You have very little space. Get rid of all this extra stuff. Then you could display some of your pretty things on the shelves, instead of just books."

"Mother—" I said, but I stopped. This was not going anywhere. She was not going to change.

But she was leaving me. She was dying, and I knew it.

The next day my mother was full of energy, and it was three thirty in the afternoon before I persuaded her to settle down and watch one of her TV programs. Mrs. Caspia had gone into full retreat and refused to take my phone calls.

Fred brought in a St. Christopher medal and hammered a nail above my mother's bed and hung it.

"They got rid of him," I said, nodding toward the medal.

"Who?" he asked.

"St. Christopher. He's not a saint. He's been discarded."

"I didn't know the Church could do that," he said.

"The Church can do whatever it wants, and that's just the beginning of the problems," I said.

A car roared into Sammy's parking pad. I heard a loud hammering at the door. That kind of hammering never means any good. I realized the car I had heard was not Sammy's car. I put down my wine glass and gripped the table.

"You've got to help me," Richard Spain shouted from the doorway. His voice was on the edge of hysteria. "Josh went to Nancy Branscomb's office, and we've got to head him off. He said she wouldn't give him his chance to have his restaurant. I'm afraid she may kill him, the way she did Fulton."

I suddenly got it. His voice was harsh and strained now. The timbre was lower pitched than when he spoke at the theater. I recognized the voice that had threatened me on the phone.

"You bastard," I yelled from the living room. "You called my house and threatened me!"

"I didn't mean any harm," he said sheepishly. "I just used my lines from an old gangster TV show I was on. I wanted you to stop poking around about my book. Now it doesn't matter anymore. Eddie's sister turned his notebook over to an attorney."

Fred swore. "You terrified Vera—"

"It's been a really god-awful day. I could use a drink," Spain said, looking around hopefully.

I went in the kitchen and poured him a shot of bourbon. He tilted his head and downed it in a two swallows. He looked for the bottle, but I put it away.

"I thought Fulton was going to use the notebook," Spain said, putting down the glass. "If he found it, I thought he was going to tell Nancy about Eddie. I thought that was his control over her. I looked all over for that damn notebook. I even broke into Fulton's house."

"So you were the one who broke into Florence's house!" I said.

"Yeah," he said. "But then I heard you say at the funeral that Fulton put some pages in a file marked with your name on it to hide them from me. He figured I might come looking."

He leaned back. "You know, the thing is, I saw that goddamn file, too. I didn't even bother opening it."

"Eddie's novel isn't what was in the file with my name. Now it's over," I said.

"Yeah, it's over," Spain said. "That's because you went and talked to Eddie's sister. Why the hell did you have to do that? Why couldn't you just leave things alone?"

I rubbed my arms. You'd think I'd be relieved having the threat of that phone call, the fear, taken off me. But my arms were covered with goose bumps.

I can't manage change all at once, I thought. I had to take this slowly, in little bites.

"That was really stupid of you," Spain's said accusingly. "Running off your mouth like that. We've got to go to Nancy's office right away. Because it's your fault. You're the one really responsible now for what happens."

CHAPTER TWENTY-FIVE

Century City, Los Angeles, California

May 28, 2007

Fred and I ran past the receptionist at archangel press toward Nancy Branscomb's office. Her jaw dropped and she started for us. Richard Spain had trouble parking because he couldn't pay the fee for the building parking, so he trailed behind us. As we ran across the slick tile floor of the empty reception room and down the hall I felt a surge of foreboding. I took a deep breath, bracing myself for what I'd find.

Nancy was sitting at her desk, a gun in her right hand. Her face was ashen. "I shot him," she said. "He told me he killed Fulton. He was coming across the desk at me."

There was a wrongness about the place.

But it wasn't until I got inside the office that I saw Josh Baggins. He was slumped back against the wall. A large and spreading bloodstain was on his left side. The blood was still coming out from under his left sleeve. He was wearing a starched white high-buttoned chef's jacket. The cuff now looked like it had been painted red.

I looked at Josh. "Wait," I said. "You killed Fulton?"

"What, you thought I killed him?" Spain gasped as he finally caught up with us.

"I am not involved in killing anybody," Evelyn fluttered over Josh. She took steps around him and pressed her hand against the wound to staunch the blood. "I need everybody to understand that. And I certainly didn't know Josh was. He and I are splitting up; I can tell you that."

She wore a blouse and skirt for the visit to Nancy's office. She must have supported Josh at one point, because I could see she had blood on her. She stood next to him, but clearly tension existed between the two of them.

Josh looked up dully. "So you finally got here. Took all of you long enough."

"As a nurse, I'm only staying to help;" Evelyn said. "We need to get him to a hospital. He's losing too much blood."

"Fulton got in my face," Josh said. "He wouldn't help me. It would have been so easy for him, but he insisted he wanted to use the information he had for the damn Chinese leaseholders."

"Fulton was killed because of something he knew," I said. "I didn't understand what, because he certainly didn't have any money. That seemed to rule out his using his knowledge for money. But a blackmailer's demands can be other than monetary. He can use his knowledge to force somebody to do something. In this case it was to force the queen in the chess game he talked about. And when Fulton was looking in the cabin for the old Chinese lease, he saw the old photographs."

"But you didn't realize what the photographs in the cabin meant, did you, Josh?" Fred said.

"No," he said. "Only that it was bad."

"What did Fulton know?" I asked.

"Her," Evelyn said, pointing. "Fulton said he'd tell the police."

"For God's sake, tell them what—" I sputtered.

"You know that old man in the newspaper," Evelyn said triumphantly. "The one they found at the pagodas in Venice Beach? He's her father."

"What?" I said, stunned. There it was: the motive stronger than a few pages from Eddie's novel.

"And Fulton, your co-author, your big buddy," Evelyn spat at me, "he saw a way of using what he knew to make her do what he wanted."

"Shut up, Evelyn." Josh said, lifting his head. "Just shut up." He turned to Nancy. "We could still do it, Nancy. I could call the police and say I was wrong."

"It wouldn't work," Evelyn said.

For some reason, she seemed oblivious to the strains in the room.

"Goddamn it, I told you to shut up!" Josh said, using his last strength to push Evelyn.

"She's really stupid, isn't she?" Nancy said.

"I'm stupid!" Evelyn said. She stepped away from Josh, who sagged against the wall without her. She jabbed a finger at Nancy. "She went up to Simi Valley. She checked him out of a rest home. She took him to Venice Beach, and she left him."

"I couldn't," Nancy said, shaking her head. "I couldn't afford it anymore. It was $5,500 a month just to keep him. Plus there were extra charges every month. They had gone through his fortune, everything he had. Four years ago they told me he was going to die. They said he only had a few months left. But he didn't die."

"She just left him there," Evelyn said, not stopping. "Her own father. When Fulton found the photos of the two of them in the cabin, he could prove it."

"I don't make that kind of money. I don't know who does, but I don't," Nancy mourned.

"Rolled him under the pagodas. Stuck a note on him. And diapers. Bitch!" Evelyn said. Her voice rang with satisfaction.

"Then the rest home did a property search in his name and found out about the cabin," Nancy said. She got out of the office chair, took the picture of the cabin off the wall, and stared at it. "They insisted, just insisted, that I sell it and give them the money."

"Everybody wanted something from Nancy," Fred said. "Richard Spain wanted her to take on his new novel. Stix Chimenius wanted her to consent to the Docklands project. Josh wanted her to consent so he could have his restaurant. And Fulton wanted her to withhold her consent in order to restore the rights of the Chinese leaseholders. The difference was that Fulton suddenly knew something that could force her to do what he wanted."

"The cabin was the only thing left of his," she said. She frowned, then dusted the top of the frame with her fingers. "He loved it. He always said that when he was old, when he was alone, he'd live there some day. Well, life is a big joke. That's not where he wound up."

She rolled her head, from left to right, and transferred the gun to her left hand. She rubbed her right fingers at the right side base of her neck. "I just thought the government would take care of him if they didn't know who he was. Christ knows, he paid enough taxes for fifty years. They take care of all kinds of illegals. Why not him?"

"But Fulton recognized the picture of your father in the newspaper," Fred said.

"Well, I never expected a picture of him to wind up on the front page of the newspaper, did I?" Nancy said. She sat back down. "Somebody wrote a human interest story about him. The whole thing just took off. Fulton said he thought he recognized the man in the picture, but he had no proof until he found the old photographs of my father and me in the cabin. He would have ruined me."

"Is that what Fulton was going to do?" I asked. "Tell the police who your father was?"

"No," Nancy said, shaking her head. "Fulton had his own agenda. He had this ridiculous moral streak. He said he'd been a defense lawyer for years. He didn't want to be one anymore, but now he was going to make one thing right."

"Fulton told Josh he was going to the cabin in the Delta. There's only one copy of the original lease, and he was convinced that's where your father hid it," Spain said.

"I told you," she said, looking up wearily. "Fulton had lousy judgment with friends. He was in the car with Josh. And he just told him he had something on me. Announced that he now had clout with me. Of all people to tell, Josh, that shit."

I looked at her face and realized the woman was coming unglued. The façade was cracking.

"Then you decided this was an opportunity," I said, whirling on Josh. "You wanted Fulton to use what information he had to pressure her for you."

"Stix Chimeneas," Josh said. He stopped and coughed. Blood spattered on the front of the chef's jacket. Josh closed his eyes, gathering strength. "He said he'd give me the restaurant immediately if I could get Nancy to agree to the Docklands project. And Fulton could have forced her to do it!"

"Stix Chimenias," I said. "He was behind everything, pulling the strings."

"But Fulton had another way to use his new clout," Fred said.

"I told you, that it was my life!" Josh said. "I'm a gifted chef. I'm good at running a kitchen. It's the only thing I've ever been good at. I have lots of ideas. Signature dishes that would only be available at my place, Delta crawdads, and fiddle ferns. People would come from all over. It would have been a wonderful restaurant."

"But Fulton wasn't having any," I said.

Josh said, "I said to him, 'I can't make her do this, but you can.'" Josh shook his head in wonder at Fulton's obstinacy. "I told him, 'They'll give me a chance at the restaurant if I get Nancy to let them develop. You can make her do it.' But he wouldn't do it. It would have been so easy for him, and he just wouldn't do it. Can you imagine anything so selfish? Just mean. Just indifferent."

"But I can't see Josh planning all this—" Fred said.

"Wait," I said. "That's it. He didn't plan it. He had to make a plan right there on the spot when Fulton said he had clout."

"Josh reacted to opportunities," Fred said.

"My God," I said, stopping and thinking. "Fulton said he grabbed the moment. Not a chess player."

"There's one thing I don't understand. Why did you go up to the cabin with Fulton?" Fred asked, walking in front of Josh.

"Because I knew Fulton was looking for something there," Josh whispered. "He said he had to find it right away, because next month would be too late. The project would already be dead and it wouldn't matter. Whatever it was, it had to be in the cabin. I thought it was what he had on her. And when he found it, I knew I had to be there or he wouldn't share."

"But what Fulton was looking for was an old lease," Fred said as he turned to Nancy. "He thought your father had it hidden in the cabin.

It was the only copy left, the copy that guaranteed the rights of the original Chinese leaseholders or their heirs."

"Ridiculous, ridiculous idea," Nancy said, shaking her head. "My father received the copy of the lease in a battered old envelope filled with original documents for the Docklands project. He immediately checked and found out the lease was not recorded. He knew he had the only copy and that everybody involved with that lease was dead. My father told me he simply burned the lease."

"The Delta project," I said. "That's what was hidden in the file folder with my name on it. All those numbers. They were the assessor's parcel numbers of the properties for the Docklands in the Delta that Fulton was researching."

"So when he went to the cabin, he and Josh tossed the place," Fred said.

"Fulton didn't find the lease, but what he found was almost as good," I said. "Photographs, taken maybe twenty-five years ago, of Nancy and her father fishing. And he decided to use those photographs."

"I really think he was round the bend," Josh said indignantly. "He said he could control Nancy. He kept rambling on and on about this land law that kept the Chinese from owning property in 1913, and how unfair it was. That California really wasn't the Golden State for those workers. For God's sake, we're talking before World War I!"

"And the developer was running out of time," I said. "For his project. So he would have agreed to anything."

"That's what Fulton said," Josh said. "He said the land was very valuable now because of the new project and the leasehold. He was crazy on this nut idea of what he called justice for the Chinese leaseholders. At the end, I even begged him to do both. To tell me what he knew, make her protect the Chinese lease holders, and also help me get my restaurant. But he only wanted to force her to protect the rights of some old Chinese. And it doesn't matter. Anybody can see it doesn't matter. Most of them are dead!"

"Checkmate," Fred whispered. "He had her."

"And I said, 'Why won't you do this? This is my chance,'" Josh said. "I explained and explained and explained."

I looked at Josh and said, "And then you got in a rage. One of your well-known snits."

"I didn't plan to kill him," Josh said. His voice rose. His face looked bewildered. "But we sat in the car and we argued. I got so angry with him. He wouldn't agree and I was furious. I always carry a chef's knife. And I don't remember doing it. Honest to God, I don't. But I stabbed him."

"It wasn't planned," I whispered. "You grabbed the moment. It fits."

"And the garment bag?" Fred asked.

"Well, then I didn't know what to do," said Josh. "I couldn't lift him. Fulton wasn't a big man, but he was dead weight. I had a double garment bag in my trunk and I figured out if I put him in the garment bag and zipped it up and tied on a rope to pull it, I could drag him so I could move him. I got him in the bag and in the back of my car and started driving home."

"How did Fulton get in the slough?" I asked. I placed my hands on the back of one of the two side chairs to prevent them from trembling.

"I took the J-Mack ferry," said Josh. "It was the middle of the night. It was only the ferry operator and me, and he was in the operator's cabin watching the cable guide the ferry to the dock. So I just pulled the bag out of the back of my car and pushed it off the back loading platform. The operator didn't hear me. The ferry is clanging noisy. I figured the current would take it. I saw that there was a very strong current. Just my luck, the damn rope twisted around the cable. Now, would you believe that?"

"I can't believe I got it wrong twice!" I said. "All along, I thought this was either about Eddie's book or about Howie Willow's bomb. For God's sake, Oliver was right. Two different things can be going on at the same time and involve the same people. But this murder was to force Fulton to pressure Nancy. Eddie's book and Howie's bomb had nothing to do with Fulton's murder."

"We were trying to figure it out as we went along," Fred said soothingly. "Investigators deal with stuff they don't get right all the time. You don't get perfect vision forward, just backward."

"I also thought Fulton was using Howie as a model," I said. "Because of the bomb being in the book. But he wasn't. He put Howie's bomb in the novel, but he was using Josh as the model for the murderer. Two things at once, again unrelated."

"That body in the wheelchair—that wasn't my father," Nancy said. "You should have known my father. All of you. Bright, alive, and witty. He could be a real bastard, but he could charm anybody when he wanted to. He could make anybody laugh." She was speaking slowly. The thought brought something like animation back to her face. She smiled at the memory. Her lipstick made a grotesque slash against her white face.

Once again I got a sense of foreboding that echoed her words.

"My father's body kept living. What was left of him ate up all the money he had made. A whole lifetime of money. And it was eating me alive. Do you know," she asked bleakly, "they told me he could live like that for ten more years?"

"We've got to get help for Josh," Evelyn insisted. "Now. He's dying."

I looked at Josh. His face was pale gray, the color of modeling clay. His features were glistening with sweat. His head began to tilt over his chef's jacket, as if his balance was failing. His eyelids were nearly half closed. His upper lip half curled, as if permanently set by his tendency to whine.

I was having trouble breathing. Nancy's office was charged, like an electrical force field.

"I wanted to come here and tell her," Josh said. His voice was hoarse. He stabbed a finger at Nancy. "I wanted her to know I called the police about the old man. So she'd know she should have helped me." Then he crumpled, graceless, an inert heap on the floor.

"Ms. Branscomb," the receptionist said. She was at the door of the office. "The police are at my desk. They insist—"

"It's fine," Nancy said, waving an absent gesture. "Show them in."

She put the gun back in her right hand. She reached down and lifted a voluminous leather handbag and put it on her desk. She tenderly placed the photo of the cabin in it.

"I knew a family in Davis once. They had a tragedy, a car accident," she said. Her voice was singsong, as she cited the story. "They were first-generation Italians. Later, when people tried to call and offer condolences, they'd say, 'The family clothes itself in silence and requests silence from the world.' I always liked that as a final statement. Dignified."

Then she raised the gun.

"Wait!" Fred said, springing at her.

"No," she said.

I tried to move to her as she put the gun in her mouth and fired.

The blast knocked me back. I hit my shoulder on the wall. Her mouth was a ragged bloody hole in that emotionless face. Her head fell on the desk. Two little pieces of white landed on the carpet near me. I stared at them, stupefied.

The gunshot blast was so strong, it blew the caps off her front teeth and across the room.

CHAPTER TWENTY-SIX

West Los Angeles, California

May 29, 2007

"I couldn't figure it out," I said. "I knew Fulton was using something he knew, but he didn't have any money. I didn't understand. He didn't want money."

Fred and I were sitting in Oliver's office on Wednesday, May 29.

"So now I suppose you think I should congratulate you?" Oliver said.

"No, Oliver, you don't have to congratulate me. You're going to have to deal with me," I said.

"Vera, I really don't want hysterics," he said.

"The murder was about the Docklands project in the end," I said. "All about the project."

"Vera, there's something you need to know," Fred cut in. "The newspaper article on Nancy's death said she put her shares in a trust for Eco Delta, the ecology group she was part of. So it's over, Vera. The whole damn Docklands fiasco is over."

"You insisted on an appointment with me to tell me that?" Oliver said.

"See, our relationship has gone wrong, Oliver. It's gone wrong because of clout," I said. "It hasn't been a partnership. It's been you telling me. I listened to you because you were surer than I was at the time about what would be good for my writing."

"I have set aside this time in my very busy schedule today," Oliver said, moving his desk calendar, "because you asked me to. Could we get to what you want to say?"

"I'm just explaining that I understand a lot more about clout now. How valuable it is. That's what Fulton's death was about. And Nancy's death, too. And even Josh's death. He died because he didn't have clout. Three people dead, for lack of clout."

"I have explained what I have had to do," Oliver said." I have tried to achieve a fair solution—"

"I think you'd better listen," Fred said.

"I know now which character Fulton intended as the murderer in our book," I said. "He revealed himself with that opportunist remark. The killer in the book was modeled after Josh Baggins."

"I am less than impressed that you now know who your murderer is," Oliver said. "You're near the end of a mystery. You, the author, didn't know who the murderer was. It's an untenable situation, and I can't believe you allowed it."

"It's the tone, Oliver, the goddamn tone," I said. "When you say I should have known better, it's like I'm just an empty vessel to be filled with your wisdom. But authorship does not reside in the testicles, Oliver. So I finished the last chapter of the book." I took the manuscript out of my canvas tote and handed it to him. "I uploaded it to your computer. Here's the hard copy of the finished manuscript."

"What?" He asked, rearing back in his chair. "What are you talking about? I can't believe this—"

"You're going to submit the novel to the publisher," I said. "We have two days before the June 1 kill date."

"I am not," Oliver said. "We've already been through this."

"Fulton is dead, Oliver, so I don't need him to sign off the book," I said. "What I'm telling you is that things have changed."

Something was very wrong. Oliver should have been bellowing.

"So we're going back to the original book deal, Oliver," I finished. "We, as in you and me."

"Oh, Vera," Oliver said, shaking his head. "We are not."

"Yeah, we are," I said. "If not, I'm going to sue you for switching authors on my contract without my permission. I figure this whole thing brought out the worst in your ethics."

He stopped, stunned.

I'd finally got to him.

"But— that's not the way it works," Oliver said. "I explained about our contract. You'd lose legally."

"Right. I'd lose," I said. "But I'd make a helluva stink. The buzzards at that publishing company, your tormentors, they'd certainly know what's gone on. Meanwhile, you sure wouldn't be able to transfer my deal to Mark Huntsinger, so you'd lose him. Unless maybe you think he'd remain loyal?"

"That's outrageous!" said Oliver. "We have worked together for *years—*"

"I enjoy that reaction, Oliver," I said. "Nine tenths bullshit and one tenth hypocrisy."

"You are making a working relationship impossible," he said. He slammed his hands down on his desk.

I tilted my head, considering him. I said, "Right. I'm uncooperative. I've been reading about women my age, Oliver. What happens physically is, our levels of estrogen drop, which unmasks existing levels of testosterone. It means there's a hormonal reason why I get bitchier as I get older."

"This is sad." Oliver said, shaking his head regretfully. "You just want to show off. You now have a letch for this—this loser in cowboy boots." He waved at Fred. "But, Vera, maybe you'd better take another look at where he's coming from."

"Hey, come on, Oliver," Fred said. "I think I'm worth a letch."

"All this attitude is from him, not from you," Oliver said, jabbing an index finger at Fred. "Vera, you've never been able to make a decision in your life without flapping around. You can't even decide what to do about your own mother."

"And you think my decision about my book has to come from Fred. That it has to be from a male. But I did decide about my mother, Oliver," I said. "Maybe that's her last lesson to me. I'm not an amenable woman, and that's all right. That's acceptable."

"And you propose to take this kind of posture with me from here on in?" asked Oliver.

"Oliver, you know the story of the princess and the frog? The Grimm's fairy tale? Everybody thinks the princess kissed the frog to turn him into a prince. But she didn't, Oliver. Read the original story. She smashed him against the wall. That's how she got him to be a prince," I said.

"Does that mean you're going to throw Oliver against the wall?" Fred asked, interested.

"No, but he and I are going to be a partnership. A real one," I said.

"Vera, you must know," Oliver said, rolling up his eyes as if praying, "Fred has serious boundary issues. He keeps inserting himself into our business. You know we always had a good relationship."

"Oliver, that's because I always did what you said."

He sighed sadly. I knew Oliver. He knew something. And he was so anxious to tell me, he was practically pissing his pants. Oliver made a tent of his fingers. He meticulously examined his cuticles. He had only one bombshell left. But it turned out to be nuclear.

"I hope you'll take what I'm about to say in the spirit in which I tell you," Oliver said. His voice was avuncular. "Which is as a friend and colleague."

I looked at him.

"You've been regarding Fred's advice as disinterested," Oliver said. "I hate to disrupt a budding relationship. But I've done some checking. Did you know Fred works for the developer of The Docklands at the Delta?"

I felt like someone had taken all the oxygen out of the air.

I looked at Fred and asked, "Is it true?"

I don't know how, but I kept my voice level.

"Fred was obviously generating problems between us," Oliver said. His voice was sonorous. "So I had someone look into him."

"Come on, Vera, it's not the way he's putting it," Fred protested.

"Is it true?" I repeated.

Fred sighed and said, "Look, you were right. Stix Chimineas walked in on Fulton at the cabin. He needed to know what Fulton was up to, and he hired my agency."

I want to believe you Fred, I thought, I really do.

"So you gathered the information I was paying for, but you didn't give it to me. You gave it to Stix Chimineas," I said.

"No, now that's not true," Fred said. "I started looking for Fulton, and then in a crazy coincidence, you showed up in my class. We obviously had the same interest."

"That's when you showed up at my door," I said.

"You didn't pay for time you didn't get," Fred said. "In fact, he paid for time you got."

Oh Fred, why did you have to say that? I thought our time together was pure mutual pleasure. I didn't think anybody was paying.

"And you didn't think you should tell me?" I asked.

"I couldn't tell you," Fred said. "I had a confidentiality agreement."

"Oh well, that explains it, then," I said. "All this information on Howard Willow came from you. Willow is a miserable shit, but you came up with him to prevent me from getting a line on Chimineas."

"Vera—" he started.

"That's why you were stunned when I actually found Howie." I said. "Because he provided himself with an alibi."

"Well," Oliver did his voice of God imitation, "if you will continue to take up with these unsuitable people."

"I couldn't understand why I went so wrong on Eddie's book," I said to Fred, "Then on Howie. Then on who was my murderer. I went wrong because I was skillfully led."

"So that's where the advice you're acting on is coming from," Oliver said, slipping the last word in.

I fought the urge to smack the smug look off his face.

"I'm in the middle of fixing your wall," Fred protested.

"I'll hire somebody," I said.

My world was crashing. But ordinary day-to-day existence, to the point of the banal, errands like fixing the damn wall, intruded on my plans for the rest of my life.

Fred said, "When I met you, I liked you. That was not part of my planning. What we had together wasn't part of any job."

One thing I've learned. When you've been cut off at the knees, you can't let others see it. Like wolves, they zero in on weakness.

I gathered myself and turned to Oliver.

"You haven't gained anything, by telling me about Fred," I said. "The deal I offered is still the deal. You submit the manuscript to the publisher. We become a real partnership."

"Vera," Fred said, moving to stand between me and Oliver, "don't do this. I don't get it. Are your instincts dead? Don't you go at all by what you're feeling?"

"I thought I had a gut instinct about you," I said. "But you know what? Wishful thinking, coupled with hormones, could color my gut instinct."

"That's not what's wrong with you. To you, wanting another person is a sure sign of weakness," Fred said. His expression was bleak. "This is convenient. You're going to use Stix Chimeneas to put a wedge between us. Then you don't have to worry about me getting close."

"And there's your mother," Oliver said, piling it on.

"I've been thinking about what happened to Nancy and her father, Oliver," I said. "My mother will go back to her own apartment, and we'll work it out. I'll hire Mrs. Caspia. Or I'll hire some other old lady in that complex. She'll use up what money she has left. I don't know how I'll make it work, but I will. This life is my only life, and I'm not a nurturer. And I'm not going to change."

I walked to the door. "I don't blame my parents anymore for painful events in my childhood," I said. "And I accept that I'm not going to give up my life to be a caregiver, like my cousins. And I accept that if I do care about someone—" I looked at Fred, "I can be used."

"Vera!" Fred said. "Stick with me. Give us a fucking chance. Think about it. Have dinner with me. We seriously need to talk."

"I don't know if I can," I said and then paused. He was right. I ached for him. I still wanted him. I wanted him so bad I didn't know if I could ask pointed questions. How the hell could I work that out?

Well, I thought, all right. I'll have dinner with him. I never claimed to know everything in advance. Maybe I could handle Fred, with this new confidence. And handle Oliver. Or maybe I'd at least be able to fake it.

I turned to Oliver and asked, "Are we in agreement?"

Oliver's square face was bright red.

"Yes," he said, exploding.

"Good," I said, standing up. "That's all."

ACKNOWLEDGMENTS

To the wonderful people of Courtland, Isleton, Locke, Rio Vista, Ryde and Walnut Grove for their endless directions and wonderful stories of the Delta life and history in the Sacramento Delta. To Nicky Suard, owner of the Snug Harbor Resort in Walnut Grove for her generous time and tour of the Delta area towns.

To the Los Angeles Police Department Officers Drake Madison, Pete Llanes and Heidi Llanes for answering endless questions and Detectives Mike Depasquale and T.L. Gipson for their help in clarifying information for the book.

To Dr. Richard Jang for his wonderful stories and memories of his childhood and the Chinese way of life in the Delta.

To Alex Rosales for his endless patience and time with all of the computer questions.

And most of all to Kathy Owens, Vincent D'Alimonte, and Charles Del Monte.

www.ingramcontent.com/pod-product-compliance
Ingram Content Group UK Ltd.
Pitfield, Milton Keynes, MK11 3LW, UK
UKHW040602210726
13854UKWH00008B/1830

9 780595 481941